THE HUSBAND HOAX

Accidental Love

Book 1

SAXON JAMES

Christian

Being invited to my cousin's wedding really shouldn't be a big deal except, oh yeah, I haven't seen my family for a decade. My parents turned their backs on me and I've done everything since to become successful and show them what they lost. Only, it's kinda hard to be a success when you're a walking trainwreck.

So I'm going to fake it. Hire a guy with an online presence so impressive they'll be desperate to welcome me back into the elitist fold, and roll into the wedding with the kind of confidence I've never felt a day in my life.

The plan's a knockout.

Until my fake date cancels minutes before the ceremony.

Émile

One letter from my dearly departed grandfather, and suddenly
I'm on a husband hunt.

He's reworked his entire will so I'm set to inherit far more than
I'm entitled to, and all because he's asked me to use that money
for "good".

In order to get that inheritance, though, there's one stipulation:
marriage.

Even with his request, I'm tempted to stick to my original plan
of getting as far from my wretched family as possible, and
letting them fight it out.

But then I run into a tall drink of scattered mess outside of a
wedding who's in desperate need of a date, and the pieces click
into place.

I help him, he helps me.

Marriage, money, then go our separate ways.

Easy.

Now all I have to do is stop myself from falling for the guy.

CW: Homophobic Families

Chapter 1

Émile

Like a vampire walking into a church, I feel like my body might combust as I step foot into the Regency. Not because I don't belong here—the opposite, actually. I've been raised with extreme wealth in places like this all over the world, but I don't see the glamour in it anymore.

I wish I'd stayed in Amsterdam.

Giselle, my sister, waves wildly from down the chandelier-lit hallway, and at least *she* brings a smile to my face.

"Elle, what ... what have you done?" I barely hold back my laugh. But it's not at my sister's expense, no, I'm *impressed*. Giselle's long blonde hair has been completely shaved off, she's got a septum piercing, and there's no way those rags she's wearing are designer.

"Gran said to look our best today. I just got it done." She clasps her hands demurely in front of her.

"Feeling rebellious, are we?"

"What the fuck does it matter?" she asks, dropping the act.

"I'm not getting any of the money so she can't hold it over me."

Until recently, that's exactly *why* I played their game.

Now ... I can't help wonder if it's worth it. Unlike Elle, I *will* inherit a sizeable chunk, but the majority of the inheritance will go to our father and uncles. As always. What the hell do they need all that extra money for? What do *I* need it for?

"You okay?" Elle asks.

"I'm back in Seattle, surrounded by family. What's not to love?"

Her lips twitch, but she keeps the English composure we've been taught to hide behind our entire lives. "Literally every part of that sentence. I'm sorry about Pa. You two were so close."

Emotions threaten to take over again, because we *were* close. The closest. He was the one person I could always rely on growing up, who gave me time and attention because he *wanted* to, not because it looked good.

I glance back over my shoulder to check we're alone, and step closer. "I almost didn't come back for this. If it was anyone but him, I probably wouldn't have."

She nods. "After this, we'll go back to your apartment for a drink."

I'm going to need many, many drinks.

"Ready to go in?" I ask. "Because I'm going to have to insist it's lady first." For no other reason than I can't wait for my parents to see what she's done. It might even startle a reaction out of our zombie mother.

Elle pretends to brush the hair from her shoulders and pushes her way inside.

Even though the memorial hasn't started yet, the room is in full motion. Waitstaff are busy with table settings, and the smell of tea is already heavy in the air. Heaven help them if they get it wrong. Or god forbid—use bags instead of leaves. Gran's always complaining about the uncultured Americans, but I must be an abomination of an Englishman because I really don't give a fuck about tea.

We've lived in America for the better part of my life, so while I was raised an Englishman, I'm a bastardization of every country we hopped between while I was younger, until we eventually settled here for good.

My gaze finds where my father is following the house manager, and then flows to my mother. Face perfectly passive as ever, she shakes her head slowly, and the woman in front of her hurries to rearrange the centerpiece. Like the placement of flowers is somehow of the utmost importance.

Kill me now.

My family is … well, they're the worst product of generational wealth. They're obsessed with maintaining status and order, believe the rest of the world is beneath them, and think that because they have money, they deserve to be revered.

I'm convinced my mother believes she's the American-based version of the monarchy.

We've been approached multiple times to film a reality TV show, but thankfully, that sort of thing is beneath the Cromwells.

If it wasn't for Pa, I'd probably have turned out the same.

Since graduating from Cambridge, I've taken a gap year, and then another gap year, then … well, I'm twenty-six years old, and I've only been home for the occasional birthday party or milestone.

My parents believe I'm gaining *life experience* before I learn the family business, but the only experiences I'm having are how to live away from them all.

And now I'm back.

For the funeral of the one family member I've ever looked up to. My heart squeezes in on itself for the thousandth time since I got the news of my grandfather's death, but I tuck the emotion away and try to remember the Émile that I am here.

If I hadn't wanted to show my respects for Pa, I never would have come. I've been working on myself while I was away, figuring things out, and one of those things is that I don't want to inherit C.W. Shipping. As one of the largest shipping companies on the planet, I'm supposed to be desperate for the position. It was founded by great-relatives in England, before they opened locations all across the globe. Gran was set to inherit none of the company until she married Pa and he stepped in and took the reins.

Which means their direct descendants have first dibs on prime position.

I don't want any of it.

I'd have told them all already, but Pa's funeral isn't the place to go into all that.

I'm here now, and that means playing this pompous game.

I fix my smile and open my arms wide. "Mother."

I swear her eyes brighten, just a touch, but nothing else on her face changes. "You're home, Émile. How was your flight?"

"Comfortable." It's a total lie. I swear coach was created as torture for the masses. The first time I flew in those cramped quarters was a shock to the system, but I refuse to be a hypocrite. The only times I touch my trust fund is when I'm stateside, or need to keep up the Cromwell appearances.

Mom leans in to press a kiss to my cheek when her gaze drifts to Elle.

"Giselle Cromwell, where is all of your beautiful hair?"

Elle shrugs. "The trash by now, I'd presume."

Mom pales so fast she looks ready to faint, and the fact I take pleasure at her annoyance makes me as bad as the rest of them.

"You ... your ..."

Oh, okay, she's actually in shock. It's not often Mom is lost for words. I step forward and wrap my arm around her. "It's only hair."

"Only hair …" she repeats faintly. "What will your grandmother think?"

"Who's this random person at my party?" I manage in a bored voice.

Elle snorts a laugh. "I love how everyone's assuming she'll pay me a second of attention in the first place."

"Ah, so that's why you're acting out? Attention?"

Before Elle can reply, Dad's booming voice crosses the room. "Giselle Cromwell, tell me I'm not seeing what I think I'm seeing."

The spark Elle held while she was facing down Mom fades. The same blank Cromwell stare comes over her, and my gut twists at having to stand there complicitly while Dad orders Elle to leave and make herself more presentable.

Perception is the most important thing. No one gives a shit about feelings when we're not supposed to have any.

I learned to shove mine down from a young age, but the older I've gotten, the less room I have to hide everything.

Dad's attention slides from Elle's retreating back to me. He looks me over, then, when I apparently meet his approval, he holds out his hand. "I'm glad you made it back in time."

"Wouldn't dream of missing it."

"Excuse me, sir," the house manager murmurs. "Further to our discussion yesterday, I wanted to confirm that we've relocated the wedding ceremony from next door to an outdoor area farther down the hall."

"Excellent. Any issues?"

"None. We were very accommodating."

Dad gives his curt nod and the house manager scrambles away.

I frown. "Did I … please tell me I'm misinterpreting, but it almost sounded like you asked for a *wedding* to be relocated."

"Of course I did. Damn rowdy things. They'll be in and out all day, I didn't want your grandmother having to deal with that kind of headache."

That ever-present knot in my gut twists tighter, and I mimic Dad's nod. "Excuse me."

Today is going to be horrendous.

Chapter 2

Christian

Some days, all I wish for is a Prince Charming to *fix* me.

And yeah, yeah, you don't need a man to do that and whatever, but fuck, it would be nice if one could. I'm a mess. A hot mess. No matter how hard I try, I cannot get my shit together, and it's getting to the point where I'm worried that I never will.

Maybe *DatesforRates* will help me—with more than being my date to this wedding. I mean, sure, he's little more than a professional conman but even those fall in love. I assume. It's not like I meet a lot of conmen to actually ask one of them.

I've been a wreck for a solid week about finding a date to the Most Dreaded Wedding Ever, so having found *someone*—a very expensive someone—is helping me breathe again. And yes, the wedding gets capitals. That's how important of an event this is.

I don't know why, but today has that weighted feeling of an upcoming milestone. One of those events that stick with you. It's not even my wedding.

It's my cousin's. Where my parents will be. The same

parents I haven't seen since they *politely* suggested that if I wanted to date boys, I should find my own place to do it from.

That day still leaves a filthy taste in my mouth.

I groan, looking myself over in the mirror. The tux fits perfectly, it's the most expensive thing I've ever worn, and I'm going to spend the entire night highly strung over something happening to it. I'm already sweating.

"Just don't eat anything with sauce," Auntie Agatha says, perched on the side of my bed. She lives next door to Big Boned Bertha—the house my friends and I rent—and isn't really our aunt, but she's the closest thing to an elderly family figure we have. She calls us her lost boys and we call her our aunt. She's in her late seventies, with dark gray hair and a shiny black cane, and we do whatever we can to help her out, and she returns the favor by checking in on us to make sure we're looking after ourselves.

My best friend Gabe sniggers. "Probably best if you don't eat anything at all."

"You want me to starve?" I ask.

They answer as one. "Yes."

The confidence they have in me, I swear.

That said, based on past evidence, they're probably right.

"Fuck, I'm nervous."

Agatha scowls. "Those parents of yours have a lot to answer for."

"I know."

"The fact they could let a sweet boy like you go because of who you love is baffling. *Any* of you boys." She pats Gabe's hand. "We're all rooting for you, but I swear I'd like a word or two with them."

Gabe's normally happy, dimpled face darkens for a second. We'd all like more than a word or two with the people who abandoned us. Unlike most of my roommates though, I'm still holding out hope that my parents will come around.

It's one of the only reasons I'm going to this wedding.

"You look so handsome," Agatha says, gripping her cane as she gets up and walks over. "This internet man will be beside himself when he sees you."

"Doubtful, but as long as he's good to carry on my lie, that's all I need."

"I wish I didn't have to work today," Gabe says. I know it's eating at him, he'd call off sick if I asked him to. It's what he does. Helps people. Gabe doesn't know the word "no" when someone needs him. A month ago, a couple he rescued from a house fire asked him to officiate their wedding, so he went and got himself registered so he could do it. Even though saving them was literally his job, Gabe always goes above and beyond for people.

We've been best friends since high school, and I'd be lost without him.

"I think it's better this way," I say, trying to convince myself. "I'm just lucky you're always here for me after I screw up."

I catch his cringe in the mirror.

"Unless you'll be working late?"

"Ah, no. But you don't always need me, you know? You're a lot stronger than you think."

That's a joke if ever I've heard one. "Yeah. Right. I would have fallen apart by now if I didn't have you."

And like he can sense my throat getting tight, Kismet, a ginger tabby, bounds into the room. He's a stray, with a squashed grumpy face who won't let anyone touch him but me, and always shows up when I need him the most.

Exactly like my roommates.

Gabe and I were lucky to find the room here. We all were. The owners offered cheap rent for anyone in the arts and that's how the six of us came together. Me and Gabe. Xander and Seven, who met in foster care. Then Rush, and Madden. Gabe might not sketch as much as he used to, but it's in our blood.

I'm sure the owners didn't mean to fill the house with people who are outcasts because of their sexuality, but if that wasn't their plan, it's a pretty big coincidence.

I lean down to give Kismet a rough scratch behind the ears. He looks entirely unimpressed, and after giving me a once-over and making sure I'm fine, he sneaks out of the room again.

When I straighten, I catch sight of Gabe in the mirror. His knee is bouncing up and down, a sure sign he wants to say something.

"You okay?"

"Ah … yeah. Just making sure he didn't get too close. Allergies, you know." He joins Agatha in inspecting me. "You look like a real winner."

"I'm not sure about that."

"I am. And you'll see it one day."

Thumps and curses fill the hall, giving us a brief heads-up before three of my roommates appear. The only one missing is Rush, but I swear that guy doesn't know what day it is half the time.

"We wanted to wish you luck," Xander says. He's a blue-haired, freckled twink who's a total sweetheart.

"I'm fine?" I assure them, but it comes out more like a question.

Seven pins me with his "stop lying" look. "You're not fine. You don't need to be fine. You need to go to that wedding with DatesforRates"—he even keeps the judgment out of his tone—"and show them all what a successful human you are now. Right before you take a dump in the middle of the dance floor and give them a two-fingered salute."

Urg. "No more advice from you."

Xander sniggers. "Imagine if he dropped trou, squatted down, and … nothing happened?"

"Make sure you up your fiber and water intake," Madden

says, standing there buck naked, as always. "Or I've got some natural laxati—"

"I *will not* be taking a dump. Jesus. I want these people to respect me."

"Respect is overrated," Seven says, crossing his huge, tattooed arms and leaning against the doorframe. "And since you don't plan to shack up with DatesforRates"—this time he sneers over the words—"it's the perfect time to let your true self out."

I sigh. "My true self will be locked up tight. No mistakes. No missteps. I've rented an *insanely* expensive tux, cut my hair to an acceptable level, and fought tooth and nail to get a play I helped choreograph into a real, professional theater, and I will *not* be seen as a *joke*." I suck down a sudden breath, cheeks feeling hot from the flare of indignation.

"It'll be awesome," Madden says, flipping his cap backward, and he almost sounds convincing.

"All right, everyone get out," Gabe says. "You're smothering him."

And it's a testament to our friendship that they don't argue. They know I'm getting overwhelmed, and Aunt Agatha follows their wishes of good luck with a kiss on the cheek before she leaves.

Then it's just me and Gabe. Like it's always been.

He walks closer, wrapping his arms loosely around me and propping his chin on my shoulder. He's a few inches taller than me and his body is like an enormous wall of solid muscle. "You okay?"

"I wish I could fast-forward twenty-four hours and know that I pull this off," I murmur.

"It's okay if you don't—I want to put that out there. But I really think you will."

My eyebrows jump up. "You do?"

"Of course. I know you're … umm, absentminded. Sometimes. But you're also sweet and big-hearted and you've worked your ass off to perform in a stage show *you* helped choreograph. If they're not impressed by that, there's no getting through to these people."

"I'm in the ensemble."

"You're performing in the *Moore Theater*. Dude, stop discrediting yourself. You could be in one scene shining some bastard's shoes and I'd still be impressed as hell. You're living your dream. It doesn't matter if you're not some famous big name." He waves a hand toward my door. "None of us are. We're all working to get to the point where you are now."

I shift my weight, uncomfortably aware that he's right, but it's not enough. All my life I've loved acting, loved performing, and over the last few years I've had this image in mind of my name in lights and my parents seeing that and knowing I've made it. I might be a walking disaster in real life, but on that stage, under those lights, doing something I've rehearsed until I've bled, muscle memory takes over. It's the only time I'm graceful. The only time I feel put together.

It's a pipe dream. I know that. But it doesn't stop me from hoping.

The show runs for three weeks and starts soon, but after that I'll be back to children's parties and whatever minimum-wage position I can find, while I volunteer until something else comes along.

"If it helps … pretend you're not you today," Gabe says.

I turn to look at him. "What do you mean?"

"Well, you're an actor. You haven't seen these people for like, what? A decade? None of them know who you are now."

My bottom lip curls between my teeth and I think through the possibility. Act. Like in a role. Of myself. A brand new, highly successful and confident Christian Kilpatrick. A guy who has his shit together and doesn't live with five other roommates because he can barely scrape together enough jobs to cover food and utilities, let alone rent.

The idea ... isn't the worst one. The only time I'm good on my feet is when I'm on stage. When I've cemented the steps into my muscle memory so solidly I don't have to think. I just go through the motions. Because when I think, I fuck up, and that's what I'm worried about happening.

I've always been a screwup. Absent-minded, with my head in the clouds, walking through life and bumping into all my problems.

I'm not the guy who gets to win.

I'm not the guy who comes out on top.

And normally that's okay.

"Breathe, Chris," Gabe says, holding back a smile.

"I think you're onto something."

"Well, I am incredibly smart."

"No, I mean it. Datesfor—*Jordan*—said to flick him a message with some info about me and I've been holding off, but I could ... well, not *lie* but maybe stretch the truth a little. Give my personality some oomph. Who *really* knows what an ensemble cast member earns anyway?"

"No one."

"Exactly."

"But please tell me you're not planning on introducing yourself like *Hi, I'm Christian, and I make a billion dollars a year* because I've gotta say, it's trying too hard."

I laugh. "Of course not. But maybe I could rent an insane car, like a Ferrar—"

"*Nope.* You've already spent too much money on this thing. Today, Christian Kilpatrick will be impossible to intimidate in his fancy clothes and priceless confidence. He'll hold his head high and won't get flustered ... and he'll do it all without a goddamn Ferrari."

As much as I want to huff, he has a point.

"And you're *sure* this Jordan guy is solid?" Gabe presses. "He's not going to fuck up your story?"

I quickly shake my head. "Hundreds of reviews and he hasn't messed up yet."

Gabe hums like he's trying to be confident for my sake but doesn't quite believe it. "Sorry I couldn't come."

"It's fine, you need to work." His twenty-four-hour shifts at the fire station can't be easy, and the last thing I want to do is add more pressure to his life. Gabe is a *good* guy. If he wasn't scheduled to work, he wouldn't have given me the option not to take him.

But honestly, no one I live with would impress the Kilpatrick family. Wannabe elitist snobs. Seven doesn't know how to make it through a conversation without saying something crass, Rush would probably show up halfway through the ceremony since he's never on time for anything, Xander would talk himself into an allergy halfway through the night, and Madden would have to put on clothes for the event, which is something he hates in general.

Hence, why he never wears anything at home.

The rest of us barely notice anymore.

And Gabe, sweet, sweet Gabe, wouldn't be able to hold back from standing up for me and saying something that would probably close the door to my family for good.

No, I need someone steady. Professional. Someone who has experience doing this kind of thing regularly.

DatesforRates will be my savior.

I'm going to get through this.

And my asshole parents are going to regret ever turning their backs on me.

Tonight, I've planned everything to a tee. I'm ready. I'm rehearsed. It'll be like a performance.

Tonight, maybe just for tonight, I'll win.

I mean, fuck. The universe owes me one—at least.

Chapter 3

Émile

The reading of the will happens before the afternoon memorial, sequestered away in a small room apart from where everyone will be arriving in the next hour. It's depressing, sitting here and being reminded that Pa is gone. The one person in my family who had time for everyone. It's like I can hear his heavy French accent grumbling about how formal this whole thing is.

Dad is on his phone and Mom is staring vacant-eyed at the wall. My uncles and aunts and cousins are all here, and for the first time ever, Gran seems reserved. I know they loved each other even if I'm not sure why.

As always, I feel like I'm on the outside looking in, and it's a bizarre effect to all be mourning the same person for so many different reasons. Even though the majority of the people in the room are hoping to be given the biggest slice of the pie, I know none of us actually wanted him gone.

Elle sighs. "I don't know why I need to be here. Heaven

knows I'm not getting anything." Her voice is loud in the reserved quiet.

"He may surprise you."

"Hundreds of years of evidence suggests otherwise."

She's right. The money in our family has always been handed down through the male heirs. Sure, Elle has a trust fund as healthy as mine, but when it comes to inheritance, it's "not needed." Her husband is supposed to provide for her.

Even if Pa had wanted to change things up, there's a lot of red tape around what can and can't be done with the money.

Generational wealth at its finest.

"Thank you all for coming today to the reading of the last will and testimony of Jean Cromwell. He was a smart man, much loved by his family, with considerable assets to be distributed. First, I would like to distribute the letters written by Jean Cromwell. I have one here for his wife, his daughter, his grandsons Clifford Cromwell, Émile Cromwell—"

My head jerks up as he continues reading and when the assistant brings my letter to me, I take it stiffly. It's in a sealed envelope, unmarked except for my name, and yellowed slightly from age.

That deep ache returns to my chest as I stare at it, dying to open the letter, but not able to make myself. This will be the last of Pa's words. Ever. And without knowing what it says, I don't want to read it here with so many people around. I might need privacy to cry or grieve.

A soft tearing noise drags my attention to Neil, one of my other cousins. His gaze flicks over the paper and he frowns, then shakes himself out of it and stuffs the paper into his pocket.

I zone out as the executor talks, not particularly interested in hearing about how the wealthy people in this room are going to become even wealthier. My thoughts are so consumed by what the letter might say, and it's embarrassing to admit that all I'm hoping for are kind words.

I'm trying so very hard to forget how much I hate this life, just for today, but it's eating at me, that these people can think they're good people and walk away, congratulating each other on their swollen bank accounts.

I fucking hate it.

I hate the games and the expectations. I simply want to break free of it all. To go back to Amsterdam and lead a simple life where I'm no longer Émile Cromwell.

"And for Jean's considerable finances, the amount will be distributed equally between his male grandchildren. Clifford Cromwell, Neil Cromwell, Émile Cromwell ..."

The voice is drowned out by the ringing in my ears.

His *grandchildren?*

The room stirs with surprise. My dad bristles, trying to figure out what's going on. The will is usually straightforward, distributed predictably between family members in the exact way every other one has been before it.

That money *should* have gone to Pa's sons and sons-in-law, with a much smaller portion coming to me and my cousins.

He skipped a whole generation.

Holy shit, *all that money.*

My mind races with the thought of it. The things I can do. The way I can benefit people.

I'm getting so ahead of myself that I almost miss what the executor is saying, but I catch the end. And it crashes all my fantasies at once.

"The above listed heirs will receive their inheritance after marriage."

―――

THE MEMORIAL IS every bit as ridiculous as I was expecting. To get myself through times with irritating extended family, I like to play a game. To see how far I can take my stories before someone catches on to me.

"Is your sister okay?" my aunt asks in her syrupy sweet voice. "Because I remember when Britney Spears shaved her head and—"

"She's fine. Simple matter of hair lice but it's rectified now."

My aunt's face twists like she's sucked on a lemon. Unlike Mom, she doesn't keep everything masked behind indifference.

"Are you sure there are none left?" She absentmindedly scratches behind her ear. "I was just talking with her and no one told me."

I shrug. "I hear they're notoriously hard to be rid of, so it's possible she's missed one or two."

With a strangled sound, my aunt hurries away, and I walk over to where Elle is eating a slice of cake.

"There is every possibility no one will want to come near you tonight," I tell her.

"I could be so lucky."

I grin and take the seat next to her. "I may have told Sheryl you shaved off your hair because of head lice."

"Ohh, good one." She takes another bite and talks around it. "I told Rupert it's because I was tired of men coming in it."

I almost choke on air. "You did what?"

"Well …" She mimes jerking someone off. "I more *alluded* to it. It's not like I'd say the actual words, he probably would have had a heart attack. How crass do you think I am?"

I smirk and gently wrap my hand around hers and lower it back to the table. "That's enough imaginary hand jobs for today."

"I figured it was cum or gum so I went with the option most likely to get me out of the conversation."

"And yet we're all clueless why you're the black sheep of the family." She's at least changed into an "acceptable" dress. "Has Dad seen you again?"

"Yep. I've been keeping an entire room between us."

My conscience twinges at me. "Sorry I didn't say something."

"Why? I don't need you to fight my battles for me."

"Yeah, but—"

"Nope." She pushes her plate away and then meets my eyes. "You have more *important* things to focus on."

The will. The *marriage* clause. I still have no idea *what* Pa was thinking. "Seen Clifford?"

"Nope. But I assumed he's crawled inside Gran's ass, and I had no desire to look for him there."

I shudder at that imagery. "Do me a favor and don't tell *him* the cum story."

"I'll tell him I shaved it to match my feminist pussy."

"The American in me hates that word."

"And the Brit?"

"The Brit in me wonders what makes a pussy feminist?"

"It's the teeth, darling." Elle pats my arm. "Tear an unwanted cock to shreds."

"Have you been hanging out with frat boys again? You're mouthier than usual."

"Lots of toxic types at the office. Their brains can't handle it when a pretty girl speaks sailor." Unlike me, Elle is putting her university education to good use.

"So I assume you do it all the time."

She hums. "I heard Mom and Dad talking about Darcy earlier."

I try not to groan. "I'm surprised they haven't locked us in a cupboard together yet."

"It'll be coming. *You're almost thirty, Émile. It's time you settle down, Émile. Clifford The Perve is ahead of you—*" I snort because there's no way my parents would call Clifford that. "Oh! And the new one they're sure to add: *don't you want your money? Blah blah blahhh.*"

"It's not like he's engaged either."

Elle's gaze snaps to me. "You didn't see?"

"See what?"

But the look on her face is easy to read. "The giant rock on Martha's finger. He's been in negotiations with her family for *months* now."

Wow. Never in my life did I think he'd find someone rich enough to marry who'd actually go anywhere near him, let alone *accept* a proposal. Sure, women find him attractive, but it's his wandering hands and slimy words that act as a repellent. What poor soul agreed to be saddled to that for their entire lives? And how much goddamn money exchanged hands to make it happen?

"Well, now they really will make my life miserable about settling down, won't they?"

"Maybe it's time to give Darcy a shot?" Elle suggests.

Even I can acknowledge there's a lot of sense to her words. We're friends in the loosest sense of the word, he's sensible, hot, probably would be a decent husband. But marriages aren't a fairy tale in this family. They aren't a product of love. They're a product of many months spent laboring over income statements, while our lawyers assess assets and draw up contracts, before the engagement is announced in The New York Post.

I don't want a part of any of that.

Fucking Clifford.

"So what did the letter say?" Elle asks.

"Haven't read it yet. I want to wait until I'm alone later. It's clearly only meant for me and I want to be able to get through it without being interrupted or pestered by nosy gossips."

"How did you manage to be such a softie in *this* family?" She squeezes my hand. "I guess I better—Ah, fuck." Elle drops and slides from her chair so quickly, I barely see her move. All I hear is her hiss from beneath the tablecloth. "*Clifford.*"

Whelp, that'll do it.

He's heading in this direction but hasn't spotted me yet, so I straighten as casually as I can, and turn to head for the doors. A few people attempt to stop me, but my desire to get away is stronger than my desire to be caught in a conversation with him. I don't need to hear about his yacht or his work or the new house slash car slash stocks he's bought to know that nothing has changed there. And I definitely don't need to see that smug face as he tells me about his engagement.

Not only is he creepy, but he's the one person in my family who's openly homophobic toward me—*all in jest, of course*. Well, I'm not laughing. It's hard enough being around people here knowing that the only reason they've decided to tolerate my gayness is because it looks good for the family. I'm an *asset*.

My gut turns again.

I need to get out of here.

As soon as no one is looking, I slide out through the side door and in the quiet of the hall, I suck in a huge breath. The uptight, obedient son act melts away and it's a relief to feel like *me* for the first time all day. I need to get home, get out of this suit, and wash the gel from my hair. Then I'll read my letter and hopefully put this day behind me.

I head for the front doors to get some fresh air when they open and what can only be wedding guests spill inside. Regency staff are directing them to the new ceremony location so I duck my head and turn in the other direction until I find a set of doors that lead to the back of the building.

They're silent as I push them open and slip out into the enormous gardens.

Pure peace settles over me, until one word rips through the air.

"*Fuck.*"

Chapter 4

Christian

Oh no, no, no, noooo.

I gape at the message from *DatesforRates* and my stomach drops through the ground. This can't be happening. This *can't* be happening.

Sure, I didn't know the guy, but having someone else here, someone to share the attention and act successful and rub my gayness and great life in their faces with was the one thing I had to hold on to.

It's like I can feel the false confidence I'd conjured retreating way down deep and being replaced by my true self, a pathetic, clumsy loser. A loser who's going to make my parents and the rest of my extended family glad they got rid of me when they had the chance.

My gaze falls helplessly on the message, the words *food poisoning* jumping out over and over again, and even though my throat is tight with the need to cry, I type out a reply: *hope you feel better soon!*

Then I shove my phone in my pocket and let the anger

take over. "*Fuck!*" I kick the gravelly dirt on the footpath. "Fuck, fuck, fuck, *fuck!*"

"That word's a favorite of mine, as well."

The voice startles me so badly I jump, swinging around and almost losing my footing. A blond man is standing at the top of the short stone staircase, casually leaning against the side of the building. Everything from his styled hair to his suit to his loafers screams money, but there's something in his expression that screams trouble.

"Sorry," I choke out, heart hammering loud enough I can hear it beat in my ears.

"Don't be. It's a delightful fucking word." His pink lips hitch on one side.

I manage to force a short laugh, still feeling wrong-footed. "Are you … are you here for the wedding?"

"No. I take it you are?"

I hesitate because *am* I? Now that my date's canceled, I'm not in a hurry to commit to going. But I nod, because if he's not a guest, what would he know?

"And by your thrilling performance, I take it you're not happy about that fact. What's the matter? Bride an ex of yours?"

I hurry to shake my head. "Cousin."

"So …"

My heartbeat has slowed, and I finally look at the guy with interest. "You want my life story or something?"

"Or something."

What the hell? "My date canceled. He just texted me."

"Oh."

"Yeah. Pretty upset, if I'm honest."

"Does he do that often?"

I shrug. "Wouldn't know. I've never met him."

The guy chuckles. "Then that was one fuck too many over the cancelation of a blind date."

"Actually, it was the appropriate number of fucks considering I haven't seen my family in a decade, and now I'm going to be walking in there, completely alone, being judged by every single one of them …" Shit, my throat is doing that thing again. I turn away from the guy slightly to try and hide the fact that I actually might cry.

When I glance back up at him, the light he was radiating has dimmed. His arms are tight over his chest, pale blue eyes locked on me.

"Why haven't you seen them in a decade?"

I blow out a breath, shoving a hand through my product-heavy curls. "It doesn't matter. Sorry that I unloaded on you, I think I'm gonna … it was a dumb idea to come here anyway."

"Maybe. But you obviously came for a reason."

Well, shit. I'm in this now. I shake my phone his way. "I was going to rub this guy in their faces. He has this whole online life set up to make him look super successful and important, and I thought if they could see I was dating a guy like *that* … I dunno. Like I said. Dumb."

"Wanting validation isn't dumb."

"Yeah, well it is when your family has made it clear they want nothing to do with you."

The guy pushes off the side of the building and trots down the few stairs between us. He's light on his feet, with a tall, slim build and wide shoulders, and when he looks at me, he *actually* looks, and the closer he gets, the more unsteady I feel. Which isn't a great thing when my body feels too big and awkward at the best of times.

"Did they disown you because you're attracted to men?" he asks, point blank. There's no accusation or judgment in his voice, which is why I build up the courage to nod.

A smile bursts across his face. "Well, joke's on them, because I'm the queerest man-loving homo they'll ever meet." He holds out his hand. "Émile. I'm your date today."

My jaw drops. "W-what?"

"I think you're incredibly brave showing up here, knowing what you're walking into, and you seem like a sweet guy. Plus, I have questions. *So* many questions. Like why you were invited and what you've been doing with your life and why you think you're some epic disappointment." He sucks in a breath, body vibrating with excitement.

"And you're gonna … pretend to be my boyfriend? Because you're *curious*?"

"It's also a much better use of my time than going back to …" He waves his hand toward the building. "All that."

Confusion slowly builds because I think … I think he means it. I step forward, more out of shock than anything. "Are you sure?"

"I wouldn't offer if I wasn't."

"Oh, man. You'd be doing me a solid. Like, I'd owe you *big*."

"Why don't we start with your name and take it a step at a time."

"Christian." I cringe when it comes out as a grunt. "Sorry, I'm nervous."

"You mean you don't usually speak like a Neanderthal?"

My face heats and I stuff my hands in my pockets. "I wish I could say I didn't but I get nervous and embarrassed easily."

"Noted. I don't get embarrassed at all."

"After a night with me, we'll see if that's still true."

"The more you talk, the more curious I get."

"Awesome. I'm like a sideshow monkey."

He chuckles. "Correct me if I'm wrong, but they don't talk."

Is it possible for me to screw this up before I've ever started? "See? Nervous."

Émile tilts the hand he's still holding out. "Are we going to shake on it or not?"

"Oh." I take another step, eating the distance between us, and close my hand around his. His skin is … *so* soft. And warm. And … and … I tear my gaze from our hands to his face and find him already watching me. His lips are quirked like he wants to laugh but is holding it in.

"How long until the wedding starts?"

"Less than an hour. I was gonna use this time with Jordan to go over a few basic get-to-know-you facts."

"Well, we're running low on time now, so why don't you give me the CliffsNotes."

"I'm suddenly having second thoughts about this."

"You can have as many thoughts as you like, we're committed now. I'll go first. I was born in America, basically country-hopped most of my formative years before my parents and grandparents settled here rather than England, but I was sent back there for university. I'm … in business management. Have a large, invasive family, and think you're completely adorable."

My gut flips over at the word adorable, but I remind myself that of course he wants people to think that if he's my date. "Yes. Right. I think that too. Obviously. Christian Kilpatrick. I live in George Park District with, uh"—my cheeks blaze, but I press on because while it might be embarrassing to share a house with other people at twenty-seven, Seattle is *expensive*—"five roommates because rent is fucking expensive around here. And I'm an actor, I guess. I'm in a play right now."

"Theater?" His face lights up.

"Yeah. Just in the ensemble, but—"

He squeezes my hand before dropping it. "We're going to have to work on your confidence. Firstly, remove the word *just* from your vocabulary." Émile springs onto the bottom step and flings his arms wide. "I'm a dancer in an incredible perfor-mance full of talented thespians, and my work has allowed me to house five others under my care. I'm a real Mother fucking Theresa."

I grab his arm and drag him off the step. "First, no swearing. They're, uh ..." I pull a face. "Uptight. Religious. Think a lot of themselves. Take your pick."

"Let me guess, they come from money?"

If only. "Dad and his brothers invested in Cryptocurrency when it was first a thing and made a shitload. That was before ... well, we moved into a huge house and then when I came out, suddenly the house was too small for the three of us."

"Your family sounds charming."

"Please don't judge me based on them."

"Oh, I certainly am."

My face falls.

"I'm wondering how you turned out so seemingly nice. Tell me, you're into some hardcore sadism, aren't you?"

"W-what? No?"

"Hmm. Pity."

My eyes almost fly out of my head. "Are *you*?"

"I so badly want to tease you and be mysterious, but I don't think you'd survive it. I'm relatively vanilla for someone with a French name. My forefathers would be disgraced."

I chuckle but that twisting anxiety doesn't let my amusement get far. "What if they figure us out?"

"How could they? If what you said is true, I probably know you better than they do at this stage."

"That's a good point, but ..." I glance at him, at those steady eyes, before I quickly look away again. "We have to be ... boyfriendly. I told Josie—my cousin—that I was bringing a guy I'd been seeing for two years." I still can't believe those words slipped out. How am I supposed to have that kind of connection with a complete stranger? "Oh no, they're gonna know, they're gonna—"

"Assume you're being restrained around their bigotry."

I latch onto his words. "You think?"

Émile moves closer until our chests are a breath apart. "I'm not afraid to touch you." His fingers lightly dance over my cheek. "What are you comfortable with?"

"In front of them? Probably nothing. But …" I swallow and settle my hand on his chest. "It's not because I'm afraid."

"Nervous and embarrassed, then?"

I huff a laugh. "Exactly. Basically my natural state."

"Well then, why don't we settle for holding hands? It's a very boyfriendly thing to do and because we're both men it'll be as scandalous as if we stripped off naked and dirty cowboy danced on a table."

I cock my head. "Dirty cowboy danced?"

Émile swings his hand over his head like a lasso. "Like this. With you bent over in front of me."

Holy fuck, now that's an image. And while I've been way too distracted to check him out, with one sentence he's put it in my brain, and I'm looking at him with a whole new appreciation. Dirty cowboy dancing with Émile—in *private*—actually sounds like the perfect way to end the night.

But … we have to get through the night first. And given past experiences, I'm not hopeful that after whatever is coming, he'll want to see me again.

So, screw it. I'll take whatever time I have to pretend to be boyfriends with someone so … *charismatic*.

I slide my hand into his. "I'm about as ready as I'll ever be."

His grip tightens around mine, then he boops me on the nose with his free hand. "Don't worry, love, I've been preparing for this night my whole life."

Chapter 5

Émile

Well, this is a direction I didn't see my day going in. The only thing stopping me from cackling like a madman is the look on Christian's face. Sickly, almost green. The hand I'm holding is getting clammy too, but I have no desire to let go. And not only because Christian is the kind of guy I'd immediately approach on the dance floor.

Hair short at the sides with a nest of brown curls on top, facial hair that's longer than stubble, but not quite a beard, and a sneaky little nose ring. His hands are curiously large, fingers long and thick, and he'd look like the type of guy who doesn't give a shit about anything, if it wasn't for his eyes.

He's broadcasting his vulnerability and uncertainty to anyone who sees him.

"You look like a kicked puppy."

"What do you mean?" *Dear god, the way his forehead crumples sweetly makes me weak.*

I chuckle. "The vibe you're radiating is like you're walking to your execution."

"I'm nervous." His voice goes up a notch.

"I know, but we don't want *them* to know that. You're a highly successful actor with a highly successful boyfriend, remember? Now …" I finally release his hand to clasp his shoulders, loving the feel of muscle under my palms. "Think of something happy."

He looks like he's going to question me, but a second later, his eyes fall closed. That cute concentration line is still there, but after a moment it clears. "Okay."

"Now think about *why* that makes you happy. Think about the last time you felt that way, think about how we're going to walk out of the reception tonight feeling exactly like that."

His face screws up again and I quickly jump in before he can.

"Because we will be. I'll be the greatest date you've ever had. Whenever you feel nervous, I'll do the talking, we'll dance and act completely overjoyed to be in each other's company and then once the night is over, I'll loudly announce to anyone nearby that I need to get you home and under me."

Christian's eyes snap open. "Umm … maybe we should leave the last part out." But as uncertain as he sounds, his lips twitch like he's trying not to laugh.

"That will all depend on how they treat you."

"Okay, deal."

I study him for a moment as he shifts under my scrutiny. I'm struggling to pinpoint exactly what it is about him that made me offer to step in. I have enough of my own problems with my own family to worry about someone else's, but maybe that's why. With my family, I have to play nice. I have to bite my tongue and meet the expectations that have been set out for me, but with Christian's family, I don't have those same constraints.

And looking at him rears up something *protective* in me.

I may have only known him for basically a minute, but I can already tell he didn't deserve what they did to him.

No one does.

I can't right the wrongs of my own shitty family, but I can make things easier on this sweet man.

"Feel better?" I ask.

"I think so ..."

"More definite."

"Yeah. Yes, I feel better."

"Good." I take his hand again and give it a quick pump. "Whenever I do that, it means your answer needs more confidence behind it. Sound good?"

"I thin—ah, yes. It does."

"Ready to go in?"

He lets out a shaky breath. "I'm nervous."

"That's understandable."

"What if I fuck it all up?"

"Then you fuck it up and nothing can be done about it, but in my experience, the anticipation is often for nothing. It's a wedding. We'll sit in the back for the ceremony, make polite conversation during the reception, we'll eat, dance, tell everyone how amazing you are, and then leave. There isn't exactly a large margin for error there. Or do I need to remind you that at a wedding, most people are focused on the bride and groom?"

"You're right." He nods emphatically. "I'm making a big deal out of nothing."

Given how nervous he is, I'm reasonably confident he'll stumble over what he's saying at some point, and I'm sure it will seem like the end of the world to him. But I'll be there to cover any blips. I can talk my way through these things in my sleep. "Now, do you remember my name?"

"Yeah, Émile."

Damn, that sounds nice in his slow, deep voice. "Perfect.

And if you forget or panic or whatever, make up a pet name. I'll go with it."

Christian lets out a long sigh. "You're seriously saving my ass. There has to be something I can do to thank you. I'm poor as shit but I could take you out for burgers, or … if you've got kids or whatever, I do birthday parties, or … or … fuck, need someone killed?" He waves a hand awkwardly. "Obviously, I'm joking, but that's how grateful I am."

"Let's see how tonight goes before we decide if there's anything to repay."

"I suppose that's smart." At his uncertainty, I squeeze his hand and he lets out the most adorable, deep chuckle. "Yes. That sounds great."

"Ready to go?"

"Nope, but we're running out of time so I better suck it up."

I give his hand a quick squeeze and his head that had been drooping forward snaps upward.

"Yes. I'm ready." Christian shoots a nervous smile my way. "Better?"

"I like a man who can follow instructions."

He manages a short laugh as we make our way toward the doors. "You *sure* you're vanilla?"

"Well, I don't think a bossy streak and some light spanking is all that kinky these days, do you?"

"Yeah, I guess not."

I squeeze his hand tighter this time.

"No. *Not* kinky."

And while I'm proud of how easily he's taken to my strategy, unfortunately for him, he manages to get those words out far too loudly, just as we've stepped back into the hall inside.

Where a group of people are passing.

One woman throws us a disgusted look, while two others come to a complete stop.

I can feel the tension rolling from Christian without even needing to look at him. If that's the worst that happens today, this is going to be easy.

"See? Next time you'll listen to me. I *told* you there were no kinks in your jacket." Then I turn a pleasant smile on the suddenly awkward-looking people around us. "Here for the wedding? Us too. We were told it's this way, follow me."

Then I take off at a march, dragging Christian along behind me. Whether they believe my cover story or not doesn't worry me. The worry comes entirely from the fact that if a tiny mistake like that can have Christian shutting down, he's not going to get the comfort from tonight that he's so clearly craving.

Let's face it, his shithead parents will never see the error of their ways if they've been content to go ten years with no contact, so let's hope some of his other family members have a heart.

The hallway leads to a large open courtyard where rows of white chairs are lined up either side of a flower petal aisle. There's a lovely archway on a raised platform that all the seats are facing, and comparing this to the stuffy ceremonies I usually attend, this definitely comes out ahead.

Even if it is for a family of horrible people.

Christian tugs me into the second to last row of chairs. There are already quite a few people here, but none of them appear to have noticed him. While we have some borderline privacy, I lean in and ask, "So why *did* your cousin invite you? This isn't one of those situations where it was an obligation and she didn't actually want you to come, is it?"

"Nah, Josie's cool. She's …" He scrunches up his face. "Twenty-four now? Anyway, we ran into each other a month or so back, and she kinda insisted. Said the family had to wake up and get over it."

"And yet she still invited them all."

34

His lips turn down, and I immediately regret bringing it up. If she's his only family support, I should respect that. I suppose it can't be easy to do something so blatantly rebellious.

I tilt my lips to his ear. "Tell me, do you think I'm going to be the only one checking out your arse all night?"

His laugh is louder than either of us are prepared for, and when the people a few rows ahead turn around, Christian slaps his hands over his mouth to cut it off.

"Sorry, that was … unexpected."

"What are you apologizing for?"

"Ah … being loud, I guess."

"It's not like it was on purpose."

"Well then, drawing attention to us, maybe."

"Is it your fault people can't mind their own goddamn business?"

An exhale rushes from Christian. "What do you want me to say?"

"Nothing." I look him over. "Well, you *could* say you're planning on checking me out as well. I like compliments too, you know."

The look he gives me, like he doesn't know whether to be amused or confused, is adorable. He leans over as the rows in front of and behind us fill up. "Who says I haven't been already?"

Well, hello. My meek little petal has a spark in him after all.

His eyes hook mine and I almost wish I *was* meeting him on a dance floor where I'd be able to do something about this building want. But Christian drops my gaze and straightens.

I'm feeling like a king as I reclaim his hand and settle back in my seat. It's far too crowded to attempt a personal conversation now, but as Christian recognizes the people walking in, he fills me in on who they are.

I have fuck all chance of remembering names so I take note of his tone, and assign them to categories instead.

Assholes, Strangers, and Tolerable. The *tolerable* people are the ones I dislike the most, because they're too weak to stand up for Christian, but I'll bet they consider themselves to be allies anyway.

My heart hurts for him. This cute stranger who I can already tell is a better person than anyone else visiting this damn venue. Maybe if more people were like him, this world wouldn't be such a fucked-up place.

Christian inhales sharply and leans closer to me, almost like he's seeking comfort. "My parents."

And like that, I've found a fourth category: Blind Hatred.

I press my shoulder against his in solidarity. "Quick question, is your father wearing a rat on his head?"

"W-what?" His attention breaks from them and finds me again.

"I'm just saying, that's the most awful hair piece I've ever seen. And I've seen quite a few in my time."

"Last time I saw him, he had all his hair." The wistful note in Christian's voice isn't good.

"Well look at that …" I ruffle Christian's chaotic curls, then attempt to smooth them down again. "You've already got one up on him. We're starting the day a point in your favor. I have a good feeling about this."

Christian drops his head, but he's smiling. "Thank you."

"You have nothing to thank me for."

Still, he's reserved as the groom and groomsmen take their place up in front and we wait on his cousin. She's right on time too, so she gets props for that, and when she appears, the family resemblance is strong. All throughout our side of the guests, I spot the same strong jawline and dark curls.

As far as ceremonies go, it's a lovely one. There are a few sniffles, the officiant makes a couple of jokes, and if I hadn't known about the heavy homophobia ingrained in these people, I'd be enjoying myself.

Christian twitches beside me.

"You okay?" I whisper, eyeing him.

He nods, but halfway through the nod, he twitches again.

Oh no, please tell me he's not epileptic or something. It's been far too long since I brushed up on my first aid skills.

This time his whole head and shoulder moves.

"Christian ..." I murmur.

"It's fine." His words are a barely discernible grunt. Still, even as he tries his hardest to sit silently, his body gives the occasional twitch. And then I see it. A small black insect buzzing around his head.

He bats at it as a second arrives.

"Jesus ..." he mutters, too low for anyone but me to hear.

"Need help?"

"They ... won't ..." He shakes his head and they fly into the air before landing again.

"What's in your hair?" I ask.

"Dunno. Some kinda gel I borrowed from my roommate."

"Well, whatever is in it is attracting them."

He huffs. "Of *course* it is."

A third fly arrives and it's nearly impossible not to laugh. Somehow, I hold myself together and bat that one away, but like the others, it immediately redirects and lands on his head.

Christian shakes his head harder. Then harder again.

"Why, why, why ..." he chants.

"It's almost over," I reassure him.

"They ... tickle."

"Only flies."

"Annoying ..."

"I know."

"They ..." A flick of his head. Again and again and—

"*If there's anyone who objects to this couple being married—*"

A loud scrape of metal against stone cuts off the officiant's words as Christian jumps up with an "*Urg!*"

Every head snaps in our direction. Christian freezes. The entire courtyard balloons with the tension of unspoken words, and I swear I can feel Christian shriveling up inside.

I jump to my feet and pretend to clap my hands over my face. "Oh, that *smell!* How dreadful."

I nudge Christian out of our row, and he follows my lead like a puppet. Every single eye is on me as I shove him into a seat across the aisle and inhale deeply. "That's much more pleasant. Sorry for the interruption, but staff really should look into that. Carry on! No objections from us."

When people begin turning back to the front, I drop into the seat beside Christian, hand still pressing against his shoulder to keep him slumped forward and out of view.

It's not until I'm sure there's no attention on me that I spare a glance his way. His face is buried in his hands, ears red, with those three stupid flies still circling.

"Just kill me now."

Chapter 6

Christian

"Technically not your fault," Émile shouts over the hand dryer, fingers raking through my hair. As soon as the ceremony was over, he dragged me down the hall to the bathroom and steered my head under a tap. The gel Madden gave me is long gone and now Émile is attempting to tame a head full of cowlicks and wayward curls. I'd let him know it's hopeless, but … it feels nice. And it's helping distract me from bringing a whole fucking wedding to a standstill.

"Thanks for trying to make me feel better about this, but I didn't have to jump out of my chair like a moron, I just … I couldn't stop. It was getting overwhelming."

"Understandable," he says in that sexy accent of his.

I'm literally kneeling at his feet, hot air beating down over my head, while Émile massages my scalp. Every second that passes in this bliss makes it harder and harder to worry about what happened.

I still can't believe the way he effortlessly took the heat off me, though there's still a lot of wedding to get through, and by the end of it, I wouldn't be shocked if all he wants is to put as much distance between us as possible.

But for now, this is nice.

"Thank you." I raise my voice so I can be heard, and his pink lips curl up in the corners. There's something about the way his face is put together combined with his natural charisma that is making me so damn attracted to him with every moment that passes.

It also doesn't help that I'm kneeling face-high with his junk.

I'm not about to pull it out in a public restroom, but I can't say it's not tempting.

He holds out a hand and helps me to my feet. The hand dryer cuts off a few seconds later.

"Come on, the reception will begin soon."

"Yeah, no. Not going to that." I'd rather slink away into the night and pretend today never happened.

"Okay." Émile crosses his arms. "That makes sense considering everyone saw you out there and will be expecting to see you later, and when you're not there they're all going to know you ran away embarrassed. Perfect plan, really."

I narrow my eyes at him. "I know what you're doing."

"Stating facts?"

"Trying to use reverse psychology on me. It won't work. Peer pressure never has."

"I wouldn't dream of peer pressuring you, I'm simply stating the logical thought process most people will have. With complete honesty though, I'd much rather ditch this place and go get burgers, however I get the feeling you'll obsess over tonight for a long time if we do."

Go get burgers? I blink at him for a moment. "You'd want to go somewhere with me after that? I just embarrassed you in front of everyone."

"It was my choice to get involved, and like I told you earlier, I don't get embarrassed."

I eye him, because no way is he being serious. Everyone gets embarrassed. It's … a natural instinct, especially for people who spend time with me.

Émile's hand closes around mine again. "You want to go back in there, I can read it on your face."

"They'll all be judging me."

"Probably. So why don't you prove them all wrong?"

I don't know how he does that, just throws logic back at me. Most people would have assured me that everything is fine, and yeah, it's not like he needs to worry about some random stranger's feelings, but if he didn't care at all, he wouldn't have made a scene to take the attention off me.

"Proving people wrong isn't something I'm good at."

"And the only way to improve things we're no good at is to *practice*."

I duck my head. "You're like Yoda."

"I don't follow Trek Wars so I have no idea what you're talking about."

"Trek …" My hand tightens around his and I pull him from the bathroom. "We're gonna have to get through tonight in one piece because I have some serious educating to do."

"So we're staying?"

"On one condition."

"I'm listening," he says.

"If I fuck up tonight—and I will—you're not allowed to laugh."

And as though my words prompt him, Émile does exactly that. "I can't make that promise, are you kidding? If you do something ridiculous of course I'm going to laugh. But if it helps, it won't be mean-spirited, and I swear there will be zero judgment."

He really is the strangest person I've ever met. "Close enough."

———

THE RECEPTION IS every bit as extravagant as I thought it would be. Waitstaff in bow ties, huge ballroom, colored lights, and big-ass table decorations. Even in a tux that costs more than my weekly rent, I don't fit in.

I'm not sure whether to be grateful that most of my relatives avoid me like the plague or not. My parents are at a table on the other side of the room and neither of them have made an attempt to come and talk to me. Every time I glimpse them or think about them, the pit in my gut grows.

I shouldn't have come.

People are making today about me and not Josie, and while I might not be an expert at weddings, I at least know that the spotlight's supposed to be on the bride and groom.

"Christian!"

I glance up to see Josie jogging across the room, arms open, huge dress ballooning out around her.

"Hey, congratulations." I push to my feet to try and meet her hug, and my chair jerks backward then loses balance. Before I can stop it from hitting the ground, Émile has caught it and set it safely behind me.

My cheeks heat, and I'm about to apologize when Josie slams into my side.

"I'm so glad you came," she squeals in my ear. Clearly, she's a few drinks in, but it's nice to know *someone* is happy to see me.

"Even though I interrupted your vows?"

She pulls away. "No, that was perfect timing. Gotta keep Sheppy on his toes somehow, huh?" Her blue eyes slide to Émile. "You must be Christian's date?"

He stands smoothly, in a kinda elegant way I'd never be able to pull off. "Émile Cromwell."

Oh, fuck.

In all my word vomit, I forgot to tell him not to give his last name. I can guarantee anyone within earshot will be looking him up, and yeah, business management is an awesome job, but it's not the kind of awesome that's going to impress anyone here.

Ah, well. Beggars can't be choosers, and maybe Jordan would have been the better option on paper, but I can't imagine Jordan having my back as wholly as Émile has.

"Nice to meet you," Josie says, shaking his hand. "I'm glad my cousin's had someone to look out for him."

"You mean besides the five other people he houses?"

"He what?"

"Oh, I guess you wouldn't know about his philanthropic endeavors, what with the entire family turning their backs on him."

My eyes shoot wide. Sure, we're all thinking that, but like hell would anyone say it out loud. Those are the types of conversations you're supposed to skirt around and pretend don't exist for the sake of keeping the peace. I'm stuck on what the hell to say now, but Émile tucks his hands casually into his pockets and offers Josie a polite smile. Like he didn't just call everyone here an asshole.

I almost want to laugh, but the lack of oxygen in my lungs is making it impossible.

"I wasn't even fourteen when Christian was kicked out, and before we ran into each other, I'd been trying to get into contact with him," Josie says.

"You *were*?" I ask.

She shrugs. "I told you how fucked-up I thought the whole thing was. But you don't have social media, so …"

"It's under my stage name," I explain. Keeping everything

43

as *Chris Patrick* is easier. Plus, it's helped me get some distance between who I am as a dumpster fire of a human, and who I am when I walk on stage.

"My mistake." Émile's polite smile turns warm. "Apparently not everyone in the room is a homophobic dickwad."

Josie snorts. "No, we're not." Then she pointedly looks at my parents who hurry to act like they weren't watching us. "But *some* people have zero critical thinking skills and believe everything the media force-feeds them."

"True."

Aunt Barbara approaches to whisper something to Josie, then leans over and squeezes my forearm. "Lovely to see you, dear."

"Ah, thanks …"

"Gotta go," Josie says. "Bride stuff."

She walks away, and I'm expecting to go back to being ignored again, when a group of second cousins approach. Then my uncle. Then the groom's parents. They're all … unexpectedly warm.

"Émile Cromwell," Sheppy's mother says. "So lovely for you both to come. How did you meet?"

I jump as Émile's warm arm wraps around my waist. "It's a funny story, but we don't have all night. Let's just say one four letter word started this whirlwind romance, and I haven't looked back once." He turns to me and the look in his eyes makes my gut flip. "I've never met someone so incredibly self-deprecating and kindhearted."

"Aww, that's lovely." She rests a hand on her chest. "And has, uh … *Christian* met your family?"

"Of course. They adore him as much as I do."

She starts fluttering about something as more people crowd around us, and a prickle of *wrongness* creeps over me. Are people seriously this interested in me all because Josie came over to say hello? Are they forgetting the last ten years of cutting me out? Suddenly interested in and supportive of my relationship with a man? What the hell is happening here?

"So, Émile," someone on the groom's side asks. "How the hell did Christian reel you in?"

Émile's hand tightens on my waist and he angles away from them to tilt his lips to my ear. "Quick, what's our escape plan?"

"Ah … we could dance? That's something I actually *am* confident doing."

He shifts, nose pressing against my temple and lips brushing my cheek. It's calming. His closeness. Émile addresses the people around us without looking at them. "I'm sorry to interrupt you all, but I'm dying to get my sexy man on the dance floor. Excuse us."

And without waiting for a single reply, he pulls me through the crowd and into the center of the room.

Dancing is something I've been doing for years. Sure, most of it's choreographed, but pulling Émile into my arms, swaying to the music, seeing the kindness in his eyes as a smile touches my face, settles the knot of anxiety that's been strangling me all day. It's the first time I've felt totally relaxed all night.

"Tell me something happy about you," he says.

"Happy? Uh …" Focusing on the positive isn't something I do a lot. "I love my roommates. I love living with them and hanging out with them. Sure, people are always saying it's weird that a bunch of grown men live together, but …"

"How judgmental of them. Some days I wish we could go back to the ideals of communities where we share resources and a support network. Humans are social creatures, even the introverts. We all want to find our people." He dusts his thumb over my cheek. "I think it's fucking impressive you've found yours."

My cheeks heat at the compliment, because I've never thought about it like that. Most people think we're lazy or momma's boys or refuse to grow up. Émile's spin on it makes me oddly proud.

"What's something happy about you?" I throw back.

"I escaped what would have been a hellish afternoon with my family to spend time with an incredibly good-looking man who doesn't know how sweet he is."

Aw, shit. Butterflies race through me, but I play dumb, because no one just says things like that to my face. "W-when was that?"

He laughs, stepping in closer until our bodies are pressed together. "Don't fish, love. We both know I'm talking about you." His warm breath tickles the spot on my neck, just beneath my ear. It heats the skin down to my shoulder, my collarbone, blood burning from there, all the way down to my cock.

"I'm not completely sweet, you know," I murmur. "Just having an off-day."

"Somehow I doubt that."

"I can be … salty? Is that the opposite of sweet?"

"You tell me." That sexy British accent in my ear is making me lightheaded. It's also draining the blood in my body south, which is a super gay thing to happen in the middle of family who are uncomfortable with all my gayness.

And the way we're standing now, with Émile's hands bunching the fabric of my shirt at my hips, his nose in my hair and my thigh almost between his legs, is broadcasting that gayness loud and clear.

I want to get out of here. To show him through a full night of sexual favors how thankful I am that he did this for me. Even though I didn't get my *Pretty Woman* moment, even though no one is leaving here impressed by my life and what I've made of it, and even though they likely think I'm a regular guy with a second-rate boyfriend, I'm finding it so hard to care about any of that with Émile this close.

"I, umm ..." Shit, how do I say this without sounding like a thirsty idiot? Sure, he offered to do this with me and called me cute and is playing his part perfectly, but what if it's all an act? Fuck, maybe I shouldn't ask. Maybe I shouldn't make this weird, when things are actually going okay.

"You're suddenly tense," he says. "What is it?"

"I don't wanna say."

"Why? Because you've done so well to keep your thoughts bottled up so far?"

I huff. He's got me there. "Fine, I was just ... I was thinking ... well, tonight's been great and ... and I ..."

"Want to get out of here?"

Relief seeps through me. "Exactly that."

"Your place or mine?"

"I don't care, but maybe yours? Roommates, remember?"

"Oh, I remember. I'm almost desperate to meet them, but my place is probably best. I'm curious to see if your embarrassment extends to the bedroom or if I'll be able to make you scream."

"Jesus ..."

"Forget Him. The only thing you'll be worshiping tonight is my cock."

A bolt of lust shoots through me, bringing every nerve alive. I'm shivery and excited and so fucking hard it's a struggle to think with my top brain and not the one between my legs.

"Let's go." I step back quickly, needing the distance from Émile to reorient myself before I come in my pants. It's been a long time since I've been with someone who wasn't a transactional Grindr hookup, and I'm desperate to see this incredible man naked.

I swing around to head for my things as fast as humanly possible, and that's when it happens.

A kid darts across in front of me from out of nowhere and I sidestep to avoid colliding with her, nearly run into another dancer, who I narrowly miss by jumping aside, hit someone's leg and then … the ground disappears from under me.

My gut leaves my body for a second as I fall.

On instinct, I throw my hands out, catch the side of a table, but instead of helping … it comes down with me as well. All I'm aware of is a loud crash, pain shooting through my hip, and a splatter of *something* hitting my face.

Then an echoing silence.

Holy. Fucking. Shit.

I lie there for a moment, squeezing my eyes closed like if I stay as still as possible no one will notice, but the stifling silence disappears and voices start to swell.

Hands close over my arm.

"Are you okay?" an unfamiliar voice asks, and as I'm pulled out of the mess and to my feet, I catch a glimpse of wedding cake everywhere and the remains of the ice castle shattered across the floor.

My gut sinks. Tears build in my eyes.

Through my swimming vision, Sheppy peers at me in concern, and behind him … every person from the wedding is staring at me.

"Fuck. Shit. I'm sorry." I yank my arm out of his grip and go to flee, but my shoes slip over icing and I fall back into Sheppy.

I'm all flailing limbs as we both go down hard.

Chapter 7

Émile

What. Just. Happened?

My feet are frozen, mouth and eyes wide, the sudden silence ringing in my eardrums, and when I finally recover from the shock enough to get to Christian, he goes down *again*.

A laugh bubbles in my chest at his flailing and the fact that he was right. He's a walking disaster.

I think I'm in love.

Holding back my amusement is possibly the hardest thing I've ever done as I slip and slide through the icing to get to him. His tan face is flaming red and when I offer him my hand, he shakes his head so fast it looks in danger of falling off.

"Come on, up you get."

He still makes no effort to climb to his feet so I duck down, grab hold of him, and drag him up with me. He's covered in icing, jacket askew, hair standing every which way on one side, and slick to his head with white buttercream on the other.

His dark lashes lower in a glare. "Don't laugh."

"I'm trying incredibly hard not to."

The groom groans from beside us and I glance over to see blood smeared beneath his nose. Not much, but enough to send his mother into a fit. While she wails about whether or not it's broken, I duck down and grab a piece of shattered ice castle and offer it to him.

"Thanks," he manages weakly.

"I'm so sorry, so, *so* sorry," Christian chokes out, over and over, like he can't stop, and *dear lord*, he sounds like he's heading to his execution.

I swear, the day people stop taking themselves so seriously, we'll all be a lot happier.

"Jesus fucking shit," Josie finally manages.

"Language," her mother snaps, like this isn't the perfect excuse to let all the colorful expletives fly.

At least Christian's stopped apologizing now, though he looks in danger of passing out, which won't help matters.

Time to go.

"Jesus fucking shit, indeed," I agree, wrapping my arm around Christian. "Beautiful wedding, Josie, thank you so much for inviting us, though I'm not thrilled over one of your guests pushing my poor boyfriend into the table." I squeeze him tighter. "We're feeling rather unwelcome after that, so I'm going to take him home and look after him." I'm talking out of my ass, but I couldn't care less if they spend the rest of the night trying to figure out who apparently pushed him after how he's been treated. Even when people approached us earlier, they were more concerned with discussing me and my family than him, which leads me to believe they know exactly who I am, and they're every bit as shallow and self-involved as I thought.

Christian's better off without them.

"Is … is he okay?" Josie asks.

"Fine. In fact …" I lean in and lick a long stripe of frosting off Christian's face, which ignites some life back into him. "He tastes *delicious*. Excellent choice of cake, by the way."

And with that, I turn on my heel and carefully maneuver Christian out of the mess, to our table where I scoop up our discarded jackets and all but march him out the door.

While I should be knighted for not laughing at his family's reaction to one little spilled cake, my amusement dries up the second we step into the hall.

Christian immediately slumps forward over his knees. "I just ... I just ..."

"Come on." Gently, I pull him back upright and help him outside. It's slightly cooler than it was earlier, the night well and truly set in, and even under the streetlamps and covered in frosting, Christian is beautiful.

I need to reassure him.

"Look, it was—"

"I ... I have to go." He backs up a step.

"Please don't."

"No, I ..." He sucks in a rattly breath. "I just—"

Before he can do something dramatic, like run off, I step forward and cup his face in my hands. His beard is scratchy against my palms. "I wish you wouldn't."

"You're getting cake on you," he points out.

I don't mention that I already licked most of it off him anyway. "I don't care."

"Did you see what happened in there?" he asks through his disbelief.

"I did. It will make a funny story one day. *Not* today. But one day."

Christian eyes me like he's worried about my sanity. "Why are you still here?"

"What do you mean?"

"Well, what happened in there would be a hard limit for

most guys. I should know. I'm surprised you haven't taken off yet."

Jesus. How horrible have the people in his life been if he thinks I'm going to turn my back on him after that? Sure, I might not think that was a big deal, but he does, so he needs support right now. Not abandonment.

"I'm not going anywhere. The way I see it, you made their day memorable, and isn't that what weddings are about?"

He chokes on a laugh that doesn't sound at all amused. Then he steps back from my grip and runs a hand through his hair. "Thanks for tonight, but, as I expected, I'm a lost cause."

"I disagree."

"You don't pay attention well, do you?"

"I'm just incredibly stubborn in my belief that accidents are accidents."

"I once fell over the barrier and into the Puget Sound."

"There are places you can swim in the—"

"Where the boats come in."

I … have no words for that. "I didn't even know that was possible."

"With me, anything is possible." And I know he means it in a self-deprecating way, but I'm inclined to believe him.

"I can only hope so." I offer him my hand. "Want to go and get those burgers?"

Surprise takes over his features, and he stares at my hand for long enough that I think he's going to accept. "Nah, I think I'm going to order an Uber and head home."

I do my best not to look disappointed. "At least let me drive you."

And just when I think he's going to disagree, he nods. I'm clearly terrible at reading him.

"Okay. Yeah, thanks. But, umm …" He holds out his arms and looks down at himself. "I'm a fucking mess."

"Good thing I have leather seats. Though I wouldn't be opposed to you stripping off if you're worried."

Finally, I get a real grin. "So eager to get me naked."

"I'm a red-blooded gay man, and you're incredibly gorgeous." I eye him shamelessly. "Figured I'd try my luck and see what happens."

The cheeky bastard throws me a wink and heads in the direction of the parking lot. "Then let's see what happens."

Well, *hello.* I follow Christian around the corner and take the lead when it's clear he has no idea what direction to head in. Pity. I'd been enjoying the view of his ass. I can only imagine that all that dancing and rehearsal and whatever else his job requires, keeps him fit, because the way his pants mold over those plump cheeks is criminal. The thought of being able to unwrap the entire package? Button after button? Want slithers through my bloodstream, and I tap the button on my keys to distract myself from picturing him naked.

"*This* is your car?" he asks, hands suspended over the hood as he rounds it, like he wants to touch, but is too scared. "An E-class?"

Bribe gift from the parents to stay in town, not that I'm going to say that. "Management pays well."

"Very well." He lets out a long whistle. "Now I really am considering getting naked."

"If you want me to get you home safely, you won't distract me like that. Come on, get in. A little frosting never hurt anyone."

He mutters something as he pulls open the passenger door and climbs into the car. I watch the way he pinches the seat belt between his fingers and tries uselessly to plug it in without touching anything.

"One day you'll listen to me when I speak." I pretend to sigh, before reaching over and clipping him in. This close, I can see the dark ring around his blue irises, even in the shitty light from outside.

"I don't know how to take you," he admits.

"I told you I wouldn't lie."

"Yeah, but most people who say that still do it to spare people's feelings."

If there's one thing today has taught me, it's that I'd never want to hurt this gorgeous man. "I don't think it's possible for me to hurt your feelings when you do it enough on your own."

Another small smile. Beautiful. "So maybe I have some confidence shit to work on."

"Which is wild to think about considering you're a performer."

"Yeah, I hear that all the time."

I start the car, wanting to ask him so much more. Where it started, is it linked to his family, how he can perform when he so clearly struggles on the day to day? It's eating at me to hold back all of the questions, but he's little more than a casual acquaintance at this point and just because I helped him out this one time, it doesn't give me access to every part of his life.

Christian directs me to George Park District, an area of Seattle that's known for being artsy and alternative, and is surrounded on three sides by the University District, George-town, where all the tech-people are, and Maple Park, which is known for being a snobby and wealthy area. It's also, unfortunately, where I live.

Got to keep up those appearances.

But when we pull up out the front of a beautiful Victorian, I'm impressed. My modern, cold apartment has nothing on this. It's on a large lot surrounded by enormous trees and gardens, in a way that looks purposely unkept. The entire street has similar residences, with centuries-old oak trees lining the road, and a feeling of organized chaos all around.

"This is it?" I ask, leaning forward for a better look.

"Yep, this is Bertha."

"Bertha?"

Christian shoves a hand through his hair. "The owners have a plaque next to the door that says Big-Boned Bertha and we left it up. Our neighbor calls us Bertha's boys."

"Cute." I eye the enormous house. "And after all that talk of not being able to afford Seattle prices."

"With my mountain of debt, I can't." He laughs, rubbing his bicep. "There are six of us, though, and the owners apparently have a few houses that they rent out cheaper to people like us."

"Like you?" I'm expecting it to be related to being gay and disowned when he surprises me.

"Starving artists."

I let my gaze slowly travel over that gorgeous body. "Doesn't look to me like you're starving."

Then he completely surprises me by leaning over the console, mouth so close his breath puffs against my lips, and says, "Why don't you come upstairs and find out?"

Chapter 8

Christian

After how epically I screwed up tonight, I'm going to go ahead and assume there's no way it can get worse. And if it does, well, Émile can't say he wasn't warned. The cake down the front of me is exhibit A.

I fling my jacket over my shoulder then reach out and take his hand as we make our way down the long front path.

"Just a heads-up, my roommates kinda overstep boundaries sometimes." All the time, more like it. "Figured I'd apologize in advance."

"They're not going to walk in on us, umm, *inspecting* your body, are they?"

"I wish I could tell you no."

Émile lets out a quick laugh. "Somehow my excitement over meeting them has dimmed. Just a touch."

"Yeah, about meeting them. It's in our best interests to make sure that *doesn't* happen."

"Why?"

"Because the second they see you, there'll be a million and one questions and we'll never get away."

His warm hand tightens around mine. "In that case, should we throw open the front door and make a run for it?"

My feet pull to a stop in front of the stairs and I turn to him. "You'd do that?"

"Christian." His lips quirk as he steps closer. "You're underestimating how desperately I want you out of these clothes, love."

It's dark with all the tree coverage around us, but someone is home because golden light is spilling out of the front living room and setting Émile's blond hair alight. I swallow roughly, gaze skimming his clean-shaven face, the tilt to his lips that always seems to be there, like he's holding on to a laugh. "Yeah. I'm kinda desperate for the same thing."

And like the confident fucker he is, Émile's grip on me tightens as he bounds up the stairs and pulls me after him. "On the count of three."

"One."

"Two."

I tap the *Big-Boned Bertha* sign beside the front door for luck, then throw the door open. "*Three.*"

The pair of us hurtle into the house, me taking the lead as I all but drag Émile toward the large staircase and take the stairs two at a time. Movement catches my periphery from the direction of the living area, but I don't glance that way.

We reach the landing and before I make it to my bedroom, Émile tugs me to a stop by the bathroom door.

"Maybe we should deal with all that first?" he suggests, gesturing to my suit.

"We?"

Something glints in his eyes. "I'm not very well going to let you shower without me, am I?"

I swear my cheeks heat. That's not at all what I was expecting, but hell yes, I'm in. "Good point." I hurl the jacket through my bedroom doorway and nudge Émile toward the bathroom. "I'll grab us some clothes, go in there and close the door behind you."

He thankfully doesn't argue, and by the time I've grabbed us both a pair of sweats and a towel, I turn to head back to the bathroom and find my doorway blocked.

"Evening," Seven says, casually inspecting his nails.

"Ah, hey."

"Nice night." Unlike Seven, Xander isn't trying to cover his excitement. His grin is stretched over his paint-splattered face and he's bouncing on his toes.

"Can you guys get out of my doorway?"

"Why?"

I pin Seven with a look. "You know why."

"I thought you weren't planning on sleeping with Datesfor-Rates." He finally looks up at me and his eyes fly wide. "What the fudge happened to you?"

"That's a long story. I'm not going to sleep with Datesfor-Rates"—he opens his mouth to argue, but I talk over him—"because that's not Jordan. But that's all I'm explaining, because judging by the sound of the shower that just came on, I have a very sexy, very naked man waiting for me and you're in my way."

"Think he'd be okay with a third?" Xander asks.

"First, fuck no. We have that *no sleeping together* rule for a reason. Second, if you didn't constantly think you were sick and dying, you'd get out and meet more people and then you probably would have lost your V-card by now."

Xander sighs. "So it was only heartburn *this time.* You never know. It's not my fault the symptoms are the same as many, *many* other things."

I step toward them. "Move."

Seven's lips twitch and he straightens. "Or what?"

"Or I'm not going to tell you what all this is about," I threaten, waving a hand down my body.

"Rude!"

"You want the tea, you better move so I can get tea bagged. I'm a whole lot more chatty when I've just gotten off."

"Fine." He takes a step back and Xander does the same.

It's not until I'm at the bathroom door that I call back, "I better not catch anyone listening at this door!"

There really are no boundaries in this house. Sure, most of the time it's a joke to crowd around the door right as the hookup walks out, but I've heard every one of my roommates having sex at one point or another. As a horny dude, it can be pretty hot, but not something I'd ever do on purpose.

And considering Émile's words earlier about seeing how vocal he can make me, there's a good chance there's about to be a lot for them to overhear.

"We're going," Seven assures me, tugging Xander after him. I wait until they've descended the stairs before I step inside. There's no guarantee they're gone and haven't just run off to collect the others, but while Seven is a bit of a gossip, he's also my friend, so I'd like to think he'll respect my wishes.

The bathroom is already steamed up and *fucking hell*. Émile is in the shower. Completely naked.

Plump, white ass cheeks stand out against his tan.

My mouth is dry as my gaze follows the rivulets of water running down his back.

Holy shit he's hot.

"Sorry for the holdup," I say. "I was ambushed outside."

"The running didn't work, huh?" he calls over the sound of the shower.

"Not with having to duck into my bedroom." I start to unbutton my shirt, but I'm only halfway down when Émile turns to face me.

His gaze darkens as he looks me over, but my attention

immediately zeros in on his dick. Flushed red and standing at attention. Nest of pubes at the base, and right above them is a pair of sexy fucking cum gutters.

"Damn." I reach down and adjust my rapidly thickening cock. "You're a thousand times sexier than I'd been imagining."

Émile gives himself a long, slow stroke. "I look even better up close."

And that's all the encouragement I need. It's a fight to strip out of my sticky shirt and tight pants. Clothes that cost an absolute fortune, and I should be worried about never getting my deposit back on them, but I'm too lust drunk to care. I ball them up and toss them into the corner before shoving down my briefs and kicking them to the side.

Émile sucks in a breath that makes his chest expand dramatically. "I'm going to need you to hurry up now."

You and me both. I step into the shower and pull the door closed behind me and then we both stand there, under the warm water, taking each other in.

His pink nipples, his light dusting of chest hair, the way his narrow waist funnels downward.

Émile reaches out to run a finger over the lines between my abs, causing the muscles to jump at the contact. I hold back my moan, gaze following the paths of his fingerprints over my skin. It's blissful torture. Even under the heat of the shower, my skin is prickling, aching for his next move while begging him to touch me everywhere.

I can hear my inhales and exhales over the beat of water, see the stuttered way my chest is moving, and when Émile turns his eyes up to catch mine, he's so close I can make out flecks of green and brown in them.

"No starving artist here," he says, voice dipped and husky.

"Sorry to disappoint."

"Trust me when I say there isn't a single thing disappointing me in this moment."

I pinch his chin, angling his head a little. "Can I kiss you?"

"Well, I'm not here to watch you shower."

A short laugh falls from my lips before my mouth covers his. It's tentative at first, like a sip of something hot, a toe dipped in water, but the instant his mouth opens for mine, my tongue drives forward.

Émile's body collides with mine, back hits the tile, and I hold his face and kiss him like I've been desperate to all night. His tongue is strong, firm, warring with mine, even as he nips and bites and sucks, deepening the kiss until I can barely breathe.

I'm no stranger to hookups, to one-night stands, but this … this feels like more. I'm not an idiot, I know what's happening here, but after everything he's done for me tonight, getting to do this with him feels like a huge fucking reward.

His mouth curls upward as he drags deft fingers down my back.

"Not what I was expecting," he murmurs against my lips.

"What do you mean?"

"You've been playing the part of this timid little thing, and now you're ready to eat me alive."

I groan at his choice of words. "You have no idea." A tiny sliver of insecurity kicks in. "Is this okay?"

Émile answers me by grabbing my hand and wrapping it around his cock. "I'm obsessed. All night you've been this sweet, sexy man who's needed rescuing, and now you're completely owning me. You're fucking with my head, and I've never loved anything more."

I huff a laugh, kissing a line from his jaw to his ear, and I tighten my grip around him. "I promise that once I suck you down the back of my throat, you're going to be eating your words."

"I'd rather eat your ass, if I'm perfectly honest."

And that's one of the great things about him. He is. Honest. Always. His lips brush my neck before landing on my collarbone and it melts me. That spot. Massive weakness.

"Who says you can't do both?" I ask.

A strangled moan builds in Émile's chest as I drop to my knees. The water immediately cascades down over my hair and he fumbles for the showerhead to angle it away.

"Thanks."

"Least I can do."

I snort. "I'm sure you'll be doing a lot more than that later."

"You can bet on it."

This time it's my turn to smirk as I lean in and drag my tongue from his balls, all the way up to the tip of his cock. His dick jumps at the contact so I do it again, and again. Each time listening for the hitches in breath, the twitches in his limbs, and the way he shifts as though trying to get his cock closer to me.

I've always loved giving head. Teasing it out, gagging until I can hardly breathe, watching the man I'm with lose his damn mind, but when my gaze flicks up to see Émile's heavy-lidded stare locked on me, I realize it's never been like this. Because seeing a man as confident and put together as Émile slowly starting to unravel is addictive.

Goddamn, I hope he meant what he said about staying the night, because a quickie in the shower isn't going to cut it.

Without warning, I dive on his cock. He's long and thin, with a dark red mushroom head that immediately hits the back of my throat. I relax and suck him down, swallowing around him, and I'm rewarded for my efforts when his fingers dive into my hair.

"*Urg*, you're going to kill me," he gasps out, as I draw back enough for air before swallowing him down again.

There's nothing like the feel of my lips stretched around a

cock, the weight of it on my tongue, my chin hitting his balls as his thighs bunch and flex under my grip. The tighter he clenches my hair, the harder my cock gets, until I have to pull right off him and tug on my balls to get myself away from the edge.

"Look how swollen your lips are." His exhale is heavy with lust. "You look so fucking good on your knees."

The praise pools in my belly, and I can't resist giving myself a firm stroke. "Wanna see me on my knees with your cum all over my face?"

Émile curses and guides my mouth back to his cock. This time he doesn't try to hold still, doesn't let me take control. He fucks my face unapologetically, and the way he's taken over has me spinning.

My cock is *throbbing*, eyes rolling back in my skull as I gag my way through the filthiest blowjob I've ever given. His cock is sliding into my throat over and over, cutting off a good amount of oxygen. The world is disconnecting from my consciousness, and all I'm aware of is the burning beneath my skin, my hand flying madly over my cock, and the pinpricks of pain in my scalp from his grip on my hair.

Émile's rhythm hitches, becomes erratic, and my free hand flies to his balls.

"Oh, shit." He grunts, and his cock jumps in my mouth, releasing the first salty spurt.

I hurry to pull off him, and Émile wraps his long fingers around his shaft, the other hand holding my head in place.

I open my mouth just in time. His cum paints my face, my neck, my tongue. And the sight of him towering over me, covering me in his release, has my balls drawing up. My hand moves faster, the tingles at the base of my spine take over, and I shoot my load onto the shower floor.

Sheer relief crashes into me, and when my limbs stop shaking their way through my orgasm, I look back up at Émile.

The dark, hungry gaze has softened. He's panting. Hair askew. His grip on me loosens as he shifts his hand to drag his thumb through the mess on my cheek.

"I can't get over how sexy you look right now."

All I can do is nod. Brain pooling in post-orgasm bliss. Wishing I could tell him that was maybe the single hottest moment of my life, but there's a good chance that's the orgasm talking anyway.

Émile yanks me to my feet before turning the water back toward us. It feels hotter than before, but then, I can barely catch my breath.

"I didn't go too far, did I?" he asks.

A lot of guys I've been with aren't too worried about getting rough, but it doesn't surprise me at all that he's the kind of man who does.

"That was fucking perfect. Might not be able to give head again tonight—or talk tomorrow." Even now, my voice sounds raspy. "But it was so hot having you use me like that."

His arms wrap around me, steady and comforting, before his lips ghost over my neck. "Good thing there's plenty of other ways I can use you." He pulls back with a smile. "And plenty of ways you can use me right back."

Chapter 9

Émile

My limbs are tight as I roll onto my back and stretch out like a cat. It was a long, long night, and I lost track of the number of times we had sex, but, *damn*, it feels as though I spent the night working out instead.

Christian was insatiable. And despite what he said, he did have another blowjob in him, which he gave me, upside down on the side of the bed, while I ate his ass.

Turns out bendy dancers are full of surprises. Even bulky ones like him.

And between all the sex, we just lay here and … talked. Joked. Laughed until my side had stitches and he distracted me with a hand job.

I glance over at where he's sleeping. His arm is thrown over his face, scruffy beard visible beneath it, along with a glint of his nose ring in the early sunlight. He's still naked, sheets tangled around one leg, leaving the rest of his exquisite body on display. Including those defined, elegant collarbones that are going to fucking ruin me, and his soft, thick cock that's resting against his thigh, which will play an equal part in my demise.

Given how late we were up last night, it's creeping close to ten, which means I should be finding my clothes and getting ready to leave.

I just … don't want to.

The magnetic pull he has over me is getting ridiculous at this point, but I almost wish I was still sleeping, cuddled up to his chest.

In my defense, it's a glorious chest. All hard muscle, smooth skin, and minimal hair. I'm contemplating whether waking him with a blowjob is an option, when he starts to stir. Just a low groan at first, then a large inhale, and as he lets it out again, his powerful legs stretch toward the foot of the bed.

His arm slowly rises from his face so he can peek out at me, and I'm scared for a moment that his wake-up was all an act and he's going to ask what the hell I'm still doing here.

Christian shamelessly checks me out. "Morning."

I can't help my chuckle. "You sound like you smoked a packet of cigarettes last night."

"Hazards of being a gold star cock sucker."

"I don't think gold is high enough of a merit, if I'm honest." I roll onto my side, trying to read whether he wants me gone, but he only mimics the movement.

"You weren't bad yourself."

"Well, that's what every man strives to hear the morning after sex."

"Eh. Maybe you can try harder next time."

My surprise must be obvious because he nudges me with his foot. "Unless there is no next time and that's fine too. Last night was fun."

"It really was. If I'd known what I was agreeing to when I offered to be your date, I would have skipped the whole wedding and taken you home instead."

Some of the amusement dims in his face.

"Nope." I boop him on the nose. "No thinking about it, remember?"

"Kinda think that'll be burned into my brain forever."

"Mine too. It was hilarious seeing you go arse over tit."

Thankfully, Christian laughs like I'd hoped he would.

"See?" I say. "You're laughing over it already. Not long until it's forgotten entirely."

"I'm not sure it's that simple …" His eyes meet mine as he runs his index finger over the back of my hand. "Thank you. Seriously. I don't think there's any way I could ever repay you, and while the night was a total fail, thanks to me, you were amazing. Like, I probably wouldn't have made it to the ceremony at all if you weren't there."

"And going was a good thing?"

He frowns for a moment. "Yeah. I think so. I mean, the whole thing was fucked up, *but* I got to see people I haven't seen in a long time. I opened that door for if they ever want to reach out to me, and …" he sucks in a sharp breath, "… it's clear my parents still don't want to know me. Which hurts, but now I can stop kidding myself that they've been trying to find some way to come around."

My heart hurts for him, and I flip my hand over to take his. "They don't deserve you."

"Yeah, I get that. Just would be nice to have parents that did."

"I hear you." And while I'm not an expert on pillow talk, I'm confident it's not supposed to be so melancholy. "Mine aren't winning any awards either."

"Fuck, I swear we only talked about me last night. What's up with yours? Why are they shitty?"

"You really want to do this?" I ask skeptically. Because, while I'm glad he hasn't kicked me out yet, and that he wants to see me again, I'm clueless if he only means for sex or …

more. Would I want more? Could I offer it? Given I'm planning to run out of the country as soon as I can, a relationship isn't exactly in the cards for me.

But I can't deny there's a vulnerability, a goodness to him that I don't often see.

"My mother is completely blank," I say. "Emotionless most of the time, and when she does show emotion it's disapproval or disdain. My father is happy so long as everything goes his way. If it doesn't, the metaphorical shit will hit the fan. Mostly, I'm something to brag about at parties and heap expectations on."

His face pinches. "Sorry. That sucks. I'm not sure which is worse. Having parents who want nothing to do with you, or having parents who view you as, like, a trophy or whatever."

"I'm inclined to say you still win."

"But …?"

How much can I tell him? He's still practically a stranger, and while he's told me a lot about his own life, I'm not used to talking about mine with anyone but my sister.

Fuck it.

"My family wants me to get married."

His thumb lightly runs along the outside of mine. "Makes sense. Most do, right? How old are you?"

"Twenty-six. And I assume most parents do, but they don't usually bribe them to do it."

"What do you mean?"

"My inheritance. To get it, I have to be married, but the man they've always tried to push me toward settling down with …" I don't have the words to finish that sentence without sounding like an entitled twat.

"Don't like him?"

"It's not so much that. More … I have no real opinion on him. He's nice. Handsome. Richer than the monarchy. And I've known him since we were little, but there's no click there.

Not even as friends. We've never been able to hold down a conversation or see eye-to-eye on most things, so the thought of us being married is laughable."

"Do you have to marry him? Like, could you go out and marry whoever you wanted?"

"Yes and no. One of the clauses in the will is that I have two family members attend to witness the wedding. Elle would be one, but I'd struggle to find a second if my family didn't approve of the marriage. Second, *if* I somehow found two people, I still need to make it to the wedding. Unless it was someone rich, there's a good chance my family will try to scare them off long before. While my parents might be bad, my grandmother is terrifying. She'd likely pay whoever I was dating to leave and never come back."

"There's no way anyone would accept that."

I pin him with a look. "Most would. Everyone has their price."

"Not me."

"*Everyone.*" I shrug, not able to meet his eyes. "Maybe not money, but there's always something people would give up everything for."

He hums, not sounding convinced, and I get it. Until you see it first hand, it's hard to conceptualize. Guys like Christian are the easiest targets too. Struggling to make ends meet, big dreams, no family. My grandmother would eat him for breakfast.

"Maybe I should go," I say, but his hold on my hand tightens.

"Do you need your inheritance? You're in management, right? So you'd be making a bit on your own."

I hesitate, because I really don't like lying, but talking about trust funds is a tricky subject. "Technically, no. I have more than enough to live off without needing this inheritance."

"So …"

I sigh and climb off the bed, grabbing my pile of clothes from where I threw them on the floor. "I want to walk away from it all. No marriage, no anything. Just go back to Amsterdam for good this time. Leaving my sister is hard though, and—"

Something stiff crumples under my hand when I move my jacket and I reach into the pocket and pull out Pa's letter. "Shit." I'd been so swept up in Christian last night that I'd completely forgotten.

"What's that?" he asks.

"A letter from my Pa. The one who passed."

His mouth forms an "O," and I drop back onto the bed, staring at the paper.

Christian shifts closer. "Have you opened it?"

"Nope."

He doesn't say anything, doesn't push to know what's inside, simply places his hand on my back and rubs warm circles against my skin.

I hesitate for a full ten seconds before I realize I actually *want* to open it now. Yesterday, around my family, I hadn't felt safe, but for some reason, in this room, with this stranger, it's like I can be whoever I need to be when I read this, and I won't be judged for it.

He won't hold me to any expectation, because he has none of those where I'm concerned.

"I'd like to open it now." I see him nod from the corner of my eye.

"Want me to leave?"

"No. It's your room. Just …" I force some confidence. "Please keep doing that, it helps."

His fingers swipe my neck gently on the next upstroke, and I lean into his touch.

Time to do this.

My thumb slips into the corner seam and I drag it backward, tearing open the seal. The paper fills the quiet room with a satisfying ripping sound and then there's nothing left standing between me and whatever was important enough for Pa to stash away until his passing.

Just seeing his handwriting makes my eyes sting.

Emmy,

My little free spirit. Gone are the days where I could throw you over my shoulder to play airplanes, or toss you into the river when you annoyed me. I guess, if you're reading this, gone are the days where I can do anything at all.

Since my diagnosis last year, I've had time to reflect on a lot of damn things, least of which is the way our family operates. I look around and I see blood relatives staring back with one thing in their eyes: how long before the old fool is gone and we can have access to his money?

And then I see you, and you still look at me the same way you did when you were younger. Only there's sadness there now. I want to tell you not to be sad for me, but it's pointless to harp on about your feelings, and honestly, I'm sad for me too. I imagine the bugs are feasting on me about now, so at least they're happy.

Where I'll end up has no money. Where I'll end up is somewhere I'm going much too young. It's a nasty thing, this Alzheimer's. The way my brain is slowly turning against me. Even writing this, I'm paranoid the letter won't end up where it belongs.

If I could have my time again, I'd think of more. I'd leave my toys and my house and pay attention to the rest of the world. I'd use the money for good.

Do you know how frustrating it is to be one of the richest men in the world and have no damn access to your own money? To not be able to give it all away to people who actually need it? None of us are taking it with us beyond this life, so what's the point of hoarding it all now?

I'm rambling. I'm frustrated, Emmy. But beyond everything, I'm proud. Of you. Of who you've become. Of your ability to look outside of the family in a way I never could.

In my last act of rebellion, I completely overturned my will before they thought to start locking me out of the accounts. I caught on to what they were doing and I got there first.

By now, you should know all the money is yours—well, as much as they'd allow me to give you. I had to split it equally between my male grandchildren—I've given my apologies to Elle because I tried and failed where she's concerned—and I had to make up stupid conditions so they'd take me seriously. Skipping an entire generation isn't an easy thing to do, especially when your lawyer is old enough to have worked for your own father. But at least with marrying, they assumed that would bring in enough capital to balance the request.

The thing is, I don't give a toss who you marry.

Marry that Darcy fellow, or a beggar, or the queerest poof you can find in Europe and spend your days loving each other and doing good.

Because that's all I'm going to ask of you.

To do good.

Be the man I wasn't.

I love you the most, Emmy.

My throat immediately clogs up, and I drop my hand to my lap, head spinning with all the words.

"You okay?" Christian asks softly.

I numbly hand him the letter and after he finishes, he utters a soft, "wow."

"Yes."

"I'm not going to pretend to understand any of it, but he clearly thought a lot of you to want you to have all of his money. The whole lawyers and stuff makes my head spin, but overall, he must have really loved you."

"He did." I swipe at my nose to keep myself from crying. *This* is why I wanted to wait until I was home. Christian doesn't need to witness my breaking down. "*Fuck.*"

"What are you gonna do?" His face falls. "I mean, you don't have to tell me. Obviously. But if you need to talk it out, we can."

"Thank you. I just ... I was *so* ready to leave. To walk away. But how can I walk away after that?"

He hums in agreement. "Makes it a bit harder."

"I'm not sure what to do next."

"You could always marry someone. Anyone. Get the money. Donate it or something and *then* disappear."

"Marrying someone isn't that simple."

This is the part most people don't get. In my family, there *are* no divorces, no escape plan if this doesn't go well. I shake my head. "There's a whole process for courting someone in my family, and I don't like anyone enough to go through that process." I take a breath. "Besides, anyone I marry will want that money tied into clauses in our prenups. No one wants to marry a rich man who'll gamble it all away, for example."

"Hmm ..." His eyes go all unfocused as he stares at the wall. "You could marry someone already in on your plans? Someone who'd be happy to cut ties with you once it was over."

"There isn't a single person I know who'd allow that."

"Yeah, but there are people who *would*. You might have to pay them ..." He shakes his phone at me. "But given the guy who stood me up has a thriving business as a date for hire, I'd imagine you could find a, uh, *husband* for hire?"

"They'd know immediately if the person's family didn't have money."

"Could they stop you?"

"Me? No. But someone like that could easily be bought off."

"What if it was someone they couldn't?"

I cock my head, watching as a smile stretches over his face. "What do you mean?"

"Look, I'm going to throw this out there, and I swear I have no ulterior motives, but it's up to you if you want to believe me or not. My parents have a lot of money, yeah? Most of my family does. And sure, I have no access to any of it, but would your parents actually know that?"

I narrow my eyes. "What are you saying?"

"Marry me."

"*What?*" I damn near shoot from the bed.

"Not for real. I'm not going to ask you to trust a stranger, and you can make whatever contracts are needed to make you comfortable with the whole thing. Your family will think you're marrying a rich guy, you'll get your money, and then you can give it to whoever you need to. We'll do the annulment thing or divorce or whatever after."

I … don't even know what to say. "What do you get out of it?"

He looks legitimately surprised. "Me? Why would I get something?"

"Because you're pretending to be my fiancé so I can inherit an insane amount of money. Most people would want a cut."

Christian shrugs, looking uncomfortable. "You helped me without wanting anything back for it. I wanted to repay the favor."

"Pretending to be my almost husband is far larger in scale than a boyfriend for one night."

"True, but I wanna do this for you." His gorgeous, vulnerable eyes meet mine. "I knew you were a selfless person the second we met, but your grandpa clearly thought the same."

I can hear the truth behind his words, and I'm blown away. How can one person be so wholly *good*? Sure, he doesn't know we're talking millions here, but this whole conversation should have given him a hint that I'm not dealing in short change.

I know he wants to repay me, but I also know what a position I'd be putting his already fragile self-confidence in.

"I'll pay off all of your debt."

He jerks up to sitting. "What?"

"I'll pay—"

"I heard you, but I don't want it. I just want to help."

"I know you do and it's incredibly sweet, but I don't think you know what you're offering. My family will look into yours. They'll check that everything we say about your finances are correct, but I doubt they'll do more than that. They don't care enough, to be frank. They'll leave the details to their lawyers to finalize. But they're not pleasant people, and if there's anything I learned last night, it's that you're incredibly hard on yourself when you mess up."

He's playing with his hands, still looking uncertain, and I want to make sure there's no room for mistaking me. I sit opposite him, folding my legs beneath me and wait for him to meet my eye.

"Either you take the money, or I'll be forced to reject your generous offer."

Finally, a little amusement lights up his eyes. "You do know I don't actually want to do this *or* take your money, so it'd be easier for me to say no."

"I know. And you're welcome to it." But if I've read him like I think I have, feeling like he's in my debt isn't something he'll be able to easily brush off. "Think of it as compensation pay. Your family may be homophobic, but mine will be outwardly horrible to you. Don't take it personally, they're like that with everyone, but knowing you're the one in the way of what they view as the *perfect union*, you'll certainly be on the receiving end of some nasty shit."

Plus having all that debt he's drowning in suddenly gone? It's like I can *see* him fighting with himself.

And after one minute, that feels more like ten, he draws a shaky breath. "Okay. We'll do it."

I offer my hand. "I'm holding you at your word here."

His warm palm slides into mine, but doesn't move. "Dude, you just offered to pay off everything. I don't think you know how much I owe in student loans, credit cards, the money I borrowed for my car …"

Whatever it is, I can afford it.

"Shake my hand, Christian."

I feel the weight of his relief when he does.

Chapter 10

Christian

What the hell just happened? One minute I'm offering to do a good thing, and the next … I warn myself not to get too excited. All my debt, gone like that? Unlikely. I can't remember what life was like before the crushing pressure of overdue payments and bank phone calls. Working on this show is a godsend because it pays decent, but once I cover all my repayments, I'll barely have enough left over for food and utilities. I'm drowning. I trashed a suit I'm going to be up hundreds for, and while I desperately want to be the bigger man and turn down Émile's offer … I just *can't*.

Frustration builds in my gut and behind my eyes that I've gotten myself into this position, but it's not like I had much choice. Well, my career was my choice, chasing my dream, wishing I could show my parents that I didn't fail, that they didn't crush me, that was all my choice. Maybe if I hadn't been stubborn, if I'd gone after a useful degree I'd …

What, Christian? You'd what?

Likely be competing for a cubicle desk, still strangled with more loans than I can manage.

And while my dignity might not extend far enough to turn down his money, it does niggle at the back of my mind that taking money from the guy I'm sleeping with is crossing lines.

"We can't sleep together again." The words are so fucking hard to get out, I'm worried I'll choke on them. And not in the good way like I did with his dick.

His disappointment is obvious. "It's not like I'm paying you for—"

"No, and I know. It's … well, this is important to you. And I can't lie, it's important to me too. I'm a trainwreck most of the time, and I don't want to fuck this up for you."

"What? You think a little thing like being clumsy will fuck this up? Not possible. In fact, I invite you to knock over all the cakes you like. Those people need some excitement in their life."

How do I explain this? "I can't take money from you and be … I dunno. Going on real dates? Hooking up? I'm not sure what's going on here, but if we do this, I want to keep those things separate."

He sets his hands on the bed behind him and leans back into them. "Well, shit."

"I bet you think I'm being an idiot."

"No, actually, I see your point." His eyes travel slowly over me, and I can read on his face how torn he is. "You have no idea how desperately I want to say screw it all and turn this into an all-day sex marathon and not worry about the money or Darcy or my family but …" The conflict on his face tells me that fixing whatever horrible thing his family has done is important. I don't even know the whole story and it's already important to me too.

"I wish you'd never offered the money or that I could push back and not take it from you, but I'd be lying if I said I didn't need it." I scrunch up my face. "Sorry. You're always telling me the truth so I wanna be honest with you as well." The lump building in my throat makes me mad. Mad at myself for putting all my energy into an unpredictable career. Mad that I'm twenty-fucking-seven and still can't stand on my own two feet. That I have to take money from a man I think I could really be interested in.

"You don't need to hate yourself for that, love," he whispers, reading me perfectly. "Money isn't everything."

"Which is easy enough to say when you have it."

"Ouch."

I'm about to apologize when he speaks.

"You're totally right. Thank you."

I'm not expecting that. "What?"

"I appreciate you reminding me to be humble."

Yep. I could very, very easily be interested in him. My gaze trails over his long limbs, his tight stomach, those cum gutters that are going to be my undoing, before Émile lifts my chin with two fingers. "I'm going to have to ask you to stop looking at me like that."

"Right." I clear my throat. "Inappropriate."

"Not at all. But if I'm going to keep my distance, you really shouldn't be eye-fucking me."

My laugh is louder than I expected, and I cut it off quickly. "Sorry. I have a hot naked guy in my bed. Checking you out is my default."

"Well, take a last look." He stands up, glances at his suit on the side of my bed, then tugs on the sweats I loaned him for the walk from the bathroom to my room last night … right before I promptly stripped him out of them again. They hang loose around his waist, and my gaze stays with him as he crosses my room to steal a T-shirt out of one of my drawers.

"Sure. Help yourself." I grin.

"You're my fiancé now. It'd be basically illegal if I didn't wear your clothes."

Fiancé. Damn. That's … scary. Getting engaged wasn't supposed to hit my to-do list for the next decade at least and here I am getting hitched to a guy I haven't even known for twenty-four hours.

Sympathy crosses his face and Émile approaches to run his fingers through my hair. "Look, you're getting into a lot without much knowledge, so this is what we're going to do. I'm going to put my number in your phone and leave. Once I'm gone, you're going to search my name and look me up on social media. Look into who my family is, recent marriage and engagement announcements—because yes, we're going to have to do those things too. It's going to be a lot of attention, and I want to make sure you're ready for it."

"Wait … are you like, famous or something?" I numbly unlock my phone as he hands it over, then he takes it from me and punches his number in.

"Or something. You good?"

I stare at where his name is lit up on my screen. "Yeah. I think so."

"Good." He brushes a long, lingering kiss across my mouth. "And if you decide you want to back out, I'll be right over to screw you silly."

Goddamn, I almost blow this whole thing off here and now. "You don't fight fair, you know that?"

"Just wanted to make sure there was no confusion."

He picks up his letter and his clothes and I watch him all the way to the door, reveling in last night and this morning and wondering what the fuck I've gotten myself into. His hair is still a mess from my pillows, my skin is still tight with his dried cum, my room coated in the smell of sex, and I'm *aching* to pull him back down under me until I know what every inch of his skin tastes like.

Émile opens my bedroom door and pauses. "Huh. Christian? There's a naked man in your hall."

I groan. "Jesus, Madden. You know you're supposed to wear clothes when we have guests!"

He steps into view, hands raised like a busted perp. "In my defense, we were pretty sure he snuck out this morning. Like, it's almost eleven, dude." Madden eyes Émile. "Since when do hookups stay that long?"

Ah, crap. What do I say here? Boyfriend? Fiancé? Fellow con artist?

Émile blows me a kiss. "At least next time I'm here I'll know that clothing is optional."

"Next time?" Madden echoes as Émile disappears down the hall. My roommate turns his gaze on me. "There's a story here, isn't there? Should I get the others? Popcorn? Pizza? Or is this a rum situation?"

Might as well get it over and done with. "Let me shower and I'll meet you all downstairs."

"So is that a yes or no on the rum?"

"It's *still morning*."

He raises his hands, lifting each in turn, like scales.

"It's a no."

"Gotcha."

It's going to be a long day.

The guys aren't known for being patient though so I grab a towel and some clothes and shower as quickly as I can. The last thing I need is them gathering in the bathroom because I'm taking too long. Again.

———

THEY'RE ALL HERE when I get downstairs, and as much as I'd like to be relieved that I only have to relive this once, I know what them being here means. They organized to be home

SAXON JAMES

because they're expecting me to be a mess today from fucking up last night. And hey, they'd be right—if it wasn't for Émile. All night he completely distracted me from the horror I'd lived through and somehow made it not so bad.

I've barely sat down in the spare armchair when Xander jumps in.

"How bad was it?" he asks, huddled close to Seven.

"Basically everything I was dreading … but worse."

Madden cringes. "Well, that's not ideal."

"Thanks for pointing that out."

"I just don't get it. I'm assuming you were careful, and tried to fly under the radar, so how did it go wrong? What did *DatesforRates* do?"

I give him a dry smile. "Jordan canceled."

"That asshole," Gabe mutters. He would have only gotten home from work a few hours ago, and I kinda want to tell him to go to bed.

"Which should have been my sign to abort the entire thing then and there."

"So why didn't you?" Seven asks.

I sigh, remembering Émile and how he swooped in like a savior. "An angel appeared."

Seven loses his shit laughing. "Please tell me you don't mean literally because that'll be too much."

"No. I'm exaggerating, but seriously, this guy was suddenly there, offering to be my date. It felt like … like … it was meant to be."

"It might help if you start from the beginning," Rush says. "Who was this guy and why would he care about helping you? I mean, no offense. You know any of us would have done it, but he didn't even know you."

I huddle deeper into the armchair. "He seemed to really hate it when I said my parents kicked me out and I haven't seen them since."

"Congratulations," Gabe says in a dry voice. "He meets the bare minimum expectation of a decent human."

"Gabe's right," Madden agrees, stretching out on his side along the floor. "What about him made him an angel?"

Fuck it. I tell them everything. From the hair product–fuck you very much, Madden–to the flies and Émile's quick save there, rinsing out my hair, standing up for me with Josie, dancing, our plan to leave, then the gates of hell opening and swallowing me whole.

I'm met by five open-mouthed stares.

"You … you …"

"The cake …"

"And the groom …"

"What did she have an ice sculpture for?" Gabe exclaims.

"*That's* the part you're focusing on?" I throw back.

He scoffs. "Seriously, I know they're your family, but an ice sculpture? An actual *castle* ice sculpture? Just when I think they can't be the worst, they say hold my beer and have *a fucking ice sculpture*."

My lips twitch with a memory. "Émile used a smashed piece on Sheppy's nose."

"Practical guy."

"Yeah …" I try not to swoon over the influx of memories.

"Okay, I *guess* he sounds cool," Gabe relents. "What did he do when you fell over?"

"Tried not to laugh, mostly."

"*What?*" Gabe shoots to his feet. "I'll stab him. Just take me to him and I swear I will."

"Sit down, moron. It didn't … it didn't make me feel bad. Which is weird. Actually, instead of making me *more* embarrassed, it almost made me want to laugh too. Almost. If I hadn't been so fucking sick from causing a scene, that is."

"I'm surprised you're not used to it by now," Seven says.

"I don't want to think about it anymore." Though even as I

say that, the aftermath of cakemageddon solidifies in my memories. "Wait ... actually, I think Émile said something about me getting pushed." The whole thing is a blur that I'm desperately trying to forget, but I cling onto that memory, onto his voice, and how forcefully he told them off. His hand on me. His soft but firm guidance out of there.

"Are you actually smiling?" Seven asks.

"Yeah. He ... was really great."

"So you're going to see him again?" Rush asks.

And this is the part I don't know how to explain. We're gossips amongst each other, but I know I could tell them everything and they'd take that shit to their graves. I also know they'd have strong opinions about it though, and considering I'm still working through it all myself, I want to make my own decision before they all start throwing what they think at me.

"I hope so. He gave me his number, but ... he said to look him up first."

"Why?" Gabe wrinkles his nose.

I shrug. "Dunno. I haven't had a chance to do it yet."

"What's his full name?" Rush asks, pulling out his phone.

"Émile Cromwell."

The phone clatters to the ground and Rush gapes at me, wide-eyed. "You don't know who that is?"

Chapter 11

Émile

It's been hours without a text from Christian and I'm trying not to let it worry me.

Urg, who am I kidding?

The worry started ages ago. Now my gut is in knots, certain he's changed his mind. And I get it, I have a lot of baggage. My family is extreme and not only would we be lying to them, we'd be lying to the general public. To anyone who cares enough to follow my life. And there's a few hundred thousand of those people. It'd be enough to scare any sensible person off, and Christian's self-preservation gene is strong.

"So ..." Elle says, walking in and not bothering to knock. "Where were you last night?"

"Oh, come on. How do you know I wasn't jerking off in here?"

"Because you were gone all night. I'd be genuinely shocked and disappointed if you had any of those body fluids left."

For a brief moment, the bad vibes over me lighten. The

entire night was amazing, but my memory keeps coming back to that moment in the shower, Christian on his knees, lips puffy and red, streaks of my cum over his skin. I'd do anything to see him like that again.

"Well, you have nothing to worry about because he drained me dry." I flop back on my bed.

"Then why do you look like you just took a straight shot of tequila?"

I toss a pillow at her. "I do not. I'm … thinking."

"Uh huh." Elle shoves my legs aside and sits down next to me. "And is he the reason you disappeared last night?"

"Yep. He needed a date and it conveniently got me out of the rest of the memorial."

"Lucky you." She inspects her nails. "Clifford was parading Martha around like a goddamn show pony. She said my hair was a *unique* choice. Unique," Elle snarls. "Like I need her approval anyway."

"What hair?" I smirk, and she grabs my discarded pillow to hit me with it.

"Anyway, since you abandoned me, I demand to know everything."

"Okay, but remember you asked."

The more I talk, the more Elle's mouth drops.

"Was he cute?"

Of course those are the first words out of Elle's mouth.

"Dreamy." The more I think about him, the more hauntingly beautiful I find him. For a scruffy, walking disaster. *It's the eyes …*

"So when are you seeing him again?" Her tone is casual, like it's a given, and that reminder sinks lead into my gut.

"Not sure if I am."

"Are you kidding?"

"Wish I was. I told him to look up who I am and then tell me if he's still interested."

"And …"

"Radio silence."

She hisses. "Ouch."

"Thank you for confirming my pain."

"Why … I'm confused. Why does who you are have to do with anything?"

"Because he might have agreed to be my fiancé."

She opens her mouth, closes it. Opens again and then—my pillow smacks me over the head.

"Already in pain, thank you."

She hits me again, and I wrestle the pillow from her.

"You done?"

"What do you mean? *Fiancé*? Are you engaged? To someone you *just* met?"

With a long exhale, I pull out the letter and show her. Instead of clearing things up, she looks more confused than ever.

"So …"

"He offered to help me get the money. No strings. Said I can make a contract and everything."

"Emmy … what if he tells someone?"

"He won't."

"You can't know that."

"I trust him."

She splutters. "Why? Because you met him that whole one time?"

"I offered to pay off his debt."

"Yeah, but we both know his debt can't be anything compared to what you're going to inherit. What if he finds out and wants more? You can't trust people when it comes to money."

Maybe she's right. Maybe I'm some ridiculous idiot, won over by a pretty face and talented mouth.

"Can you please try to trust me?"

Some of her shock melts away but she doesn't look any less worried. "You forget I know how much you loved Pa. If you're doing this to honor him and do good things, I'd hate to see that all be ruined by some guy after a quick payday."

"I know. But he hasn't messaged me back anyway, so at this point, our whole discussion could be for nothing."

"Unless he's on his way to meet with Gran as we speak."

I chuckle, wishing she could meet Christian, because I'm certain that's all it would take for her to see what I see. "Let's all cross fingers that isn't going to happen."

Elle fills me in on everything else I missed while I try not to fidget. The buzzing under my skin won't settle down, and I remind myself that this is why I gave Christian my number rather than the other way around. I wouldn't have been able to stop myself from texting him.

"Are you listening to a word I said?"

"Yes, yes. Snobby and rude and Clifford being a perv." I sigh. "I really thought he'd message me."

Without Christian, I have nothing. No plan, no fiancé— technically I'm back to where I was yesterday when I first found out about Christian's wedding crisis, but somehow it feels so much worse. Like I've legitimately lost something. Which is ridiculous when I didn't want anything to begin with.

Elle drops her voice. "What are you going to do?"

"Honestly haven't a clue." I force a smile. "But I'll figure it out. And if not, I'm sure I can find someone *somewhere* who wants to marry me. Eventually."

Elle frowns, wrinkling up her nose. "You sound so defeatist. Stop that."

"Only trying to prepare myself."

"Well, prepare yourself during dinner. We're already late."

I watch her get up and cross to the door. "Please tell me you weren't sent here to get me?"

"Okay, I won't."

"You've been here for half an hour."

"It's not going to kill them to wait."

She leaves, and I get up with a groan and pull on a shirt. Like I expected, by the time I make it down the street to my parents' apartment, they don't look happy. Well, they never look happy, but they don't look ... emotionless, either. Both of them are brimming with disappointment.

I can't *wait* for this dinner.

"Good evening, family," I say, trying to act like I'm not suffocating under their cold looks.

"Émile. Dinner is at eight. Where have you been?"

"We got distracted talking, I'm afraid." And I might as well get their next question out of the way. "Elle asked where I disappeared to yesterday, and I explained I didn't feel well and had to leave early."

Neither of their expressions shift. No sympathy, no concern.

Dad lets a heavy exhale out through his nose. "That doesn't explain why you arrived home at lunchtime today."

Of course they'd know that. My lips quirk. "Why, father, are you spying on me?"

"That is not how a man behaves. We were celebrating your grandfather's memory and you left to go and meet up with who knows *what* kind of people."

"The queers." I nod. "It was the queers this time. I went to the land of my people and basked in the glow of glorious penises—"

Elle makes an intense choking noise as Mom gasps.

"*Émile.*" At least she's interested now. "This isn't the time for your humor."

"I don't think that was humor," Elle mutters and ducks when Dad shoots her *the look*.

"Besides," I say, thinking on the fly. My brain rapidly coming up with some bullshit before they can follow *that* conversation. "I've decided I'll stick around for a while. I want to hold a charity event in Pa's memory. To benefit Alzheimer's. I think he'd much prefer that over a pointless memorial." I'm talking out of my ass, but the more words I say, the more it makes sense. If I'm busy with that, they won't try to rope me into the business while I'm here, and while I haven't a clue what I'm going to actually do with the money once I get it, having charity contacts won't be a bad thing.

My parents don't acknowledge any of it anyway.

"Well, I'm sorry you missed it," Dad snaps, "because all anyone could talk about was your cousin's engagement. Do you want to see Clifford as the favorite to take over C.W. Shipping?"

"I'd prefer never to see him at all, if I'm honest."

"This isn't a joke."

"Really? Because him getting married seems like a joke to me."

"We've invited Darcy Ritcherson to the lunch we're having this week and seeing as you're not currently working, there's no reason why you can't attend."

"I'll have to see how my schedule looks. Planning a charity event is no easy task."

"I'm sure you'll find the time."

Well, lucky me. A lunch with my family and someone who's apathetically waiting on me to propose. Elle and I exchange a look and she widens her eyes pointedly at my phone on the table. I know she's telling me to check it. To see if Christian's messaged back. And look at that, she's suddenly on board if there's an actual chance she'll end up with Darcy as a brother-in-law.

But what are the chances he would have messaged back

during dinner when he hasn't bothered to send me a text since I got home? It's been *hours*. I at least thought he'd have the decency to turn me down with an *I'm sorry* fuck.

I guess all that talk about wanting to see me again was bullshit.

Or … maybe he actually has a life.

I hiccup a laugh at how stupid I'm being over one man. A man I barely know, even if he is the most adorable sweetheart in a sexy package.

"Something amusing?" Dad asks.

"I don't understand this fixation on Darcy."

"He's … like you." That's probably the most diplomatic way my father could say *you're the only gays we know*. "And he's set to inherit an entire media empire."

Gay and money. Fucking hell. Even if Christian does do this, I'm not sure his family's fast hit of new money can compete with all that.

I try to picture him here, sitting at the table beside me, knocking over the salt and using his cutlery with the wrong hands. Eating his soup with the dessert spoon.

It's ridiculous how much I yearn to see that.

"You know what? Maybe I will come to this lunch. I have someone I'd like to bring, actually."

My facedown phone is boring a hole in my brain though. I try to convince myself there's nothing there. He hasn't texted. I'm going to pick it up and be disappointed. All through dinner it has me so distracted that *I'm* the one who almost upends my water glass, but somehow I make it through without checking.

Dinner wraps up with more threats of Darcy and lunches and "you've known each other your whole lives, stop making that man wait" but Mom's words fade away. The second I slide my phone from the table and see an unknown number on my display, my stomach fills with goddamn butterflies. I forget about politeness as I swipe the message open and see two little words.

I'm in.

My mood immediately lifts as I look up and say, "I'm beyond excited for this lunch. I think it's going to be *very* beneficial."

Chapter 12

Christian

"Just how hard did you hit your head?" Gabe asks, swinging back and forth on my desk chair. "Like, is it possible that ice sculpture gave you a concussion?"

My loud laugh fills the room. "You're such a dick. It's been days. This is going to be fine."

"Right. You're going to be fine with the show opening coming up, as you juggle a bazzilionaire fake husband or whatever."

"Urg, don't remind me."

After Rush told me who Émile is and I spent the afternoon looking him up, my head had been spinning. We'd all gotten on the rum—thank you, Madden—and spent way too many hours combing through photos and videos of the Cromwell family. It feels like some kinda reality TV shit to me, and the thought of living that kind of life doesn't feel real.

I learned more about Émile in one afternoon than I'd probably learn about anyone during an entire lifetime. It was around the time we were halfway into the bottle of Captain

Morgan that I'd pulled out my phone and agreed to do this. I also got overexcited and spilled about the fake wedding, which they all thought was hilarious before an argument broke out over who get to be groomsmen.

Maybe not my finest moment, but somehow I woke up with no regrets and a text from Émile inviting me to a family lunch.

I haven't stopped pacing, worrying about screwing this up for him. "Do you have any rich clothes?"

Gabe looks back at me blankly. "*Rich* clothes?"

"Y'know." I hold up my ripped skinny jeans. "Something tells me these aren't going to cut it."

"Is there a reason you can't be yourself?"

"Yes. I told you. I need to play the part of a rich trust fund bunny." Oh no, my palms are starting to sweat. At that moment, Kismet bounds into the room and darts straight over to me. He winds himself through my legs and I scoop him up, cuddling him into my chest. The warm, soft weight, helps to calm my racing heart.

"Dumb cat," Gabe complains.

"Not his fault you're allergic." It's lucky for him that Kismet comes and goes as he wants and doesn't actually live in the house, otherwise Gabe would be sniffly and swollen more often than not.

"It *is* his fault he doesn't like anyone but you."

I grin. "I'm a nice guy."

"Or he recognizes a kindred hot mess when he sees one." Gabe watches me snuggle Kismet for a moment. "I'm worried."

"Me too."

The smirk he throws me is a relief because it means he's letting his lecture go. "That's basically your natural state. But seriously. You're more of a wreck about this than your cousin's wedding, and that was huge for you. Why do you care about this so much?"

I refuse to tell Gabe about Émile's plan once he gets the money. That's no one's business, and I'm kinda shocked he trusted *me* with that letter. A guy he just met. And I might not get *why* but I'm gonna prove it wasn't for nothing.

But Gabe knows me, and he knows I wouldn't put myself through this unless it was important. I walk over and close my door, deciding to give him *something*.

"This stays between us," is where I start.

"Yeah, of course."

"If I do this, he pays off everything. All my debts. Loans, credit cards, everything."

Gabe's mouth drops. "For real?"

My chest feels lighter, and Kismet jumps from my arms and walks over to sit by the door. I let him out before leaning against it. "I'm trying not to get my hopes up. Maybe he's an asshole and he's lying and won't even pay." I don't believe that for a second. But the thought of all my money problems being solved, just like that, doesn't seem possible. I'm convinced that no matter how well-meaning Émile is, something will come up that puts a stop to it.

"That's … *If* it happens, that's incredible."

"I know." My voice breaks with hope, and I try to hide it by turning away and scrubbing my hand through my hair. "Wild, huh?"

"So fucking wild. But I swear to God, if he's messing with you and you do this and he doesn't follow through, I *will* stab him."

"Threatening bodily harm on people." I hold my chest. "You really do love me."

"Well, duh," he mutters, not meeting my eye. "You're my boy."

"And I don't know where I'd be without you. Seriously. If I didn't have you, there's no way I'd be where I am now."

Gabe shakes his head. "That was all you. You don't need me as much as you think. Like, if I moved out—"

"If you moved out, there's no way I'd manage." I shudder. "Don't even want to think about it."

"You need to give yourself more credit."

"I give myself exactly the amount of credit I deserve."

His eyebrows have pulled together and he's clearly thinking about something.

"You okay?"

"This is … shit, man. I'm happy for you. I hope."

"Yeah, me too." It's obvious he's feeling what I'm feeling. The too-good-to-be-true factor. Any of us in the house would have the exact same thoughts, except for maybe Rush. Of all of us, he's the planner. The one who makes sensible decisions. Even if he somehow manages to be chronically late for literally everything.

"But even though the money is—well, a fucking dream, let's be honest—I want you to promise me you're not going to get carried away with it. If you're uncomfortable, or this guy is pushing you into—"

"He's not like that."

Gabe gives me a wry smile. "You think everyone is good. Even your shitty parents. I'm *just* saying, protect yourself, okay? You're sleeping with him and pretending to be his husband and he's offering you a fairy tale, that's a lot. I don't want you seeing him as some kind of … I dunno. A savior or something."

Gabe's right to warn me because I'm worried I already kinda do.

"We're not sleeping together."

"Yeah, right. They all heard you the other night."

I screw my face up. "Tell me they weren't listening at the door."

"They didn't need to. Seven said screaming filled the whole house. Kismet was pacing outside your door for an hour."

My face heats. "Fuck you, I don't scream."

Gabe lowers his voice and moans like a porn star. "Yes. Émile. Deeper. Use your tongue. Oh, oh, *oh*. Like that."

Jesus H Christ I did beg for his tongue.

"And I'm going to go and drown myself now."

He leans into the chair's backrest until he's almost horizontal. "You're so easy to embarrass. It's amazing."

"I'm so glad you get enjoyment out of this." I huff. "We made this whole plan, *after* the sex, and agreed that it would be too weird to continue doing *that* while we pretended to be husbands and he was giving me money and shit."

"I'm proud."

"Thanks."

"I give it a week."

I push off the door to go back to sorting through my clothes. "Fuck you. We got it out of our systems the other night, if anything else happens, it'll be once this whole thing blows over."

"You're not … *actually* going to marry the guy, are you?"

That's the tricky part. "I have no idea about that legal shit, but we'll work it out. To get the money, I don't see a way around it."

"And once it's over?"

"Annulment or divorce or whatever."

Gabe still looks worried. "It's a big sacrifice."

I shrug. "Is it? It's not like it'll have any effect on me. Once he's got his money, the both of us will just move on."

Gabe's looking at me through wide eyes. "I love you, but this is batshit crazy."

"Maybe. But I'm going to do it anyway."

Because as next level as Gabe finds it, I'm actually ... excited? Nervous as hell, and sure I'm going to screw it up, obviously, but the thought of doing something so completely different to what my life has always been sounds fun.

I've worked my ass off. I've put my head down, studied, held on to three jobs, volunteered, reduced my free time to almost nothing, all to try and make it in an almost impossible career.

Is it really so bad to want this break? To want, just for a moment, and get to see how the other side lives?

"I promise I'll look after myself," I tell him.

"Good. Now onto the important question."

"Yeah?"

"Why are you so obsessed with sucking dick?"

I burst out laughing.

"Seriously, dude, you sounded like shit. I almost wish your voice was still wrecked so you could meet his parents all 'hello, Mr. And Mrs. Cromwell. No, I don't usually sound like this, it's just that your son's cock is well acquainted with my vocal cords.'"

I bury my face in my hands. "You're the worst. Get out."

"Fine, fine, I'm going." I hear him get up and a moment later, he presses a kiss against the back of my shoulder. "Be good. Look after yourself. I'm going to see if Madden has any incense he can burn for luck."

"Ask the others about clothes."

"There's no way you're fitting into anything of Madden's or Seven's and Xander's shirt would barely fit onto one of your arms. You could call Rush though. I think he left for work already."

Rush doesn't answer, so I send him a text to let him know I'm borrowing something. In his free time, he designs and makes clothes, but some of his style is a little too out there for me. He also has an office job though, so at the very least, he should have something presentable. I mean, this is only lunch, but do I wear nice clothes? A suit? Full tails and a fucking waistcoat?

I try to call Émile but he doesn't answer either, so I'm going to have to wing it and hope like hell I get it right. Prove to him I'm capable of something.

Rush's wardrobe is organized by item of clothing and color, so I'm careful to put everything back where I got it from. In the end I settle on a pair of black pants and a navy shirt. The tan pants looked better, but I'm paranoid I'll end up spilling something in my lap and I don't need that playing on my mind all throughout lunch.

I text Rush a photo of what I'm borrowing and he sends a heart back in approval.

Émile said not to shave my beard or take my piercing out, which was a huge relief, but I'm pretty confident it's not going to win me any friends. All the photos I saw of his family were either clean-shaven or meticulously neat stubble and smooth hair.

I don't fit in. At all. Every minute that ticks by feels like a mistake, but fuck it all, I'm doing it anyway.

Maybe by the end of today I won't need to worry about this stupid plan because Émile will realize what a mistake it was, but hey, I'm gonna try.

I'm gonna be the best fake ~~fiancé~~ husband person I can be.

And hey, maybe I'll surprise everyone and his family will end up loving me.

That's maybe the most deluded thought I've had all day.

Chapter 13

Émile

I lean forward, closer to the display, taking in the row of rings in front of me. Elle and I got caught up brainstorming details for my charity event and I almost ran out of time to do this before lunch.

"I can't believe you're actually going to propose. To a stranger."

I shush Elle as my gaze snags on a titanium band with an onyx detail through the middle. It's understated, expensive, but not flashy, and I can just imagine that exact one on Christian.

We've spent most nights this week talking on the phone, catching up on details about each other's lives, while I briefed him on the members of my family.

"Found it."

Elle's disapproval is immediately diverted as she leans in excitedly. "Okay, I highly approve. Still don't love what you're doing, but you're not going to change your mind, are you?"

"Nope."

She sighs. "I hate being the supportive one."

"Dear lord, don't give up on me now. I'll be the sole well-adjusted one in the family, and I don't know how to feel about that."

"Bold of you to assume you're well adjusted."

I shove her and she shoves me back, but before we can take it any further, the jeweler clears this throat.

"Would you like to see it up close, sir?"

"Nope, I'll take that one." It's not a real engagement so I'm not going to spend hours deliberating over the choice. As soon as I saw it, I could picture it on Christian's finger, so that's good enough for me.

"And would your young ..." He eyes Elle's shaved head. "*Sweetheart* like to try it on?"

Is he ... does he think ...

Elle and I look at each other with wide eyes for a full second before bursting into laughter.

"Ah, no. My young sweetheart doesn't need to try it on. He's not here."

The jeweler looks like he's trying hard to maintain his professional face. "My mistake. I will box this up for you."

"Yeah. Thanks."

"That's single-handedly the grossest thing I've heard all year."

"Clifford's getting married," I remind her.

Her lips pinch. "I'm torn over whether to be disgusted or sympathetic."

"Why not throw in horrified and be all three?"

"Because then I'll need a very large Xanax and a very long sleep."

I snort, trying to keep composure since I already lost it once in here, and given what I'm buying, I wouldn't be surprised if this hits the Seattle gossip circles before I can even make it home. Usually the cheap rumor mills leave us alone, but the thought of a Cromwell getting hitched? Unfortunately that part of my life is going to be news whether I like it or not.

Vicious amusement hits me at the thought of my mom and dad assuming I'm buying a ring for Darcy, and I once again tilt my face toward the window to make sure any Seattleite posters are able to get a clear shot of me in front of the engagement ring display.

"Relax," Elle murmurs. "There was someone with their phone pressed to the glass a good ten minutes ago."

I hold back my urge to sigh. It's one of the things I hate most about living here. Abroad, no one gives a shit who I am, but with all the tech start-up superminds in Georgetown and old money in Maple Park, the Seattleite site is thriving. And for the people constantly featured in it, suffocating.

Sure, my family are used to having the attention of publications like *The New York Post*, but they're not spreading meager socialite gossip. You'd think those college students would have more to worry about than following around a bunch of boring trust fund kids.

The jeweler takes my card for payment, then returns with it and the fancy ring box. Elle and I thank him for his time before slipping our sunglasses back on and leaving.

"Are you getting nervous?" she asks.

"Nah. We both know the score."

"And you think he can pull it off? Lying to our family? To *Gran*?"

The memory of Christian going ass-over into the cake makes me smile. "In his own way."

"I'm not even going to pretend to know what that means."

"You'll want to go with plausible deniability on this one anyway." I check my watch. "Okay, just enough time to drop you off and pick him up."

She waves a hand. "Don't worry about me, I can get myself home."

When I give her a skeptical look, she rolls her eyes.

"Don't you dare question whether I'm sure or not."

I snigger. "Wouldn't dream of it." I *was* going to ask her how she planned to get home, but I swallow that question down under the force of her stare, and leave her to it.

While I might not be nervous about introducing Christian to my family, or even my plans to propose to him in front of them, I *am* nervous about seeing him again. The real him. Not the him that I've apparently been madly in love with for months, but the guy I only just met who I had an all-night sex marathon with and desperately wish I could touch again.

But can't.

I'll need to behave myself.

My resolve is sorely tested when he opens the door wearing a pair of ridiculously tight pants, a form-hugging button-up, with a blazer slung over his shoulder. My damn pulse rate jumps.

"Hey."

Christian blinks his sweet blue eyes at me, and answers in a voice that's gravelly and deep. "Hey." He shifts, focus dropping to himself. "Does this look okay?"

"Perfect."

"Really?" His genuine surprise is adorable.

"Remember what I said about honesty?" I step forward and brush a kiss to his cheek. "You look mouthwatering."

He laughs. "Not the impression I was hoping to leave your family with."

"By the time the day is over, it'll be the last thing on their minds."

We exchange the same shrewd expression as I step inside and close the front door. Once I've made sure none of his roommates are lurking, I slip my hand into my pocket and pull out the ring box.

"I got you this."

"Fuck." His hand immediately moves to rub at his wayward curls. "That box looks fancy and real."

"It *is* real. What were you expecting, something out of a cereal box?"

"Don't be stupid." He leans forward, tilting his head to the side to get a better look at the box. "I thought our relationship was at least at claw machine prize level."

"Silly me skipped a few steps." I crack the box, sliding both sides open, and his eyebrows nearly meet his hairline.

"Double fuck. That thing is … is … you want me to *wear* that?"

I close the box with a snap and slide it back into my jacket pocket. "Most people I know will be there today. I thought it might be a good idea if I introduced you to them, then proposed in front of everyone."

"Wow. We're going to make a real show of it."

"You're an actor, aren't you?" I ask, giving him a playful nudge. "Think you can muster up a tear? A shriek? Some display of overwhelming emotion?"

He's still staring at the place the ring was, looking uncertain, but he snaps himself out of it with a shake of his head. "You know what? I got you."

"You should know that I'm ridiculously excited about this. It's maybe the most interesting thing to happen to me in a long time."

"You just got back from overseas."

"Yes, but I wasn't vacationing. I was working." I can't resist tweaking his nose. "In a *café*, if you must know. Making coffees and waiting tables. I thoroughly enjoyed it."

"For real? You left that part out of all our talks."

It saddens me that he even needs to ask at all, but I remind myself that once this is all over, I can live whatever life I want to live. I step closer. "There's a lot you don't know about me."

He mirrors the movement, closing the gap between us until

we're close enough the toes of our shoes are touching. "Good thing I've got time."

"That would imply you actually want to know things about me, which is a wild quality for a future husband to have."

"Well, I think I've proved to you that I know how to do unexpected."

"Always going to keep me surprised?"

"Consistently. I'm going to be the best hoax husband you've ever had."

"Will you rub my feet at night?"

"Feet, shoulders, ass, dick …"

"Now I know you're teasing."

Christian winks, and seeing the amusement hit his eyes sends something pleasant swimming through my stomach. "What gave me away?"

I have to squash my smile down to pout at him. "You've already vetoed rubbing my dick. Which is a damn shame since he misses you."

"That so?"

"He literally wept for you last night."

Christian muffles a laugh. "Crying is a good stress reliever."

"You have no idea." I lean in so our noses almost brush, eyes pinned on his lips. "The memories of you helped relieve my stress over … and over … and *over*."

With a low whine, he steps back and doesn't bother to hide the way he adjusts himself. "I hate you."

"The feeling is mutual, love, trust me."

"How am I going to be able to get through lunch without picturing you jerking off?"

"The same way I'm going to get through it without picturing you on your knees with your face covered in my cum."

A throat clears loudly from beside us and I almost jump out of my damn skin. Standing in the hall by the stairs is a tall, gorgeous man with light brown hair and *dimples* of all things.

"Good to finally put a face to the stories, Émile."

Christian slumps. "Émile, this is the best friend. Gabe, this is—"

"The husband?"

I can't place Gabe's tone. It sounds pleasant enough but he's eyeing me suspiciously.

"You told your friends?" I ask Christian.

"We can trust them."

Gabe's eyes flick to his friend and back to me. "Gotta say, it's shitty of your family to want you to marry someone you don't like. Sorry, man. We all know what it's like to be related to assholes."

"Thank you." I'm borderline shocked that not only do I have something in common with Christian and his friends, but even though we've got a ridiculous plan worked out in order to *lie*, and I'm using Christian for that, Gabe doesn't appear to hate me. I don't think. Feeling emboldened, I ask, "Wanna see the ring?"

Christian groans as Gabe steps closer.

"Oh, this is too good. An *actual* ring?"

I bring it out again and show Gabe, who lets out a low whistle.

"Looks expensive."

"Nothing but the best for the love of my life."

It's the wrong thing to say because Gabe's easy expression cuts off as concern flickers behind his eyes. "You know this is batshit, right?"

"Completely."

His gaze strays to Christian again. "As long as you're both aware. And consenting to this shitshow."

"Already told you we were."

"Hmm. Kay." Gabe walks backward. "Have fun. Look after him."

That last part is clearly meant for me even though he's still watching Christian.

"I will," I say.

Gabe nods. "Love you."

"You too," Christian says, like telling your friend you love him is a totally normal occurrence. I blink at them both, mouth somewhere around my ankles, as Christian grabs my hand and leads me outside.

"Umm …" I hesitate over how to bring up the *L* bomb, and when I can't find a way to phrase it that doesn't sound like I'm a jealous, stalker boyfriend, I give up on tact. "Are you in love with him?"

"*What?*"

I have no fucking clue where Christian's shock at my question is coming from. "You just said—"

"*Oh.* That. Nah, we all say it to each other. We're pretty affectionate too, but we're like … I dunno. Probably the way brothers who love each other are *supposed* to be. Not that any of us have a frame of reference for that."

My heart aches at the matter-of-fact way he talks, and I give his hand a tight squeeze. "I think that's incredibly sweet." Because, while I was a teeny, tiny bit jealous at first, I can't deny that a bunch of grown men who live together being sweet and loving toward each other without it being anything sexual or romantic is … amazing. If only it hadn't come from a place of necessity.

He chuckles, face tinging red behind his beard, and my heart gives a little flutter. I recognize the red flag for what it is … and I ignore it anyway.

Chapter 14

Christian

I might be nervous as hell, but I'm also determined to be for Émile what he was for me. Confident—*ish*, a steady presence who takes no shit from his family, but above everything, I'll be his support. I'm here for *him*.

Their opinion of me doesn't matter, it's not like I'm going to join their family for real, all that matters is making them think that I'm wildly in love with Émile.

And as I grip his hand tighter and walk into an enormous, sleek and expensive-looking apartment, I doubt for a second that there's any way I'll be able to pull this off. I swallow down the lump caught in my throat and glance his way, only to find him already watching me. The warmth and affection in his eyes are only too easy to mistake for the real thing and when one corner of his lips tilts upward, the nerves in my gut settle.

"You ready for this spectacle?" he asks.

"Don't think so."

Émile squeezes my hand.

"Yes," I correct myself. "I am ready. As ready as I can get."

He tugs me close enough for his shoulder to bump mine. "We'll work on that execution, but good to hear."

I stay close as Émile leads us inside, and for a "lunch" there are a lot of people here. Twenty? Thirty? *Forty?* It's hard to count with people passing from one small group to the next. "Where to first?" I murmur.

"Probably the parents."

"Yikes. Getting the big guns out of the way then?"

"Oh, bless. They're the warm-up to grandmother."

Well, that doesn't sound good. "Warm up?"

"Oh yeah, they'll be more subtle in their disapproval. She'll just flat out hate you."

"Well, fuck."

His tone softens. "I did warn you. Not too late to back out, you know."

But even though it would be easy enough to walk out those doors, I'd never do it. I ... *like* Émile. I want to do this for him.

"Let's go meet the parents." I grin at him, and the one I get back holds a tinge of relief. He might not get embarrassed, but he's clearly nervous and seeing the guy who's normally so confident have this hint of uncertainty humanizes him a little.

It also somehow makes me feel like I can handle this.

Before we reach the group of people Émile is leading me toward, a tall woman with a closely-shaved head and bright eyes cuts us off.

"Christian, is it?"

I stare at her in confusion for a beat before I hold out my hand. "Ah, yeah?"

Instead of shaking it, she takes half a step back and sizes me up. "I can see why my brother took a fancy to you."

"Your—" I turn to look at Émile.

"This is Giselle," he explains. "My bratty sister who you'll get used to."

She makes a skeptical noise in her throat. "I guess that's

true since you're on your way to becoming part of the family now. Would you sign a prenup?"

I have no idea what the fuck Émile's told her. I get that I should probably be nice to her and get on her good side, but who the hell asks that so soon after meeting someone?

"I'll do whatever Émile wants since he's the one I'm here for." I want to tack on that whatever that *is* isn't any of her business, but I'm here to play nice. This isn't about me.

She suddenly relaxes. "You can call me Elle."

"Okay …"

"Sorry to jump you like that, but it's basically the first question our parents will ask you so I wanted to get it out of the way. Your answer was solid, by the way, but you might want to give your voice some *oomph*."

I throw Émile a confused look and he lightly rubs his thumb over the back of my hand. "It's okay, she knows everything."

"She does?"

He nods. "She knows my plans and supports me, and even though she thinks this is taking things too far, she'll support us in this as well."

She drops her voice. "This is sheer lunacy, but I helped him pick out the ring."

"You certainly did not," he says, sounding offended. "It was all me."

"Fine. I helped *in spirit*."

"What does that even mean?"

Watching them bicker is oddly calming. Normal. The sort of thing I do with my roommates and seeing this side of Émile is fun. He still hasn't let go of my hand, even when he starts to madly gesture, so I wriggle out of his hold and wrap my arm around his waist instead.

"You're getting loud," I point out and he immediately cuts

off. He turns to face me, his gorgeous eyes a mix of color that I want to take more time to inspect.

"Thank you."

"It's what I'm here for." And because we're supposed to be affectionate—and no other reason—I tilt my head and brush a kiss against his temple. "Now I'd really like it if we could hurry the hell up and meet your folks. I'm almost pissing myself over it."

"Yikes. Frosting I can cover up, it might be harder to do if you wet your pants."

"And since I wouldn't want to put you in that position …" I lean my body in the direction he was pulling me earlier and he turns to his sister.

"We'll be back. Can you organize us something stronger than that shitty wine? I get the feeling we're going to need it."

"I'll say," Elle agrees. "Gran and Clifford The Perve have already spotted you."

"Who?" I'd laugh if they both didn't look so annoyed.

"It's a long story," Émile says. "But we should probably get this over with."

Elle squeezes his arm. "I'll head off Darcy, he's coming this way too."

"Lifesaver."

"You owe me."

Elle leaves in the opposite direction to us, and I can't help glancing back. She comes to a stop in front of a drop-dead gorgeous man, who hugs her like an old friend, and the name Darcy prickles at my mind.

"Is that the guy …"

Émile sighs. "Don't worry, Elle will keep him at bay."

Ah, yeah. That's not what I was worried about. And sure, looks aren't everything, but that dude could be in an Abercrombie catalog.

I knew I should have taken out my nose ring. I automatically play with the piercing before quickly dropping my hand. Maybe if I don't draw attention to it, no one will notice?

Sure, dumbass, no one will notice the large silver hoop hanging off the front of your face.

Instead of doing what I want to, which is face palm, I force down a long breath. Then another for good measure. Pity neither of them are effective, because by the time Émile comes to a stop in front of five strangers, I'm convinced I'm about to hyperventilate. Or have a heart attack. I'd joke about how I sound like Xander, but it's kinda hard to do that with the heavy weight pressing on my chest.

"… this is Christian."

Cue smile. That's all I manage. I'm not sure where my hands are or how I'm standing, just *in and out* breaths and pulling my face into an expression I'm *praying* looks natural. Émile squeezes my hand, which helps me locate one of them, and the connection breaks through a little of my panic.

I find my other hand hovering at roughly head height in the Vulcan salute.

Fuck me.

I shove that tricky bastard in my pocket like that will somehow make them unsee that. Which isn't happening when they're all *staring* at me.

"Lovely to greet you." I clear my throat. "Ah, meet. Lovely to *meet* you. Obviously." I go for a casual laugh that comes out slightly hysterical. "Just got a bit tongue tied. Nervous about meeting—not *greeting*, heh—the family and—" I'm shaking out the front of my blazer to cool my overheating body before I catch up to what the hell I'm doing.

Émile cuts me off, thank god, and I wish he wasn't still holding my hand because it's all clammy and gross.

"Technically in this context, greet is correct as well. We're all greeting each other, aren't we?" He directs the question pleasantly toward a woman with an eerily blank face and eyes so light blue the color fades into the whites.

"Common usage overrides your point," she says, very obviously not looking at me.

"But just because something is always done one way, doesn't mean it's correct."

And maybe it's because I know he's unhappy with them, but I detect more weight behind those words than my earlier flub warrants.

"What's your name?" a tall, older version of Émile asks. I'm assuming it's his dad by the way the man's eyes are narrowed disapprovingly on me.

"Christian. Sir."

"Obviously. Who's your *family*?"

No one. How depressing is that? It's real work to keep the tone from my voice. "Ah … the Kilpatricks?"

Émile's mom and dad exchange looks. Somehow. Because their faces don't change much from their current expressions, but I'm definitely getting the feeling of being judged. Well done to them for making me feel so small with so little effort.

Émile steps closer to wrap his arm around me. "He's my boyfriend," he says before turning a sappy look on me. "And I love him *very* much."

The intimate way his words dip, the eye contact, the way his cologne fills my nose, makes it really, really hard to remember this is all fake. The horrible ripples of happiness that pass through me aren't real. Because none of this is. For an actor, I'm being ridiculously obtuse about a little thing called *acting*.

So I steel myself and take a page out of Émile's book by booping him on the nose. Heat flares in his eyes, a reminder of the real moments we shared together, and it makes it so much easier to say, "Love you, too, snuggle bug."

Chapter 15

Émile

"And who is this?"

My entire being stiffens at the voice, even as I do my best not to show any reaction. The knot that grows between Christian's eyebrows proves I wasn't quite successful, so I force a cheery demeanor and turn to my gran. "Grandmother, I'm so glad you're here!" And because I'll likely rethink and reevaluate the insanity of this entire plan if I leave it too much longer, I turn to Christian, take both his hands in mine, and sink onto one knee.

My heart is in my bloody throat, which makes next to no sense. We both know this means nothing, but the weight pressing down on my shoulders is trying to counteract that thought. Talking and scheming is one thing, but this is ... this is ...

I glance up into Christian's warm stare and somehow that drains the stress from the room, and I'm able to focus on him and me and the bigger picture of this entire plan.

My shoulders square and I reach in to pull out the ring.

I'm well aware of the hush that's fallen around us, I'm simply struggling to give a shit. The words come easily.

"I know our relationship may have started by, uh, unconventional means, but you're the greatest person who's ever come into my life. Good, selfless, kind toward helpless men such as myself." One corner of his lips pulls upward, a cheeky glimpse into him reading my mind. It might be overstated, but nothing I'm saying is a lie. "Would you do me the immense pleasure of becoming my husband?"

And so help me, that clever shit draws a shaky breath and a tear hits his cheek. "Yes. Oh my god, *yes*."

I launch to my feet, slip the ring on his finger, and pull him in for a hug.

Christian chuckles somewhere around my ear and says, "How's that for acting?"

"I think I just fell in love with you."

He snorts and we draw back, immediately surrounded by family wanting to offer their congratulations. And as much as I try to stop it, my gaze drifts toward Gran. Her eyes have emptied of warmth and the coldness radiating from them makes it evident why so many people are afraid of her.

Her gaze cuts to Mom who—for once in her life—looks taken by surprise. Eyes wider than I've ever seen them go as she processes the situation, but before I get a chance to marvel at a real human emotion gracing her, Clifford cuts off the sight.

"Congratulations." He holds out a hand, lips twisting as his gaze strays to Christian. "Interesting choice, but I suppose the pickings are slim for a queer."

I squeeze his hand a little too tight. "Far greater pool to choose from than men with no personality who look like an egg, but thank you for your concern."

He leers. "Imagine being so self-deluded that you see real love where there are only grubby money paws." He tries for a sympathetic look that only makes me want to check he's not stroking out. He drops his voice so the people around us won't hear. "I know what you're doing."

"No idea what you mean."

"Suppose it has nothing to do with Pa's will then, huh? Martha's family is in oil. *Oil*, Emmy." His gaze flicks to Christian. "What does your boy do? Offer cleaning services? Lap dances?"

Christian clears his throat. "Actually, my family made a *very* good cryptocurrency investment."

Clifford actually throws back his head and laughs. "I should have guessed." He cuffs us both on the shoulder. "Good luck with it all, boys."

My teeth are grinding as he leaves.

"What a twat," Christian spits, and that's all it takes to relax me again. "I can see why you don't like the guy."

He's right. The whole situation is one revolting mess and I'm playing a part in it. The propriety is so ingrained in us that I can't even tell Clifford to go to hell when he's being—as Christian said—a fucking twat. Just once I wish I could break free of all this. I'm yearning for the day. Once I have the money and work out what to do with it, I'll be able to move on and actually live my own damn life. No more playing nice.

The thought is so heady it makes my head spin.

"Émile?" I glance over at the dry voice to find Gran watching. "Come with me."

She doesn't wait for me to agree, we all know I'm going to anyway, but it's not a great sign when Mom and Dad follow.

"Ah, do you want me to come?" Christian asks.

"Probably better you don't, if I'm honest. There'll likely only be horrible things said about us both and I'd prefer if you hung out with Elle and tried the finger food." The sweet man looks worried, so I kiss him on the scruffy cheek. "I know how to handle my family, it'll be okay."

"Yeah, but I don't like the thought of you having to go in there and face them on your own."

"I've been doing it my entire life, love." I give him a soft smile. "But it's adorable you care."

His cheeks tinge red before he steps back. "Elle. I'll … find her. Yup. I'll be right here."

"You better be. I'm going to need some eye candy once I'm back."

He turns even redder which is a beautiful sight, but I force the fond thoughts down and trail after my parents. Down the hall and into the studio on the left. Paintings from long before any of us were born line the pristine white walls, and the enormous windows on the south side have a perfect view of downtown Seattle. The Space Needle stands tall against the sky, and I remember looking at it when I was younger, wondering what it would be like to be such an imposing force.

Grandmother perches herself on a settee while my parents squash onto the couch beside her.

I elect to stay standing, not that it gives me any illusion of power against the three people staring back at me.

"To what do I owe this pleasure? Want to congratulate me in private?"

"Hardly." Gran's voice could cut glass and Mom glances over at her, expression as unreadable as ever.

"I'm sorry?"

"Who is that *person* you have brought into your parents' home?"

"My boyf—well, fiancé, I should say. Did you see the ring? It's exquisite, if I say so myself."

She lifts her head, expression somehow getting cold enough to send a trickle of fear down my spine. "None of us have heard of him before today."

"That's because I didn't want to waste your time bringing every man I've ever dated around. We met in Amsterdam and have been doing the long-distance thing for the last few months. But he's it. I knew it from the moment I met him." Kind of. "He'll be an excellent addition to our family."

Dad's bitter laugh is loud. "You're kidding yourself if you think you're marrying that man."

I hook my thumb back over my shoulder. "Did I not just propose?"

"There is a system to these things. Clifford was dating Martha months before proposing. He had his and her families' blessings. They already have finances arranged, company shares negotiated, a list of responsibilities and duties in place for when it comes to things like maintenance, children, house-keeping—"

Oh, dear lord. Not only am I glad this marriage to Christian is total bullshit, but I'm doubly glad I chose not to run it by my parents. *Children negotiations*? Sure, Christian, you have baby number one, and I'll pop out the second, shall I?

Fucking hell, I don't even *want* kids.

But I knew they'd say all this. Or similar, at least, so I'm ready for their disapproval.

I nod, as though I'm agreeing with them. "You're right. I should have run this by you first. I got all swept up in the romance of it all. My entire family around, the love of my life beside me, a beautiful room with a beautiful view … it felt like it was meant to be." I drop my head. "But I understand. I'll go back out there and tell my fiancé that the whole wedding is off. Better to do it now, I suppose, while everyone is still here, rather than have to contact them one by one to spread the news …"

I don't dare look up, but the silence that falls over the room is thick, choking me with disapproval. I have the maddest urge to cackle like I always do in tense situations, and I have no clue how I manage to keep it together.

"There's no way that's happening."

If I'd been a betting man, I would *not* have picked that my mom would be the one to speak first.

"W-what do you mean?" I ask, playing perfectly dumb.

"You've done this now. You're in it. There's no way I'll have a son of mine walking away from a commitment he's made to someone."

"Carina," Dad snaps. "We cannot let this nobody get his hands on our money."

"Grandfather's money," I smoothly correct. Being left out of the will is still a sore spot for him, and damned if I'm going to walk out of here without taking a few little jabs of my own.

"What does this boy *do*?"

"He's the sole heir to a large cryptocurrency inheritance."

Dad throws up his hands. "Play money. Pretend money. Dammit, Émile, I thought you were smarter than that!"

"It's not exactly play money when we're talking tens of millions of dollars."

He huffs, clearly to mark his disapproval, because while it's a lot of money, it has nothing on our fortunes.

"New money is always a risk," Gran says, weighing her words. "There's a reason we're careful of who we marry. These … *people* know nothing of tradition or business. They fritter away their money on cheap thrills and tacky cars, and when things get too hard, they leave. We've never had a divorce in hundreds of years of family history, and I'll be damned if I allow this union to go ahead and for *this boy* to make a mockery of everything we've built."

The amount of self-control I need to keep my mouth closed is herculean, but I somehow pull it off. "Noted."

"End. It." Her piercing gaze almost has me agreeing, but luckily Mom gets there first.

"Think of the gossip. The scandal." Nothing about her face or her tone gives away that she's talking about anything other than the weather. "You know what social media is like these days, I'll be surprised if the news of his engagement hasn't already spread like wildfire."

"Social media." Dad makes a snarling noise. For a man who's supposed to be refined, he certainly devolves into animalistic tendencies while mad.

I rock onto my heels, trying to convey my sheer lack of interest in this whole conversation. No matter what decision they think they're coming to, when I walk out of here, the only thing I'm planning to do is spend time with my fake fiancé. Although, can it still be considered fake if I bought a ring, proposed, and he said yes? The semantics are making my head spin.

Gran's hands tense in her lap, the only outward sign she'll allow that she's not in control of the situation. I've only seen the gesture three other times in my life.

Once, when *that* president was voted in, a second time when a storm took out one of our shipping warehouses, and the third at Pa's funeral.

"You've made your bed, Émile. And God help you if you embarrass this family."

My smile is smugger than I mean it to be. "Don't worry, I honestly don't think that's possible at this point."

I'm feeling good that things are full steam ahead when we walk back out into the main room, and I immediately know something is up. Elle's standing by the tea table, laughing her arse off, and Christian is beside her, beet red, hands in the air like a busted perp. Hey, at least he's not throwing around Trek Wars signs this time.

I approach cautiously to the sound of Christian's stammered apologies.

"What's … what's happening here?" I ask.

My cousin, Neil, answers first. "Your little boy toy grabbed my ass!"

Oh dear lord. There's that need to laugh hysterically again.

"Umm ..."

"I thought it was you," Christian gasps, mouth gaping open like a fish.

In Christian's defense, we do look remarkably alike. And with his hands in the air like that, he's really showing off my ring.

"I do *not* appreciate unsolicited fondling," Neil snaps.

I pull a face. "Well, that's one large difference between the two of us. Maybe my fiancé's hand didn't appreciate a strange ass in it. Or a strange *buttock* for that matter."

Before Neil can catch on to what I've said, I roll my eyes at Elle and steer Christian away.

"I can't leave you for one second, can I?" I ask indulgently.

"I'm sorry. I *really* thought it was you, or I never would have——"

I cut him off with a quick kiss. Because I can in public. It's all keeping up the act and nothing else. No indulging here. I definitely don't linger for a fraction of a second longer than I mean to.

He's smiling when I pull back. "I take it I'm not in trouble?"

"Not at all. In fact, I insist that you never change."

"Couldn't if I wanted to."

"I do have one question though. How could you possibly confuse us with that massive stick shoved up Neil's ass?"

He laughs. "You're right. No clue how I missed it."

"Well, after that meeting, you'll have time to learn. We did it. Congratulations, stranger. You're stuck with me now."

His hand ghosts along my side before his fingers thread through mine. And after so short a time, it already feels like they belong there.

"That's not the threat you think it is."

Chapter 16

Christian

It feels like the afternoon is holding its breath as Émile and I walk, side by side, through Gas Works Park. Gray clouds are gathering out on the horizon, but the sun is still shining here, so families and groups of friends are sitting in clumps all around the grass. The water has started to turn, though, and only a few kayakers and boats are still out there.

We walk past the skeleton of the old gasification plant toward the lookout point, a comfortable silence wrapping around us. After the non-stop atmosphere of the last few weeks, this is exactly what I need.

Well, and a bigger spoon.

I glare at the tiny thing I'm stabbing into my ice cream cup, confused how it's possible to scoop any more than a drip with this thing. My gaze slides sideways to Émile, and I shamelessly watch as he goes to eat another bite. His tongue darts out to catch the ice cream, lips wrapping sinfully around the spoon before his cheeks hollow out as his Adam's apple bobs deliciously in his throat.

I curse, accidentally out loud.

"What's the matter?" Émile asks, his voice holding the same laugh he always seems to be repressing. I'm not sure what he always finds so funny, but I'd like a bit of that. To be able to look at the world and find the humor, instead of being so fucking scared all the time.

I groan, not wanting to tell him the things in my head, but he doesn't hold back with me. And the more time I spend around him, the more comfortable I am that he's not about to tell me I'm a loser with no future, or whatever the hell the guys I've tried to date have told me in the past. So whatever. I'll unleash. Not like I've been great at keeping things locked up anyway. "I'm still really attracted to you."

He about *dies* laughing.

Once he's calm, the silence settles around us again, only I'm smiling this time.

I stab at my ice cream. Spoon is still too small though.

Émile smirks and steals my spoon away. Then he tips up his cup and sinks his teeth into the ice cream. He comes away with it smeared over his nose.

"Much better, don't you think?" he asks.

I scrub at his nose with my thumb. "Yep, there goes the attraction." But I follow his lead and try to eat/pour the ice cream from the cup right into my mouth.

I make a mess.

He makes a mess.

But the grosser and stickier I get, the more my hearts swells.

We reach the lookout and lean against the barrier. There are stickers and graffiti and rust marks all over it, but right ahead, across Lake Union, Seattle stands proudly against the sky.

"There are still so many things that are a mystery about you," Émile says. "For example, I know you taste delicious covered in frosting, but I have no idea what you taste like covered in ice cream." Something lights up in his eyes. "And my cousin now knows what it feels like to have you grab his arse in public, but you've only ever done it to me naked. As your fiancé, I should know these things about the man I'm going to marry."

Grinning, I turn back to my cup and where my ice cream is a half-melted, half-frozen mess and tip it up so it ends up covering my mouth and nose.

"Ooops."

Émile looks fucking *gleeful.* "Let me help you with that." He grabs a fistful of my shirt and tugs me close enough that he can drag his tongue over my mouth, my nose, and when the warmth of his appreciative moan hits my face, I can't help but grab a palmful of his ass.

And he's right.

I should have known immediately that Neil wasn't him.

Because Émile's ass is one of a kind.

"My future husband isn't shy about getting frisky in public," he says. "That's a big, fat pro for our life together."

Oh, man. I turn away from him, clearing my throat and wishing I could ask for my spoon back so I could stab point-lessly at my ice cream. It's getting too easy to get lost in this lie. For weeks we've been planning wedding things and talking details and meeting with obscure family members who weren't at the lunch where he proposed. Even though most of my life right now is centered around the wedding, when it's just me and Émile, I'm able to forget.

I smack my lips and turn my attention toward the Space Needle.

Émile's boney elbow nudges my arm. "You've turned intro-spective."

"Yeah. Sorry. Whenever things get a bit too much, I always come here to think."

"Don't be sorry. There's nothing wrong with living in your head. But if you wanted to share those thoughts, I'm always happy to hear them."

"I think I share too many thoughts with you." I glance quickly his way and back across the water again. "We haven't known each other long and look at where we are."

"Standing on Lake Union? I hate to tell you this, but I've been here plenty of times before."

"Really? Here I was thinking you snobby folks from Maple Park never slummed it in the GP District."

Émile is uncharacteristically quiet as he turns a frown toward his hands. "When I was younger, my grandfather used to bring me here to fly kites. All the time when I was little, then on visits home once I was shipped off to school. We made a kite once. It was ... right before I left for Cambridge. It wasn't as busy here because the American school year had already begun. We came to fly it mid-week and he was so excited when we got it off the ground, even though it wasn't the most aero-dynamic."

"You? Not good at something?" I pretend to gasp.

"It was fine, but we were no Wright Brothers." Émile's face falls, and I don't like it. His face was made to be smiling. His lips supposed to be holding back that always ready laugh. Eyes bursting with amusement. They're locked off now. "That was the last time we went."

"I'm sorry."

He brushes me off with a shake of his head. "Kite flying. I outgrew it before I was ten, but he loved it so much. I humored him. He was the only person in my family who acted like he gave a damn."

"Your sister?"

"We were ... different back then. Always had each other's backs, of course, but we went to different schools, different colleges. She was—and still is—as lost as I am. We're bonded through family trauma, whereas Pa just … loved me." Émile's face transforms to horror. "Sorry. Here I am going on about all this, to you, when … well, you—"

"Don't have a family?"

"Well, I wasn't planning on saying it like *that*."

"Why not?" Phrasing it differently doesn't change a thing. "It's true. And actually, it's kinda a relief to know that *some* family members aren't total dickwobbles."

"I'm sorry, what?"

I shrug roughly. "Seemed appropriate."

"I'll say."

It's my turn to nudge him with my elbow. "Tell me about your Pa."

"Really?"

"I've made you listen to every thought that leaks out of my mouth. At least this is something we can both miss. My grandparents used to be great, too. Until they weren't."

With a heavy sigh, he links his arm through mine and gives it a squeeze. "Pa was … blindingly rich. Head of our family, adored Gran even though I couldn't picture two people who could be more wrong for each other. She liked that, I think. That he was so besotted with her that he was happy for her to take unofficial control of the family, while he played with his toys, and she took advantage of his absentmindedness. He hardly ever said no."

"What kind of toys?" I ask, before he can go off on a rant. "Though just a heads-up, if we're talking dildos and fleshlights, I'm out."

He leans into his hold on my arm. "Model trains. He was a collector. A trainspotter, or a, ah … *train buff*. When I'd have a few days away from campus, I'd jump on the Eurostar and send him photos of different trains, different stations. He's been all over Europe himself plenty of times, but he used to get so excited by the photos. He'd call me while I was on board to listen to the familiar hums and rattles. The train horns." Émile laughs, this one soft and private, for him and his memories. "He got diagnosed with Alzheimer's during my last year at Cambridge. Passed away a little over a month ago."

"Favorite thing about him?"

"He used to dress like a hobo whenever I visited him at home and when he got drunk, his French accent got so thick no one could understand him."

"I've got the dressing like a hobo thing down pat. No wonder you couldn't stay away from me."

"You do remind me of him in some ways, and before things get creepy, I'll preface by saying *all* those ways are fully clothed and PG." He hooks an eyebrow upward in my direction, and hey, even I know joking about dead grandpas is bad manners.

"Okay, then, what ways?"

"You're both good people."

I point at my face. "Trashed my cousin's wedding, try again."

"Not on purpose."

"Do I need to remind you that we met because I wanted to lie to my whole family?"

"Yes, but it wasn't for a vindictive reason. It wasn't to make yourself appear better than them. It was because you're dying for their support and respect, when quite frankly, with maybe the exception of your cousin, none of them deserve a second of your time."

I shoot him a cheeky look. "And you do?"

"That remains to be seen, but I sure fucking hope so."

I squeeze his arm, feeling smug, wishing I was as good with words as he is so I could tell him I think he's a great goddamn human himself. It goes beyond being *good*. He's like a light.

Shines brightest on the people around him until he burns out. Everything he's told me he does so far, he does for other people.

"I'm having a charity night soon. To raise money for Alzheimer's. I hope you'll come."

See? Exactly like that. "Of course I will."

I might have only made up all that shit for the wedding to get their respect or whatever, but it was still *for me*. My fingers absentmindedly find the engagement ring and I turn it around and around, curious if Émile ever does stuff just for *him*.

"So your Pa was a good person?" I find myself asking.

"I'm not sure. To me, he was, and I want to say yes, but then I remember the letter, and I start questioning. All his life he had all that money and did nothing with it. It wasn't until he got sick, and it was too late, that he regretted things. I don't know who he was as a father, but my mom didn't turn out great, and I have no idea who he was at work. With employees …"

Émile's right that his Pa's letter was too little, too late. He's definitely guilty of a whole bunch, even if it's stemmed in negligence, or naivety. But what the hell does it matter now? Before I came out, if one of my grandparents had passed away, the last thing I would have wanted to know is that their love for me was conditional. That they were flawed. So I push down my doubt and say, "Since there's no way you can ever ask him those things, there's no point fucking up your good memories by worrying. He sounded great. You're allowed to love him for that. Without guilt."

"Thank you." The relief on Émile's face is worth the lie. This once.

"I'm not going to see you much after Monday," I remind him. As soon as the show starts, my days will be absolutely full. I'll be tired and grumpy a lot of the time, and excited and running high the rest. My time will be limited. We've talked a lot about the next three weeks and pausing wedding planning because at the end of the day, my show, my *career* is real, the marriage is not.

I need to remember that.

Chapter 17

Émile

Christian: *Fuck, did you see this?*

I click on the link that immediately follows his message and there, in full detail, right down to his goddamn ring, is a photo of Christian and me walking along Gas Works Park the other day. Right under *Seattleite*'s encouraging heading of "Shipping heir, Émile Cromwell, slumming it in the District with mystery man." Nothing in the sorry excuse for an article mentions the ring or our engagement, but a quick skim of the comments shows it didn't go unnoticed.

Fuck.

Normally the engagement isn't a surprise and there's a photographer on hand, ready to take official announcement photos, but considering that day was a blur of family disapproval and Neil's bum, it didn't exactly sit high on my list of priorities.

But now people are speculating. Either Christian is engaged to someone else and having an affair with me, or Émile Cromwell is officially off the market. Lying to my family is one thing, but lying to the world has slightly heavier ramifications if we're found out.

Me: *You okay?*

Christian: *Think so. It's just a bit weird to see my face on some random gossip site.*

I don't point out to him that now they've run it, we'll likely be popping up all over the internet. Given no one in my family is famous—far too crass for the Cromwells—we're usually left alone by the American obsession with celebrity culture. The only time we're bothered is when one of us fucks up—thankfully a rare event—or when there's large shifts within the family. Being as wealthy as we are, holding a huge amount of power through our supplying the world, means we're always going to draw notoriety.

Pa's passing brought a whole pile of speculation onto our inheritances and who would be the heir to step up to the board, and I've seen news of my return to America, meaning I'm ready to settle down and start a family of my own. Speculation about me and Darcy has been news fodder for a while now, and I knew what I was doing when I was seen purchasing that engagement ring.

But that afternoon at the park had been private. A quiet moment. One where neither of us were pretending, where we didn't feel the overwhelming pressure of what we were doing. I shared things with him I hadn't shared with anyone and maybe he doesn't appreciate the significance of me talking about Pa, but I know that moment brought us closer.

Me: *How did you go tonight? Did you break a leg?*

Christian: *Thankfully not literally. But yeah, it was pretty good.*

Me: *Only "pretty good"? You mean I don't get to see you all week because you're off living your dream, but your dream is only PRETTY good?*

Christian: *Okay, smart-ass. It was amazing.*

I smile, this happy ache settling in my chest as I flop back onto my bed.

Me: *What's your favorite part?*

Christian: *It's kinda hard to explain. The atmosphere, maybe? It's like … this ball of tension that surrounds everything, and then you get on stage and it snaps and you fucking fly. I get to be someone else for a few hours and it's like my brain just switches off.*

Me: *No catastrophes?*

Christian: *Nah, we rehearse so much that everything is second nature. I don't need to overthink every single thing I'm doing. It's the one place I'm not scared I'm going to mess everything up.*

Me: *You don't mess everything up with me.*

My message shows as read, but he doesn't immediately respond. The absence of typing stretches out between us, and my breath catches in my chest until the dots finally appear.

Christian: *I'm starting to believe that.*

Maybe it's only a start, but I'll take it. For this thing to work, we have to trust each other completely, but it goes beyond trust. I *want* to make Christian feel good. I *want* him to be comfortable and know his worth. And before this thing is over between us, I'm making it my mission to show him how amazing he is.

For, umm, no other reason than the fact he deserves it.

I send him back a blowing kiss emoji and roll over onto my front to where my emails are open on my laptop. I'm deep into planning for this charity event, and it feels good to be working on something I care about. Something I'm good at. Whenever I'm back in the States for an indeterminate amount of time, I need to be working, and the only part of the family business I have any interest in touching is the charity offset. Sure, it was originally started to reduce our taxes and bad press, but even with the shady origins, it's the one part I actually like.

Because, you know, people are okay with forgetting that

your enormous ships pollute the seas as long as you start a charity to benefit marine life.

Let's not worry about *fixing* the problem so long as we're retroactively throwing money at it.

With the most paper thin of defenses, supplies do need to make it to other parts of the globe, but I wish it didn't have to come at so high of a cost. Still, I'll take my family's guilt money and make as much of it as I possibly can.

My charity event won't be attached to the business, but I've had enough experience now that I know what I'm doing.

I've got the venues short-listed and contacted, a list of caterers to try, contacts to reach out to for donations, and a tentative guest list. But every time I try to focus on more, my mind insists on creeping back toward Christian. I wish I could sulk and tell him I miss having him around, but I refuse. This play is important to him and it only goes for three weeks. He needs my support, not me distracting him from something he's been working so hard at.

Still, it's hard not to keep checking my phone for a reply, knowing full well he's gone out for a quick drink with the cast before he heads home to sleep it off. It's the final show of the first week before he has the next two days off, and from the phone conversations we've had recently, he's exhausted.

And his lack of presence at family meals isn't going unnoticed.

All week I've fielded questions about which school Christian attended, which families he's associated with, and whether he's a hunting or a polo man—Dad's scoff when I reminded him Americans hardly know what polo is still echoes in my ears.

I've been keeping things close to the chest, because it's only a matter of time before they work out that Christian is estranged from his family and not going to inherit one red cent.

Which means shit all to me but will cause a catastrophic melt-down for them.

Unfortunately for them, there's literally nothing they can do at this point.

Hmm … The sooner we're officially public, the less power they'll have to meddle with our relationship.

Breaking up when our social circles already know about my proposal is one thing, doing so at an international level? Might as well put Gran in her grave.

Me: *We're going to have to announce that we're together. Sooner, rather than later. I know you only have two days off next week, but could I schedule something for then?*

Christian: *What do you mean by "schedule"?*

Me: *A photographer. Maybe even someone to write the announcement for The New York Post.*

Christian: *Jesus.*

Me: *Yeah, it's a lot.*

Christian: *I know you warned me, but I don't think I understood how BIG everything would be.*

Me: *Are you having second thoughts?*

Christian: *Fuck, no. It just seems really dumb and over the top to me.*

Me: *Yeah … me too.*

Christian: *Sorry. But yeah, I'll do whatever. Just let me know.*

Of course he would. Our announcement photos could be of us launching ourselves out of a plane, and he'd do it. Still, I can't get past what he said.

It's dumb and over the top.

It *is*.

Those are the types of things I've never been able to under-stand about my family; we operate under the illusion of wanting privacy, but we're happy to broadcast all the family changes to the world. The carefully controlled narrative they spin is all bullshit.

My time in Amsterdam was chalked up to working abroad, when it couldn't have been further from the truth. I'd been hiding out, living in a tiny one-bedroom flat, making coffee and waiting tables to pay the bills and it had been amazing. It had been *real*.

It *hadn't* been a charity event charging five thousand dollars a ticket.

I chew my thumbnail—*nasty habit,* says my mom's voice— and compare all the truths to the lies. This isn't the world I want to live in. It's not the impression I want to give people. Everywhere I go people are struggling and they look up to the people with the wealth and the power and the status. They see these perfect fucking lives and aspire to reach these lofty goals, when what they're reaching for doesn't actually exist.

I'm part of that problem.

My sticking my head in the sand while in Amsterdam.

My posting from yachts and dinners in expensive suits that cost more than Christian's monthly rent every time I'm in America or visit family in England. My absolute silence and scheming while people suffer.

Even the reminder that I'm *planning* to do good doesn't help. Instead, it has the slimy quality of a cheap excuse.

Pa's will is ironclad. There's nothing anyone can do to take my trust *or* the money I'll be entitled to. I've grown up so used to my every action being watched and judged and made to measure up to some arbitrary standard, when really … what can they do?

What can they do?

Sure, there are other ways they can cut me off at the knees, but restricting my access to the properties they own, the planes they use, the business I never fucking intended to run anyway —it's all what I intend to estrange myself from.

Which begs the question … what am I waiting for?

If I don't want to play their games anymore, then all I have to do is stop playing. Might as well start now as I intend to go on, and while my marriage will be nothing short of a sham, I can at least start trying to be honest about the rest of it.

Well, *some* of it.

There's still the charity to consider, my sister and her reputation, and while I'm confident that there's nothing they can officially do about Pa's will, I'm not going to push them to contest it and tie the money up legally for any longer than it needs to be.

So, baby steps for now.

And the first of many will be claiming my engagement. Publicly.

In exactly the way I want.

Chapter 18

Christian

It's dark by the time I get home and even though I opted for water instead of alcohol while I was out, the headache behind my eyes is intense. It's been a long, tiring week, but even with the headache, even with the ache in my muscles, I'm fucking *happy*.

While I'm so much more confident on stage than off, it's not often I make it through an entire performance seamlessly, but today was like magic. Feeling competent always catches me by surprise, which is why I love performing so much. I have time to practice the moves, over and over, until they become muscle memory and I can switch off my brain.

If I don't think through my next step, I'm going to end up on the floor, but performing takes that uncertainty away. I always know what my next step will be. The music, the costumes, the makeup ... it's like I'm someone else.

Plus, the swell of applause from the crowd never gets old. My cheeks hurt from how hard I've been smiling.

One day I'd love to book a talking role—I'm not leading

guy material—but I remind myself it's baby steps. This is the first time I've ever been on stage for a show as large as this, before now, all my experience has been small, local productions and a few understudy roles. This is big for me, and I'm trying to drink in as much of the atmosphere as possible in case this never happens again. I'm still not convinced it wasn't a complete fluke. Or a mistake.

Every good thing in my life always comes with that undercurrent of *when will it end?* I'm always waiting, always preparing myself for the inevitable decline. I've been on this cycle for my entire life, every good moment is followed by a crash. Some small, like not booking a job I'd thought I'd nailed the audition for, and some large, like my family kicking me out. I'd been naive to think they'd be accepting in the first place, but I'd never thought they'd go that far.

I shake off the melancholy and remind myself that this is what I've been working toward, and while it's here, I'm allowed to enjoy it. If the rest of our performances are like this week was, I swear I'll never come down from this high. We might not be selling out the theatre, but the people who have come to see it have enjoyed themselves. It's the visibility that's a bitch. There's only so much marketing that can compete with the big productions.

It'll be sad to go back to the monotony of real life, but at the moment I'm so far removed from that it's hard to remember. Besides, I'm not sure how soon that's going to happen when I have Émile and his crazy plan to return to.

I jog up onto our shadowy front porch, and almost jump out of my skin when someone moves in the dark.

"Umm, surprise?"

The familiar British accent has a smile splitting my face. "What are you doing here?"

Émile doesn't answer at first, just takes a step closer so I can make out his face in the light coming from the dining room. His eyebrows are knotted, lines around his eyes tense.

"What's wrong?" he asks. "Don't you want to see me?"

"Of course, but we're meeting up tomorrow."

Apparently that isn't the right thing to say because the curl at his lips drops. "I should have waited. My apologies."

"Your *apologies?*" I laugh at how stiff he sounds and catch him around the waist before he can run off. It's not until I tug him against me and meet his wary eyes again that the most ridiculous and amazing thought hits me. "You didn't miss me, did you?"

"Don't be absurd. How on earth could I miss someone I'm planning to marry who looks adorable crashing into cakes and sexy when he gropes my cousin and then blows me off for an entire week because he has *passions* that he wants to follow?"

I'm smiling as I nod. "He sounds like a total asshole."

"Complete and utter twat. Who I maybe missed. Just a little, of course."

"Of course." My chest feels like it grows too big, warmth surging through my limbs and pooling in my fingers. "Maybe … maybe the twat missed you a bit too."

His smile trembles back to life and mine is still out of control. I wish I could avoid those thoughts and the way they tumble out of my mouth because *I'm* the one who set the damn rules between us. For good reason.

If it was up to him, we probably would have had a repeat by now. Maybe a lot of them. But he's not the one who pressed himself up against me. He's not the one desperate to feel his hair. Hungry for the feel of his tongue against mine.

My large inhale is filled with his sharp, crisp cologne, and it's a real effort to take a step back from him.

I slip my hand into his, my fingers slotting perfectly between his fingers, and then I tug him toward the door.

"Well, you're here now. Might as well stay over."

"Only if you insist."

I shake my finger at him. "But no funny business."

"Agreed." He drops his voice as we step inside. "But I suppose I should tell you there's nothing funny about you naked and on your knees."

I half laugh, half sob as I drop my head back. "Fuck, you're making this hard."

"Poor choice of words, Christian."

"We're going to behave ourselves, dammit."

"Of course we will."

"Because we're grown-ass adults who have self-control." I glance back at him to find him grinning at me.

"Maybe if you say it enough times, you'll believe it."

"And maybe if I jerk off in the shower before sharing a bed with you, that'll help too."

"Sounds like a solid plan to me."

Somehow we're able to sneak inside and upstairs before anyone catches sight of us. I'm assuming most of my roommates are out either working or drinking, but since the front door was unlocked, at least one of them is home. I love them, but I'm relieved I don't have to deal with any of them right now. The only thing I want to do is get through the fastest solo shower session in history and then climb into bed beside Émile.

I plant him on the side of my bed with strict instructions to strip off while I'm gone but before I turn to leave, he grabs my arm.

"There is another reason I'm here. Other than the possibly missing you a smidge."

"Oh yeah?"

He swallows roughly, and sets both hands purposely on his thighs. "I don't want engagement photos."

"Huh." My heartbeat kicks up a notch as my brain immediately spins into overdrive because if he doesn't want to do this anymore ... well, we're both kinda fucked from that angle, but at least I won't need to jerk off in the shower, I guess. "Umm why?"

"Because like you said, it's dumb. Quite frankly, I hate all the pompous rigmarole I've been raised with and I've decided I don't want to play that game anymore. And so we're going to announce this thing like any average couple would."

Well, that sounds a whole lot better than I'd been expecting. "Social media?"

"Exactly."

"I guess now isn't a great time to mention that having a couple hundred thousand followers isn't exactly 'average,' huh?"

"Please let me have my delusion."

I lean down to brush a light kiss over his lips before I've caught up to what I'm doing. As soon as it hits me, I straighten. Clear my throat. Avoid his eye. "Right, well. I'll be back once I've rubbed one out."

"And I'll be in your bed waiting."

Fuck, fuck, fuck. Émile is teaching me so many new things about myself, including the fact that I'm apparently a goddamn masochist. I grab a towel and head for the bathroom but before I can pull my door open, a *whoops* makes me stop.

I glance back at Émile to find his pants and briefs down below his mouthwatering bubble butt.

He sends me a cheeky look over his shoulder. "I got a little overzealous. Don't think of me while you're showering, will you?"

My groan carries me all the way to the bathroom.

Where I definitely don't think about him and that incredible ass while I definitely don't touch myself, and definitely *definitely* don't blow my load in world-record time.

By the time I get back to my bedroom, dry and in my sleep shorts, Émile is stretched out under my blanket, hands tucked behind his head. His lean biceps stretch enticingly under his skin and I let out a self-deprecating moan as I climb in beside him.

"This is probably going to be the shittiest night's sleep I'll ever have."

"You invited me to stay."

"You showed up at my place at ten at night."

Émile rolls onto his side and I mirror him. "I only wanted to see you. And I did. You could have sent me on my way after that."

I narrow my eyes. "Why doesn't that feel like the full story?"

And in a rare body swap, Émile runs his fingers over my bedspread, following the design, nerves displayed on his face. "I wanted to get it over with."

"What?"

"The picture. It's just … I had this revelation tonight that I'm as much a part of the problem as my family is and I wanted to change that. To distance myself. And sure, a photo doesn't sound like much, but to them it'll be catastrophic. They've been ice cold toward me since the proposal, and this will be another way I'm throwing tradition in their faces. But I want to do it. And I'm scared if I don't do it while I'm sure, that I might come up with a thousand excuses why I shouldn't."

"Fuck. Moments like this make me kinda glad I don't have to worry about family." We both know that's a total lie, but neither of us deserve what our families have put us through. I roll over to switch on my lamp. "Let's do it now then."

"Really?"

"Why not?" I shuffle back until I'm sitting up against the headboard. This is probably the last thing I wanna be doing, but oh well. It's either this or some stuffy photoshoot, and I don't think I'd be able to get through something like that without dying from suffocating propriety. Or accidentally tripping, falling, and ending up with a dick pic splashed all over TMZ.

Émile wriggles up beside me and I wrap an arm around his warm back. We're both shirtless and I know from the way he's leaning heavily into my side that he's trying to soak up as much skin and body heat as I am.

He lifts his phone and I only have a second to figure out how to do this. My hand awkwardly hovering in mid-air wouldn't be a great display of the ring. Instead, I set my hand on his bare chest, then turn my head, pressing my face to his cheek and trying for the brightest smile I can manage. Sitting here, with him in my arms, his ring on my finger, makes finding that smile a million times easier.

Émile takes the shot.

Then he laughs when he pulls it up to inspect. "Wow, you must be great at what you do. You look half in love with me."

"Gotta pull off the act somehow." The words feel empty.

I watch his face for any sign of doubt as he uploads the photo and types out a few words. "You good with this?" he asks.

"Course."

"Okay." He hits post, then turns his phone off. I still haven't let him go. "All done."

"Yeah."

Émile tilts his head to meet my eye. "You okay there?"

"Just fucking peachy. I've always wanted a fiancé I'm not even allowed to touch."

"You can touch me any time you like. But I understand why you won't."

"Maybe ... maybe once it's all over—"

"Maybe."

We watch each other for a moment before Émile leans in and brushes a soft kiss against my lips this time. "Go to sleep, love. We'll worry about the rest in the morning."

Chapter 19

Émile

"Christian McCaully Kilpatrick!"

I jolt awake at the sudden shout, and Christian shoots upright as his door flies open. An elderly lady stands there, gripping her cane, dark eyes narrowed on the two of us.

"So it's true? The dearest of all my babies trying to break my heart by not even telling me he has a man and got engaged …"

I'm trying to keep up with what she's saying, but I'm so lost. That isn't Christian's mom, or grandmother, so … who the hell is she?

Christian groans. "Auntie Agatha, this is my, uh—"

"Fiancé," I happily help out.

"Yes. That. Émile. He's my … Émile."

Agatha's eyes soften. "It's so wonderful to meet you, darling boy." Then her gaze snaps back to the man beside me. "You're bottom of the list now. You'll be lucky to even make it into the will."

"I thought Seven was bottom of the list?" Christian asks.

Agatha sniffs haughtily. "He was. Until this. You have no idea the pain you've inflicted on a helpless old lady."

"Seven's ranking at second now," another voice says before Gabe passes Agatha and joins us in the bedroom. "He helped with her groceries yesterday."

"He's *such* a good boy."

Christian *hmphs*. "You weren't saying that when his music kept you up half the night."

"Maybe I'm becoming a fan of BDSM."

Christian buries his face in his hands, ears going pink.

"I'm sorry, what?" I ask, living for this glorious conversation.

"She means EDM," Gabe explains, glee lacing his voice. "But it's more fun not to correct her."

"At the risk of sounding impolite, Agatha is your … aunt?"

"She lives next door," Gabe explains. "And is always sticking her nose into our business."

"Christian, you're back in the will, Gabriel's out."

Christian sends an angelic look at Gabe who flips him off in return.

"With the number of times you change this will of yours, there'll be no money left to leave people," Gabe points out.

"Ungrateful little turd. That's the last time I make chicken soup for you when you're sick. Not that I'll be able to do that anyway, once you've—"

Gabe's face pales and he hurries to wrap his arms around Agatha. "You know I'm only playing. I love you. We all do."

Christian rests his hands dramatically over his chest. "We'd be nothing without you."

The harsh lines in her face soften. "That's better. Now. I want to hear all about your Émile."

Oh no. I may not have many limits, but apparently I've found one. We're not strictly naked, but sitting around in my briefs, telling an old lady how I met the fake love of my life is where I draw the line.

Especially when I'd rather be wrapped back around his body like I was when I'd woken up.

"Why don't we meet them downstairs?" Gabe suggests, trying to steer her from the room, but before they can reach the doorway, another man bursts inside. He's got blue hair, pale skin, and a smear of paint by his ear.

"I need to borrow your watch." He barrels across the room, pulls open Christian's nightstand and starts searching through the drawer.

"Is that a dildo, Christian?" Agatha asks. "I can't see you having use for that when you've got a dashing gentleman right beside you."

"No!" He shoves the drawer closed, blush seeping down into his bare chest. "Jesus, Xander. Go and borrow Seven's."

"I tried. The battery's dead." Xander presses one hand to his chest, taking a deep breath that he holds for a beat, before letting it all out again. "My heart rate has been high all morning and now …" He does the breath thing again. "It hurts. I think … I think I might be having a heart attack."

"Holy shit." I grab my phone, ready to call emergency, when Christian places a hand over mine.

"Sure it's not indigestion again?"

"I … I don't know."

Gabe squeezes Xander's shoulder. "I'll go and get Seven."

He leaves and Agatha levels Xander with a glare.

"I've made it perfectly clear you're not to die before me, got it?"

"Yes, ma'am."

"If you do, who will I leave my fortunes to? You're my favorite, you know?"

Xander manages a small smile that he exchanges with Christian, hand still pressed to his chest. "Thanks, Aggy."

She hobbles out of the room and her bellow follows her down the hall. "Seven, you get your ass up and that boy to the hospital now. So help me god if he dies, you'll be out of the will!"

"I take it she likes that threat?" I say to Christian. "Also, your middle name is McCaully?"

"No, my middle name is David. Apparently that wasn't Irish enough for her."

Xander whines. "Maybe it *is* just indigestion."

"Does your left arm hurt?" I ask.

"Don't answer that," Christian says to Xander before turning to me. "Seven will take him to the pharmacy. The people there know us and will run through some basic health checks, which is the only thing that will settle him. Symptoms listing only makes him worse."

"My left fingers *do* feel a bit numb."

"And that's my cue." An enormous guy with deep red hair and about a million tattoos joins us and wraps his arm possessively around Xander. "Come on, little dude, I ain't carrying you this time."

They leave and we're finally, finally alone again. I flop back onto the pillows. "Well, that was one way to wake up. Are you sure we shouldn't be worried about him?"

"Nope. Xander is perfectly healthy, physically. But once he gets it into his head, there's no deterring him until he's seen someone." Christian's stunning face hovers over me, the remnants of his earlier blush still sitting high on his cheeks. "Sorry about all that. Like I said, boundaries kinda don't exist for us."

"You're certainly surrounded by a lot of energy." I can't help but compare it to the stifling silence and low murmurs that make up ninety percent of my life. It reminds me of the busy streets in Amsterdam, the cheerful conversations, the flood of color that everything was washed in. "I don't want to leave," I say. I'm not even joking.

"Hiding from that photo we posted?"

Well, hell, I'd completely forgotten. I suppose that explains how Agatha found out, but given she's not exactly within my target follower demographic, I suspect the announcement has traveled farther than my social media.

Christian reaches for my phone and his eyes almost bulge out when it turns back on. "Oh, fuck."

"What's wrong?"

"I just … I guess I didn't realize that it would be a big deal." He watches as more and more notifications fill the screen. "This is … wow." His inhale is shaky. "Okay. Umm … I'm spinning out a little …"

"Ignore it."

"But …" He passes me my phone and grabs his own. The breath he was holding rushes from him. "Nothing."

"Well, you don't have social media, do you?"

"I do. Under Chris Patrick."

"Thankfully it doesn't look as though anyone has linked that name to you, which is surprising." I skim some of the posts I've been tagged in. "They've figured out your real name. Do you have any photos on the Chris Patrick account that would show up in an image search?"

He thinks for a moment. "Only ones in full costume, but it's mostly the sets and backstage and whatever that I post about."

"Well, you've gotten lucky. Let's hope it stays that way."

Christian groans and face plants into his pillow. "Now I think maybe I'm the one having the heart attack," comes his muffled voice.

There's a low *meow* and then a grumpy-looking tabby cat jumps onto the bed and curls up beside Christian.

"Naw kitty …" I reach out to pat its head, when it lets out

a low warning sound, ears back, hair behind its head standing on end. My hand darts back to my side and Christian peeks out at me, bringing a heavy hand down on the cat's head.

"Shut up, Kismet. He's a friend." He pats the cat roughly, and while the creature doesn't exactly look like it's enjoying the attention, it simply narrows its eyes and deals with it.

I want to be resentful that the cat apparently hates me but is happy to be pummeled under Christian's palm, but I get it. If he was touching *me* like that, there'd be no complaints.

"So, when you said you had five roommates, what you really meant to tell me was that you had five roommates, one of whom you say I love you to–"

"Actually, I say that to all of them, just not as much as Gabe."

"Right. Five roommates *who you love*, a crazy old lady next door who's your adoptive aunt slash sugar grandma, and a psychopathic, obsessive kitty."

He props himself on his elbow, thinking. "Yeah, that sounds about right."

"I absolutely adore it all."

"Well, that's good, because I was going to suggest that we hang out here today. Maybe order in, watch a movie."

"As much as I love that idea, we should probably be seen in public together. Knowing my family, they're waiting until I get home to begin the grand jury, so if we can generate some positive news like … an art gallery outing, or a charity event–"

His soft lips land on mine. The kiss is fleeting, over far too quickly.

I glower at him as he pulls back. "So that's it, is it? Whenever we want to stop the other person talking, we'll just kiss them."

"Seems like a good plan to me."

Kismet shakes himself out and jumps off the bed.

"Thank god," I say, before wriggling closer to him. "I was beginning to get jealous that the cat was in my spot."

Christian laughs, thumb swiping gently over my cheek. "Sorry to cut you off. It's just … last night you said you didn't want to be part of the problem anymore, and isn't doing all that playing into what they want from you?"

He's right. It's startling I hadn't realized that's exactly where my thought process went. To damage control. Not the things that I actually want to do. Not the things that represent who I am and what I want out of life. No, my first thoughts were how to smooth things over with my family.

And what the hell does it matter?

They can't touch me. They can make things difficult, of course, but that's costly and time-consuming for both parties involved.

"Okay," I say. "Let's go with your suggestion. Food and movies. Maybe you can show me around the house too."

"Oooh yeah. Wait until you see Xander's paint room."

"His what?"

"Well, we used to call it a studio, but he got so much paint everywhere that the owners have told him he can do what he likes with the place. There are murals on all the walls and even a few small ones on the floor and ceiling. It's a lot and a mess, but actually looks kind of cool."

"I'd love to see it." I mean it.

Gabe walks back in without knocking, shaking his phone in one hand. "Yeah, well, you're going to have to wait. The hunt's on. We've gotta go. *Now.*"

Chapter 20

Christian

Hell yes. I'd been so worried about missing the hunt with how stuffed full my next few weeks are, but the taco gods are shining down on me today. I scramble out of bed, grabbing the first T-shirt I find to tug over my head before struggling into a pair of pants.

Émile watches me from the bed. "I thought we were staying in today?"

"We can. Later." At the confused look that crosses his face, I pick up his clothes and hand them over. "Sorry, babe, but it's *the hunt*." I widen my eyes, begging him to get a move on.

Thankfully he takes pity on me. He climbs out of bed and yanks his pants on. "What the hell are we hunting?"

"Tacos."

His hands fumble his pants button. "And here I was expecting birds, or ... or ..."

"Of course not."

"Not that I don't love the enthusiasm," he says, waving a

hand between me and Gabe. "But, uh, *why* do the tacos need hunting?"

"I'm not sure I can support your marriage if it comes with *this* much negativity," Gabe says, before tilting his head back into the hall and shouting, "*Madden*, put some clothes on. Hunt time!"

The loud *bang* above us is a clear sign Madden's fallen out of bed in his rush to get ready.

"I'm still so confused," Émile mutters, shrugging into his shirt.

"We'll explain on the way. Just *please* hurry."

The three of us barely spare enough time to brush our teeth before jogging out of the house. Once a month, on a random day, at a random time, GP District has its taco hunt. Tac'obout Tacos is a taco truck that goes way back in the GPD and when the words "come find me" hit their social media, people stop what they're doing and search. I don't even know when it started, but one day my phone lit up with a screenshot from Xander and it's been a monthly event for us all since.

"I've literally never heard of this before," Émile says, jogging after us.

"Clearly not part of the cool kids' cult."

"Yes, well, Cambridge tends to frown on cult-like behavior."

Gabe snorts. "You all still worship a king. If that's not cultish I don't know what is."

"That's the first time I've heard the monarchy referred to as a cult, and I can't help but think there's something there."

I give Gabe a shove. "No deep thinking allowed. All brain power needs to be channeled toward where the truck will be."

"How long do we have to find it?" Émile asks.

"No time limit. First person there gets free tacos for the rest of the month."

His lips twitch with that laugh that's always bubbling under the surface for him.

I pretend to be exasperated, but I couldn't be further from it. "Yeah, yeah let it out."

So he does.

And I'm not saying I *can't* look away, but it's pretty fucking hard to do.

"I got the map," Madden says, jogging over to us. Despite the cooler morning, he's wearing gym shorts, a tight T, and his Mariners cap on backward. But hey, I can't see his dick for once, so that's a win. "Last time it was over here." He zooms in on the map on his phone. We've marked off all the previous locations, like we have some sort of plan in place, but really, it hasn't been any help.

"Looks like that area down near Georgetown hasn't been popular," Émile points out. "Think it could be there somewhere?"

"It's possible. It doesn't go near Maple Park much either, though."

"Yes," Émile says, laying his accent on thick and posh. "But that's because people in Maple Park wouldn't be caught dead eating a taco, let alone one from a food truck."

"Okay, so … take a gamble on Georgetown?" I suggest.

Gabe starts typing on this phone. "I'll text the others to meet us there."

We head for Madden's truck and pile in before he tears away from the curb.

"If you're all in a race for who can find it first, wouldn't it make more sense to split up?" my poor, naive partner-in-crime asks.

"But then we'd be split up." Madden's voice holds a giant *duh* in it.

"But you can't all win, surely."

"We can't, but I don't think any of us ever have before so"—I shrug—"we don't do it to win."

"But you just flew out of the house like your arse was on fire."

"We give it a solid go," Gabe explains. "And we *want* to win. Someday. But, like, that's not the point of it."

"So what is the point?"

It's lucky Madden has pulled up to the light because the four of us turn confused looks on Émile.

"To … to hang out," I explain, wondering how the fuck that wasn't obvious. "Something to do."

Émile's hazel gaze slides from me to where Gabe and Madden have turned around in the front, and he hurries to hold up his hands. "My mistake. I guess I'm not used to people doing something just … to do it. All the people I know are only out to win."

Gabe wrinkles his nose. "But winning is so … temporary."

"What do you mean?"

"Well, so we get the free tacos, then what? We eat, the month ends, we forget about it in a year. It's the same with any award or sports or—"

"*Not* sports," Madden cuts in.

"Oh yeah? So where are all your Little League trophies?"

Madden's jaw clenches and I whack the back of Gabe's head. "Low move."

"What? It proves my point. Mads got hurt, and that was it. The sport moved on. His parents either threw his trophies in storage or dumped them. Either way he'll never see them again. They're only … *things*." He looks out his window. "Who cares about things?"

I could face palm if it wasn't so obvious. Welcome, Émile, to the hot mess that is my life and my loved ones. For someone with his shit together, I have no idea how he views our dysfunctional communal living, but I refuse to think about it too carefully. He's stuck marrying me and then once that's over, the rest of it won't matter. His opinion, like Madden's trophies, will be gone.

"We could check beneath the overpass near Madison," Émile says, and it thankfully breaks the tension that's fallen around us.

"Good thinking." Madden takes a sharp left, sending me into Émile who takes advantage of the closeness to rest his hand on my thigh.

His warm breath tickles my ear as he says, "You're sexy when you're being all sweet and sentimental."

"I'll keep that in mind."

I return to my own side, but Émile doesn't let go of my leg. The casual affection hits right in the center of my chest, and I cover his hand with mine, trying not to feel too smug that I get to have this. There might be a limit, but being with him is giving me all of the first-date jitters.

We check the overpass and by the lake, down near Gas Works Park, through some residential streets. Seven, Rush, and Xander—minus his heart attack—all join us at one point as well, and when it hits midday and we get the first clue from Tac'obout Tacos, Émile deciphers it. In our neighborhood, only a few streets away from home is the Trailer Park Markets and there, parked around back, is our Taco Truck.

We're not the first ones here, but Xander is still beside himself as he squeals and points. "We found it, we found it!" I ruffle his hair on my way past to join the line and Seven slings a heavy, tattooed arm around Xander and steers him after us.

Émile treats us all and we find a picnic table to sit at and eat. Shielded by the trailers, there's no breeze, and the sun is directly overheard, warming me to my core.

"So, how's the show going?" Seven asks.

"Yeah, awesome. Didn't fuck up once last night."

"It's a fulluping miracle."

"Fulluping?" Émile echoes.

"Seven doesn't swear," I explain. "At least not with actual cuss words. He'll swear up a storm with whatever nonsense words he's come up with, which I argue is just as bad."

"Shut your mother-fulluping mouth. Of course it isn't as bad. It's pure sunshiny fun."

"Agreed," Xander says.

"Your opinion doesn't count," I say. "You agree with everything Seven says."

"Not true. I think that *Kill Diver* show is trash and overhyped."

Seven's mouth drops, a long sound coming from him like he's been wounded. "You take that back."

"Never going to happen." Xander gives him a sweet smile that scrunches up the freckles on his nose and even Seven can't argue with that face. He slumps instead, lips trembling against a snarl.

"You suck."

"I wish."

I turn my whole body away from their bickering and face Émile. "Hey."

"Hello, you."

"You're pretty."

His whole face lights up with my compliment. "What are you going to do about it?"

"Gaze at you in despair, torturously wasting away at all that man I get to look at and not touch."

Émile palms my shoulder. "You actors sure are dramatic."

"It's in the job description." I scootch a bit closer to him. "What are you thinking about?"

"How much I'm enjoying myself."

"Really?"

He boops me on the nose. "You shouldn't sound so surprised. Your friends might get offended."

"It'd take way more than that to offend them."

"It's true," Gabe jumps in. "We've all seen the people who are supposed to love us at their shittiest. Nothing really gets to us anymore."

"Unless it's indigestion," Seven says, throwing a look Xander's way.

"I *said* it could have been that," Xander mutters.

Seven presses a kiss to the side of Xander's head. "I'm glad we got it checked out anyway. And now, we get to eat tacos."

That sufficiently railroads them back onto the topic of Mexican food as Émile lets out a soft sigh beside me.

"Everything okay?" I ask.

"Yep, it's just … don't look, but we've been spotted."

"Oh, shit."

"It's fine, I doubt they're going to come over here, they're just taking some photos."

"Well, what do I do?"

"Just keep eating." He's struggling not to laugh again. "That piece of lettuce stuck in your beard will look amazing as a headline photo."

"*Argh.*" I scrub at my face, but Émile takes my hand and settles it in his lap.

"Relax, I'm joking. Just keep doing what you're doing. Maybe amp up the love a tad. Make those fuckers believe you can't get enough of me."

I reach over and lift his taco so he can take a bite, only it isn't anywhere near as romantic as I'd been picturing. The shell cracks and half the toppings drop out of the bottom and back onto the wrapper.

"Ah, ooops?" I say.

"That was for the thing about the lettuce, wasn't it?" Émile asks dryly, swiping his face with napkins.

"No, but let's say it was. We're even now."

"Sure we are."

"Shh." I steal the napkins from him and take over cleaning his face. "Let me be in love with you. This is the kinda thing they do in those romcoms, right?"

"You'd be more of an expert in those than I would be."

"Then take my word for it. This is totally, one hundred percent, what they do in those things."

"Noted." He slides closer, closing the distance between us. "And what about this?"

Then Émile plucks a dandelion from the ground beside us and tucks it behind my ear. His fingers linger for a second, golden-flecked gaze locked on the flower, before meeting mine again. "Is that a romcomy thing to do?"

"Uh-oh."

"What?"

I swallow, and aim for a playful grin. "I hate to tell you this, but tucking a flower behind the ear is romcom code for falling in love. You've done it now. You're going to be stuck with me."

His fingers graze my neck as they drop. "And somehow that isn't the threat you're trying to make it out to be."

"Surprising, considering I dropped salsa in your lap."

"*What?*" He springs back to inspect his pants and it only takes a second for him to work out that I'm full of shit. "Hilarious joke."

"You fell for it."

"And with that, I think I want my flower back."

"Too late now." I spare him one more mischievous look before turning back to my food. "I don't make the rules."

Chapter 21

Émile

Damn Christian and his damn romcom rules. I can't get what he said off my mind, and while there's no way I'm in love with him, it doesn't stop me from wishing we'd never made this deal to begin with.

If we hadn't, would we have taken the time to actually get to know each other? The thing about spending an entire day with him, surrounded by his friends and their inside jokes, and Monopoly Monday that I'm also roped into, is that I've gotten to see more of him than, well, anyone I know. He doesn't hide behind snark and banter. He doesn't try to conceal his flaws. When his friends tease him, he turns a delicious shade of red, fidgets with his nose ring, and then hangs his head so none of us can see him smile.

Except I haven't left his side all day and I'm counting those smiles.

One, for the tacos he spilled on his shirt.

Two, for him missing the step into Madden's truck and smacking his face on the seat.

Three, for the story of them first meeting Auntie Agatha, when Christian tripped over a bush and ended up grabbing her tit.

And four, right now, when Christian's out first and the jeers and catcalls helpfully inform me that he's terribly shit at this game.

"I'll defend your honor, dear one." And defend it I do, until there's only Madden, Seven, and I left, and Christian's passed off the bank to Xander who passed it to Rush who passed it to Gabe. I'm feeling proud of myself for remembering all of their disastrous names, when Christian yawns wide and settles his arm across the couch behind me. It's such a boyfriendly thing to do that when he drags his thumb over my neck, from the cradle of my shoulder to that soft spot behind my ear, I lean into the touch. Starved for it, if I'm honest. Wishing we hadn't drawn all these lines between us so I could take that touch and turn it into more.

All day I've been subjected to the scent of his body spray, his bashful gaze, the way those defined collarbones are peeking out of the low scoop of his T-shirt.

He shifts closer, pressing his side to mine. Nose running the length of my hairline and distracting me completely from the game.

"Thanks for humoring us today," his low voice says by my ear.

"I'd hardly call enjoying myself humoring you."

He makes a non-committal noise. "Thanks anyway. It's … been nice. Hanging out."

"It has."

"And while I'm super invested in watching you kick both my friends' asses …" He shifts beside me, hips flexing forward as he smooths a hand down his sweats and pulls the material tight over–*hello*. "Help me."

I'm not strong enough to remind him of our deal. Not with

him offering me everything I've been dying for all day. "But ... the game ..." Not that I give one, single solitary fuck about finishing, I just have no clue how to get away without announcing to them all that we're going to have sex.

"I got you," he murmurs before raising his voice. "Ah, I'm so thirsty, I need a drink." Then he sets his hand on the table under the pretense of using it to stand up, and "accidentally" slips. The board upends, tiny plastic houses scattering away across the table and floor.

Madden huffs. "Seriously, Christian? *Again?*"

"Ooops?"

The others dutifully go in search of the pieces like this is a common thing and while they're distracted, Christian grabs my hand and drags me from the room.

"How many times have you needed to create a distraction like that?"

"Cute you think any other time before tonight was intentional."

"You mean you've never before staged a distraction for your friends to sweep a man off for promisingly filthy things?"

He glances at me, all soft eyes and wrinkled forehead. "Actually, ah ... boyfriends haven't been a big part of my life so you're actually the first guy I've ever brought home. Umm, properly. Hookups, obviously, but they're normally gone before my roommates can attack."

I try not to get too happy over that fact. Or feel too special. It's not like I'm here because he wanted to introduce me, and if it wasn't for an overly enthusiastic old lady barging in this morning, I'd likely have been shooed out the door as well.

Still, that's not something I'm going to focus on when Christian's hand is warm in mine, and his delicious arse is a step ahead of me, begging me to follow.

I've barely stepped onto the landing when he hauls me

against him, hands steady at my back and hard cock pressing enticingly into my thigh.

"This okay?"

My hands slide up his chest, melting at the smooth muscle beneath them. "You tell me. The hands-off rule was yours and I'm happy to go along, but I'd be a gigantic liar if I said I haven't been in a constant state of hunger for you again."

Conflict fills those blue eyes, even as his grip on me increases. "It's okay, yeah? I mean, the money is separate from … from this."

"It is."

"And things won't get all weird and mixed up?"

"Not if we don't let them." I shift so he can feel how desperate I am for him as well. "Frankly, I think us being constantly hard around each other is the problem. With all the blood in our dicks, how are we supposed to convincingly fool anyone? If anything, having sex means we'll be on top form." I'm rambling. I know I am, but the desire to stop is far less than the desire to see him naked again. "Besides, it can't be healthy to be so constantly boned up. Even Viagra comes with a warning on the packet."

"True. It's for our own good, right?"

Before I can let rational thought sneak in, I lean forward and suck on one of his deliciously tempting collarbones. "Our doctors would be so very fucking grateful."

I'm not proud of the needy hint to my words, except then his mouth comes down hard on mine, and suddenly I am. Because I'm far too horny to think about much of anything except the way he's kissing me. Strong lips, deep, sweeping tongue, one hand tangled messily in my hair as he holds me in place. I feel it, his need, from my scalp to the tips of my toes, because I'm desperate for him in all the same ways.

"Bedroom." He grunts and I swallow the noise. But now that I have my hands on him, I'm not in a hurry to let him go, and we bump and stumble our way to his door. He throws it open, blindly swipes to find it again as we spill inside and he shoves me up against the wall.

"Goddamn door." He slams it with a resolute *thud* and then instantly melts to his knees.

My thighs tremble at the memory of the last time he was kneeling in front of me and I sink back into the wall, letting him take full control. He pops my button, rips open my fly, and then his hand dives under my boxer briefs and closes around my aching cock.

Relief is pumped into my bloodstream, as heady as adrenaline, and I arch into his fist, begging him for more. And God, he doesn't make me ask for it. As soon as he pulls me out, he wraps his lips around me and swallows me to the root, just like the last time in the shower. And it's bliss. Mind-numbing bliss that I wish I could live in for the rest of my worthless life, because I honestly don't think I'm being dramatic when I say there's no greater sight than him on his knees.

Only, then he goes and proves me wrong by releasing me so he can pull off his shirt. Skin. So much skin. And muscle. I want to taste it all. Bite and lick and suck, but then he's moaning around my cock again and I can't seem to keep my thought processes from crashing into each other.

Through heavy lids, I watch him work me over with a type of enthusiasm I've never seen before. He's all unrestrained, red flushed cheeks, hand gripping the front of his sweats like a goddamn clamp. My shirt feels too tight and restrictive, but my fingers stumble over the order of buttons with an ocean of pleasure swimming through me.

My balls pull tight.

"Oh, god, you need to stop," I gasp.

Christian immediately pulls off, dark eyes shuttered and unfocused. "Why?"

"Because as much as I'd love to come in your mouth, I'm not quite ready for this to be over yet."

Focus drips into him until his eyes fix on mine. "What did you have in mind?"

"Would you let me fuck you?"

His groan comes from somewhere deep inside of him, and he leans forward to dust his lips over the crease where my thigh meets my groin. "Only if you do it really, *really* hard."

His words short-circuit my brain and I haul him to his feet. Flip us. His back hits the wall with a satisfying *thump* and our mouths crash together. He tastes like me, and like him, and I need to get off, to come, to get this consuming need out of me. He shouldn't feel like everything. He shouldn't feel like the end. He shouldn't feel like the thing I need to turn my body to static, all energy. A constant buzz of want.

"Condoms?"

"I'm on PrEP."

"So am I, love, but I'd still prefer to use one." Because of my reputation and my family and not at all because the thought of my cum running down his muscular thighs makes me never want to leave this room again.

"There's ... a couple in the drawer. Lube too." He nods to his nightstand. "There."

"Strip off, turn around, and plant your hands on the wall."

He's got his pants around his ankles before I've taken a step and it's near impossible to tear my eyes away from his plump ass. The elegant curve of his back.

Fucking dancers.

I rid myself of my shirt before grabbing a condom and the tube of lube. I'm so turned on that I'm almost cross-eyed. Tempted to just slick myself up and push inside, but I force myself to slow down. To press against his back, to kiss his neck and his shoulder and sink my teeth into that delicious dip there.

Christian takes the lube and flicks open the cap, while I drop the condom at our feet. My hands map out his delicious plains of muscle, bringing out the most erotic low sounds from him.

"I know you don't want this over with, but gonna warn you that it might not be our choice if you don't get a move on. I wanna come so bad."

I chuckle and suck a mark onto his neck, loving the way he squirms against me.

"Give me your hand," he begs.

I give it. Then wait, while he covers my fingers in lube, and try not to tremble when he presses his arse back into me. Nestling my cock in warmth.

My fingers sneak into the furrow of his ass, following the trail down to his hole, and I don't waste any time pressing inside. The sounds catching in his throat are low and needy, spurring me on and threatening to make me float away.

"That's it, gorgeous. Just like that."

He takes my finger all the way and rocks back onto it. "More."

A second finger joins the first, seated deep inside him. My free hand doesn't stop mapping out the dips and crests of his torso as I focus on working him open. Stretching his hole, knowing that in a few short minutes, I'm going to be burying myself inside of it.

After an entire day of trying to be good, I'm done holding back.

I duck down to pick up the condom and make fast work of rolling it down my length before taking the lube from Christian and coating myself in it. I employ every trick in the book to take myself back from the edge, but no number of sweaty gym socks can take away how it feels to push forward and have Christian's body open for me. The pressure, the deep suction.

The way he presses back to take me deeper with the kind of gravelly cry I feel in my chest.

His forehead hits the wall in front of him, hands searching for grip and making his shoulder blades flex. I grunt as I bottom out, steadying myself with a tight grip on his hip. Holding our bodies flush and connected.

Heat is coursing through me, all lust and attraction, and absolutely nothing else. I ignore the fullness, ignore the way my gaze fixes on his parted lips when he tilts his head to the side, ignore how I hold him against me, just for a second, just to feel the way he fits.

I'm already panting like some kind of animal in heat, and I'm almost glad his back is to me and he can't see the way I'm coming entirely undone in the most incredibly pathetic way. I could hold him and he'd let me–I know he would. And it's possibly that, or possibly how desperately I want to, that warns me it's not a good idea.

So instead, I move my grip to his neck, fingers tightening over the back of it. "I hope you're ready."

"Oh, fuck. Give it to me already."

I'm only too happy to comply. My hips snap forward in a few practice thrusts that set my teeth on edge. He feels too good. Too … consuming.

There's no point trying to play cool and smooth when every cell in my body is roaring at me to let go.

So I do.

I fuck him so hard, he collides with the wall, over and over. His grunts are short and hot, building to the melody of our bodies slapping together.

"Yes, yes, *yes*, fuck, more. *More*."

And I'm not sure that I can give him more, but I give him everything that I can. No holding back. Thrusting together in a frenzy of groans and praises, the sweat building on our skin and filling the room with the most intoxicating scent.

The nervous laugh that so often scratches at my skin builds, only this time it isn't nerves. It's relief and joy and a type of pleasure I've never known to look for. My fingers tighten their hold, nails biting into his hip, other thumb leaving a visible depression right below his jaw. I press harder, fingers curling into his hair.

I want to leave him covered in my marks and use them to count the days until we give in again. Because this need, this drive, there's no way I can ignore it for long, and I'm beginning to suspect he feels the same. The magnetism between us is unique to only him and me and the moments it builds between us.

Christian's palm *thwacks* the wall as the other disappears down to grip himself. He pushes back onto me, fucking himself on my cock, and even though my thighs and my arms are starting to complain, I double up on my efforts. Like I'm trying to turn him inside out and upside down, the way I'm suspiciously worried he's already doing to me. Without trying. Without wanting. I'm so drawn to him, he'll be my undoing.

"Yep, I'm gonna … I'm gonna …" He stiffens, head thrown back, and I loosen my hold on his hair to snake around the front. My hand finds a home around his throat and I tug his ear between my teeth, owning him, claiming him, as the tingles racing from my spine to my balls overwhelm me. My thrusts lose rhythm. My brain melting to a soup of *yes, perfect, fuck, mine*, and when I can't hold back any longer, I gladly fall over the edge. Emptying my release into the condom is a soaring high, punctured only by the thought that I wish the condom didn't exist at all.

Christian slumps and I follow him. Sweaty limbs tangled together up against the wall. We stay there, panting, recovering, fingers finding each other and linking, stroking, touching.

I laugh, so quiet only his hair could hear me, letting out too much happiness to hold in one body, and Christian cringes as I slip from him.

"Well, that should keep us going for another week, I'd say."

He pushes carefully off the wall. "Are you kidding? All that's done is make everything much, much worse."

At first, I'm worried he regrets it, and maybe I could have pushed harder to check he meant for all of that to happen, but then he steps closer and reels me in. The hurricane of thoughts stops.

"I'm gonna need a repeat. Or two? Maybe three. How many rounds did we go last time? We have a record to beat."

"We better get to it then."

Chapter 22

Christian

I'm still struggling to catch up with the dramatic overhaul my life has done. Performing nearly every day, sometimes twice a day, already takes a lot out of me, but in between the shows, I have to sneak time in with Émile. And, unfortunately, his family.

Who I was sure were assholes the day I met them, but now there's zero doubt left in my mind. Planning a wedding under the burning eye of disapproval takes more out of me than performing for two hours straight.

None of them are happy about the way Émile proposed, none of them are happy about the way the engagement was announced, and none of them are happy with literally any of the choices we're making for this stupid wedding. It makes me very glad I've never wanted to go through that for real, because I'm probably going to end up with PWSD—post wedding stress disorder.

I'm starting to get how bridezillas are made.

Thank fuck for Elle. When she's not working, she acts as a

buffer between me and Émile and the rest of them. She shuts down Clifford's opinions, reminds their dad that all his colleagues have no reason to be invited, and stops their mom from hiring someone to document the entire planning process. It also helps that Émile is deep into planning his charity event and that seems to be the only excuse his family accepts for us sneaking away from them.

It's almost a relief the show is on now, because spending all day every day talking flowers and churches and food ... I moan, resting my head in my hands.

Of course Émile is fielding all that and planning this charity thing without breaking a sweat. If that man feels the pressure over anything, I'll eat my left nut.

I'm so glad I relented to the sex. It was getting so hard to concentrate around him, and now, that's the highlight of my week.

"Christian?"

My head jolts up at the voice, and I have to blink a few times to make sure I'm seeing who I think I'm seeing. "Josie. What the hell are you doing here?"

She winds her way through the makeup stations we have set out backstage. There's a dressing room for the two leads, but the rest of us are left to fend for ourselves in the bullpen.

"Just got back from our honeymoon." She turns soft eyes on me. "What on earth happened that night?"

I sigh, not able to keep eye contact. "Yeah, not my finest moment."

"I should hope not. You ended up eating more of my wedding cake than I did."

"Hey, at least you didn't have to worry about Sheppy smashing it in your face," I try.

"I was looking forward to that, actually." She crosses her arms and leans against my dressing table. "Are you okay? I know ... I know that must have been shitty."

And when I think about the epic fucking humiliation I went through, I want to agree. But shitty probably isn't the word for how I was feeling in the moment. The thing is though, it might have only been a month or so, but it feels like forever ago. So much has happened since then that I haven't had time to dwell on that night and how terrible it was. Actually, I almost find it funny.

Almost.

"It was, *but* I was mostly ashamed for ruining it for you."

"Thanks, but you're giving yourself way too much credit. The wedding was a dream, and by that point I was so drunk everything is a bit hazy."

"Well, thank fuck for alcohol."

She turns a cheeky look on me, and it's so strange seeing someone that shares so many of my features right in front of me. I've missed this. "I heard down the family grapevine that you're still seeing a certain someone. A very *rich and powerful* someone."

Well, I guess I should feel grateful that they're talking about that instead of cakemageddon.

I decide, *fuck it* and hold up my hand.

Josie's jaw drops. "You're engaged?"

"Sure am."

"Holy shit that's amazing." She catches me totally off guard by swamping me in a hug. "I'm so happy for you. No wonder he came across as a slightly overprotective dick. He was looking out for the man he loves."

"Uh … yeah." Though I don't get how pointing out that *homophobes are bad* is dickish behavior. "Did you just come here to be pissy at me about the cake?"

"Nope. I wanted to see you perform, actually. Sheppy is already in our seats."

"Wow." I'm hit with an influx of nerves. "That's … great. So great." And not the pressure I needed before going out there, but it's also pretty amazing to know I'll have any family here at all. And I know I shouldn't ask it, already know the answer before I even let the words out, but I can't help myself.

"And … my folks. Have they said anything?"

Josie's face pinches. "No. Though I only got back yesterday. And late, too. So it's not like I've had much chance to talk with anyone …"

Which we both know is bullshit since she's already been well filled in on Émile. I force a smile. "Aw well. I tried, right?"

"Exactly."

"And you're here."

"I am."

"Which means a lot."

She chuckles. "Thanks. I'm going to head out so you can get ready, but can I see you after?"

"Yeah, of course!"

"Awesome." She leaves, calling back over her shoulder, "Break a leg …"

Knowing they'll be out there watching, I'm going to make it the best performance I've ever had. I want to blow them away with how incredible the entire show is and have them go home and talk about it with everyone who wishes I would disappear from the family tree. I want her to talk about how amazing I was until they're sick of hearing my name. Until my parents, just for fucking once, acknowledge they maybe had it wrong. Maybe me being gay isn't everything. Maybe there are other reasons they can be proud of me.

I give my nose ring a few small tugs, trying to get refocused. It's not long now until curtains up. Word has been spreading and we've had some great reviews, which makes me hopeful that this doesn't all end once this run of shows are up, even if we haven't been able to fill the theater yet. But I'm trying not to think too far ahead. Especially when ahead is a clusterfuck of unknown.

All I have to do right now, is go out there and perform for the only family who gives a shit about me. And sure, maybe it's not the right kind of shit like Émile expects, but after seeing his family, all it's done is remind me that no one's perfect. I'll take what I can get.

Still, the stabbing reminder that the hope I was holding on to about my parents was for nothing kinda hits deep. Seventeen years they were in my life. They were warm and kind and so loving.

Then one tiny part of me wasn't who they thought I was and like that … nothing. Some days I struggle to remember what it was like to have parents.

"You ready?" Sophie asks on her way past.

I jerk out of my pity party and realize everyone is already on the move.

"Yep. Totally. Let's knock 'em dead."

Josie cares. Josie's here. I'm going to make it my best performance ever, which shouldn't be hard considering the entire crew are buzzing. We can all feel it. That precipice of potential. After years of working in and out of small productions and local theater, this could be the show that takes us somewhere.

But we're only as good as our last performance, so I clear all the pressure and try to get into character. I might not have any lines to memorize, but constant costume changes and high-level choreography are more than enough for me to keep up with.

The opening music trembles through me, settling some of my nerves as my mind empties. Mostly. It's still holding to the knowledge that Josie made the effort. Josie's here.

The nerves amp up again but I wrestle them down. No time for those.

My cue hits and I run out onto the stage. The attention feels heavier today, the audience most interested. Where normally I slip into the background as an unidentifiable figure, today I *know* I'm being watched. Studied. Judged.

I push myself. Spin harder. Faster. I'm overly conscious of my footwork and end up flubbing a few steps. It's minor. No one notices. I fuck one of my rotations which puts me a beat behind everyone else, but it's okay. I can catch up. This is only the first number and starting on the back foot only gives me room to improve.

I try to sink into that nothing place I go when I perform. Where my brain empties and I let the moves take over, but reality crashes into me when I sidestep too far and collide with another dancer. Brit? Joseph? I don't stop to look.

With any luck it will have gone unnoticed. Well, for anyone but Josie. Josie, who's watching. Josie, who cares. Josie, who wants to be proud of me, but I'm making it so hard.

Sweat prickles along my brow, and my heartbeat is drumming way harder than it should be. I have one wild, ridiculous moment where I think—*heart attack or indigestion*—and it's enough to throw me off. I spring onto the bench and the second I launch off it, I know I've fucked up. I twist the wrong way, send the backflip over too fast, and my foot smacks into something. There's a muffled grunt, I land, barely, foot too far out and I throw myself back to correct before I face plant, hit a prop instead, and lose all sense of the stage around me as my feet disappear.

I fall back, hit something that slows my descent and gives off a thunderous rustle. A groan. And then an enormous bang as I hit the stage.

It takes a very long moment for anything to happen. Sound. Feeling. Sight. It's all sucked away into a *holy shit* void where I'm about to cry.

The stage backdrop is behind me, pulled tight under my weight, the cables keeping it suspended, pulled to their limits, and I'm just waiting for the entire thing to fall.

But hey, if it lands on me, at least then no one will be staring.

"Oh my god, Christian, are you okay?" Reece asks, darting from backstage as a voice announces that there'll be a quick intermission and the curtain starts to drop.

I don't answer. Because there is no answer. Because I'm dead. Surely I'm dead.

Please let me be fucking dead.

My eyes fall closed, even as an arm wraps around me and helps me stand. Tests my legs, my feet. I refuse to look. My cheeks are so hot they might burst.

If they did, at least then I'd be spared living through this. An exploding brain has to be preferable to the pit building in my gut that's making me dangerously close to throwing up.

That's making my head pound.

My palms sweat.

My pulse rate peaked at a thousand.

"You're okay. You're good," some asshole says, like it's a good thing I haven't been gravely injured.

Like they all don't hate me for fucking this up.

The arm around me tightens, coaxes me forward.

My head spins and a wave of nausea passes through, rippling out to my limbs.

And then, because none of this can possibly get any worse, I pitch forward and vomit all over the stage.

Chapter 23

Émile

Chris Patrick single-handedly brings down the show—literally.

I stop working on the table plans for my charity event as the alert for *Seattleite* pops up on my phone. Dread prickles through me as I pull up the article and the more I read, the more I'm lurching into ragey indignation.

That's *my* Christian they're talking about.

My Christian they're ridiculing.

My Christian who apparently flubbed the one thing he's always been so proud of himself for being able to pull off without a hitch. I've seen him at his worst, the way he beats himself up, and I've seen him post-performance, *radiant* under the pride of pulling off something so important to him.

His self-esteem is already tied to his capacity to get through the day without issue, I can only imagine how rock bottom he's feeling.

"Maybe put them at this table—"

"*Shh.*" I'm not even regretful at cutting Elle off as I hit his number and lift my phone to my ear. It goes straight to voice-mail. "Fuck."

Elle lifts her eyebrows. "That was an emphatic exclamation."

I toss my phone her way, and have to sit in silent horror as I watch the same emotions I've just gone through play out over her face.

"How the hell did he stuff up so badly?"

"It's sort of his thing," I tell her. "Just never normally like … like *this*."

"I wouldn't want to be him right now."

"To be fair, I doubt he wants to be him right now either." For the first time ever, I'm at a loss. "He didn't answer. What am I supposed to do?"

She pulls a face. "Don't ask me. I've never done the relationship thing for precisely this reason. People *rely* on you."

"Surprisingly, that doesn't sound totally horrible."

Elle lists her head. "Emmy, I know this is all fake and whatever, but … do you actually like him? Like, if you weren't pretending to marry the man or whatever, do you think you'd actually be dating?"

"If I wasn't pretending to marry him, I'd have had no reason to see him again."

She doesn't say anything else, just reaches over and squeezes my hand. We both watch as my phone goes nuts between us.

"Oh, joy," she says dryly. "They've caught on to who he is."

"Shit, really?" I unlock the phone and not only is there a bunch about his *show-stopping* performance, they've now linked him to me. To our engagement. Which is probably a good reason for him to have turned off his phone. "I need to get to him. The show should be over by now, maybe I'll head to his house—"

There's a knock at my front door, and as much as I want to

believe it's Christian, the air is thick with the ominous hint of a conversation I don't want to have.

"Should we pretend we're not here?" Elle asks.

The knock comes again, more insistent this time.

"I don't think that will help."

"They can't force you to answer the door."

"And if it's Christian?"

She pins me with the type of look that explicitly tells me to grow up. It's not him. We both know it, but I hold up hope anyway as I stand from the table and approach my front door. The moment I open it, Gran walks in, followed closely by Clifford.

Her watery blue eyes sweep the room before settling on me and Elle.

"Émile, my darling boy." She reaches up to kiss my cheek. "You need to fire your cleaners. It's like a fraternity house in here."

Somehow I manage a pleasant smile. I don't need to look around to know that there's nothing wrong with my apartment. "I don't have cleaners."

"We'll need to fix that." She nods at Clifford. "Message Ian and have him send someone."

"With all due respect"—it's getting harder and harder to say those words—"I'm not in the market for a cleaner."

Clifford chortles. "Perhaps his little husband is doing it for him."

"Excuse me?"

"Isn't that what they're called? Gentleman you can pay. House husbands or some such."

My teeth actually grit together so hard I'm worried I'll lose a molar. Or punch him. It's a fifty-fifty split. "I certainly hope you're not referring to Christian."

"I'm only saying, old chap," Clifford raises his hands, "he's not exactly … *our* sort of fellow. Know what I'm saying?"

Before I can answer, Elle pipes up. "Silly me being a clue-less girl and all, but I'm not following. Could you elaborate further on that?"

"Well, because … you know. He's … he grabbed a *perfectly* respectable man's behind, and—I'm sure no one here failed to notice—he *shovels* when he eats. Like he's on some kind of prehistoric expedition. I'm surprised he didn't take an eye out with those elbows. Everyone I spoke with was quite horrified."

"Unsurprising considering most of the people you speak with are like you." I keep my voice pleasant, and the fact I'm insulting him goes directly over his head. The need to punch him has slipped dangerously close to forty-sixty territory, though.

"Aren't you going to offer me a seat?" Gran asks.

I know I'm supposed to. I know it's what's expected of me, but I also think it's too much of a coincidence that they've shown up now, with the perv off on one of his rants, and honestly? I have no interest in whatever conversation they've brought to my doorstep.

"Actually, I was just heading out. I'm sure you've seen my fiancé isn't having the best day and he needs me."

"*Sit. Down.*" The sudden, ringing tone is unexpected and harsh.

I sit.

Glance at Elle who's just done the same.

Gran rises to her fullest height, which only grazes Clifford's shoulder, but there's a power in the old lady that makes it diffi-cult for me to move.

"I have entertained this ridiculous venture quite long enough." She stares me down. More power in her small frame than I'm used to her showing. "This boy does not know how we behave. He does not reflect well on our family. And you've been behaving completely out of hand since he appeared and I'm quite done."

"You're *done?*"

"I will not have this family made into a mockery after everything we've achieved. We belong in the *Times* and the *Wall Street Journal* not splashed all over whichever trash publication gossip site I've been subjected to today. It ends. Now."

The need to lash out and tell her where she can put her demands is right on the tip of my tongue, but I swallow that need down. Bury my frustrations under a mask of polite detachment. "And you don't think a failed engagement will grace those same gossip sites?"

"To be perfectly frank, I don't give a damn."

"Well said, Grandmother," Clifford simps.

I'm at thirty to seventy odds now, and if he doesn't get the hell out of my house, I'll break that stiff upper lip he's so fond of. "Well, it appears we're at an impasse. I must marry for my inheritance, so while trying to fulfill Pa's wishes, I'm going against yours. You'll have to understand, this puts me in an uncomfortable position."

"Your grandfather would be disgusted by your behavior."

I'm hit with a flash of a memory. Pa, two pairs of glasses perched on his head while he enthusiastically detailed the rail network in Europe to a local senator at one of his parties. The way his sherry sloshed over the rim of the small glass, the way his face got redder the more he drank, the way he crashed into a server and helped her scramble around on the floor to pick up the hors d'oeuvres.

"Perhaps. Or perhaps he would have been incredibly proud of me. Either way, his will is iron clad. I'm fulfilling my end of the bargain and once I have my money, I'll be flying back to Amsterdam, where you won't need to worry about gossip sites or my husband groping any respectable gentleman besides myself. Because I quite happen to like it when he gropes me."

"Émile Jean Cromwell," Gran seethes. "I will not be spoken to like that."

"Not a problem." I stand and grab my keys. "As I said, I was just leaving. I'm sure Elle would love to make you a cup of tea."

Elle gives her most angelic smile. "I'm sure I saw some tea bags around here somewhere."

Gran looks faint, and I'd worry about upsetting an old lady if I didn't think she was going to outlive us all through sheer force of will.

I make it all the way to the door before anyone speaks again.

Gran's voice is back to pleasant tones. "Very well, Émile. You do what you need to do. But you can trust I'll do the same."

My footsteps falter for a split-second, but I brush it off and keep walking like I haven't heard her. I've been over that will a thousand times. I've had my lawyer review it, assess the doctor's letter stating Pa was of sound mind when he changed it, there's nothing she can do. Without the threat of cutting me off, she has no power over me.

It's hard to convince my head of that, though, when I've been raised my entire life to defer to her judgment. Walking away leaves me with this itching sense of *wrongness*.

It's how I know I've made the right choice.

Chapter 24

Christian

Is this what rock bottom feels like? I sit backstage, senses dull and brain a blank canvas, numbing me from going over and over what the hell just happened. Reece reassures me that it was an off day, that it was one performance, blah blah blah, but it's kinda hard to follow his voice when the smell of my unleashed breakfast is clogging my nose.

"One show in a three-week block is nothing. I know it was embarrassing, but you're not hurt. That's the main thing. Tomorrow, you'll be back out there nailing the choreography like you've done every other day."

I give him the most incredulous look I can manage.

"Nope. Enough of that," he says. "You've worked way too hard on this, brother. I'm not letting you slink away in embarrassment. These things happen, and the best way forward is to get back out there. I would have sent you back on stage already if you weren't basically comatose."

"Heh." I'm not sure if the noise is supposed to be a laugh or a disagreement, but I can't bring myself to commit to either.

"Go home. Have a big dinner. Sleep it off. I expect you here tomorrow."

The sounds of the final song reach my ears and only the horror of having to face everyone makes me push to my feet. I'm still in full costume and makeup, but fucked if I'm hanging around to change, and thankfully Reece doesn't ask me to.

I sling my bag over my shoulder and walk outside. It's already night, and I have no idea if it's cold or not, because I'm in an insulated bubble of shame. Getting into the car, turning it on, pulling out onto the road, and driving home … it all exists in a vacuum, and I'm only concentrating enough to make sure I don't end up in an accident.

That'd be the perfect end to my day.

All the lights are on at the house. It's shining like a beacon in the darkness of the grounds, and I pull up on the long driveway, calculating my odds on getting inside and making it to my room without someone springing out at me.

In the back of my mind, I know I should call Émile. I know he'd make it better. Through a joke, or logic, or by coming over here and distracting me with sex, but I have no energy for any of that. I want to cry, but I don't. I want to sleep, but I know it will be impossible.

No matter what Reece said, I can't imagine my epic fucking fail will go unnoticed by investors. It definitely wouldn't have gone unnoticed by Josie. She's probably on the phone to her mom, mocking what a complete screwup I am. My parents must be breathing a sigh of relief tonight.

I scowl at the sting in my eyes and jump out of the car, making my way quickly up to the house. I've almost got myself convinced that if I walk fast, with purpose, and don't make eye contact with anyone that they'll all leave me alone.

I really should know my roommates better than that.

I've barely stepped inside, kicked off my shoes, and taken a few steps into the hall when Gabe launches himself at me. He collides with my chest, an *ooof* puffing from me, before he takes me down. My face is smothered into the antique rug as Gabe drapes himself over my back.

Footsteps—Seven, based on the Medusa tattoo over his foot —and then weight over my legs. "This is cozy," he says.

I try to answer but someone else lies down on my back, my ass, more weight on my legs. I'm hugged from all sides, crushed into the floor. Someone's stroking my hair, probably Gabe, and a rough hand that I'm assuming is Madden's rubs my arm.

That prickling in my eyes is back and I screw my whole face up against it. Refuse to let it out, to let that feeling win.

"Still think buying a weighted blanket would have been easier," Xander says from somewhere above.

"What are you complaining about?" Rush asks. "You're on top."

"It's an awkward angle, though."

"I have an elbow in my balls," Seven grunts. "Feeling little sympathy right now."

I suck the largest breath down that I can manage with them all on top of me. "At least tell me Madden's wearing clothes," I wheeze.

"Shh …" he says, the pressure running over my arm increasing. "You already know the answer to that."

Fucking hell.

Teeny footsteps come from somewhere to my left and then Kismet appears, trotting over and butting his head against mine. His ugly squished face makes him look like he can't believe he's part of this shit, but I'm glad he is. Even with the pain in my ribs and the lack of oxygen, I'm glad they all are.

It's hard to be numb when you're being crushed to death, after all. Gabe shifts away from Kismet who hisses loudly at the sudden movement, backs up a few steps, and then, when he's sure the coast is clear, creeps closer and sets one tiny paw on my head.

My eyes fall closed, a host of memories trying to take over, but I turn my focus to my friends. Their weight, their scent, their softly murmured voices. Seven is thankfully keeping his mouth closed, because as much as the advice *it was bound to happen eventually* or *you should be used to landing on your ass* is accurate, it's also not what I need to hear.

I have no idea how long we're all pancaked together, but after a while, the tension leaves me.

"There's a high likelihood this is the greatest sight I've seen in my life."

I jolt at Émile's voice. Of course he's here. And as much as I want to throw everyone off and launch myself at him, I'm also kinda hoping they'll squash me so completely I won't need to face him after this.

"Should I join the pile, or are you done?" he asks.

Gabe shifts so I can see his face. "Your call."

"Up." It comes out as a grunt, but they get it because one by one they climb off me.

"Finally," Xander groans.

Seven tackles him into the couch and pretends to smother him with a pillow, while I do everything I can not to look at Émile.

Unfortunately, he's much smarter than me because he steps closer and crouches right in my line of sight.

"How did you know?" I ask him.

"Love, everyone knows."

My cheeks *flame*. "I've changed my mind. Everyone climb back on and kill me this time."

"Oh, no. You're not getting out of marrying me that easily." His soft hand takes mine and he hauls me to my feet.

Gabe sniffs, eyes red and irritated from being so close to Kismet. "Lemme get my antihistamines."

"C'mere," Rush says, holding up a blanket. Émile eyes him curiously but I go, too drained to think.

I collapse onto the couch and he burritos the blanket around me, tucking in the sides and making sure it's nice and tight.

"Want to talk about it?" Émile asks, taking the seat beside me.

"Nope."

"Want to drink?" Madden suggests.

I shake my head. "So much for no nudity when we have guests."

"It's not my fault you keep bringing people around without warning."

"I'm fine." Émile smirks. "Not like it's a bad view."

Well, he's right, and it's reached the point where it's odd to see Madden *wearing* clothes rather than the way he is now.

"I like your almost-husband," Madden says.

I snort. "After tonight, I can't see a wedding actually happening." I turn to Émile. "Right?"

The face he pulls basically confirms it. "Let's just say, my grandmother isn't exactly happy about the attention."

"Not like I did it on purpose," I mutter, a hot, sickening dread settling over me. A small part of it is disappointment over the money, but it's easy to ignore since I never imagined that would actually happen. No, I feel sick because as hard as I tried, I let Émile down. And unlike me, he needed the money for unselfish reasons. "If you're here to break up with me, you can cut your losses and leave. Trust me when I say it will not be a surprise and there's no way I'll hold it against you."

Instead of getting up and leaving, his long fingers wriggle under the blanket and seek out my hand. "You're still as ridiculous as ever."

"Hate to tell you this, but I can't see that ever changing."

He pumps my hand. "Try again."

A small smile slips onto my lips. "Fine. That ain't changing. Ever."

186

"Is that a promise?"

My chest feels full, and I try to remind it that Émile's pretty words are for everyone else's benefit, to keep up the act, but it's impossible to believe when he's looking at me like that. "Yeah. It is."

"Good, because I'm counting on it."

Chapter 25

Émile

"Can you make it all go away?" Christian buries his face into my neck, all but nuzzling me. I'd tell him just about anything to keep him in place because the rough scratch of his beard against my throat makes me melty.

"You have to know I'd do exactly that if I could."

"Yeah …" He sighs and then does exactly what I don't want him to, and flops over onto his back. The connection between us broken, it's time to face another day we need to get through alone. "I just can't figure out why *everyone* is talking about it."

"In the nicest way possible, you almost brought down the entire set. That was going to be news whether you were tied to me or not. And unfortunately for you, since you're my fiancé now, that made everything so much worse."

He hums, staring at the ceiling, too much going on behind his usually bright blue eyes. "Is this what it's always like for you?"

That's a hard question to answer. "In a way. While I was at

Cambridge no one really gave a shit who I was, except for the few people I already knew to keep my distance from. In Amsterdam, I was able to blend in with the crowd, mostly, but here … the States are a world of their own. Gossip is currency, and being heir to an enormous fortune apparently makes me a somebody … when it's all bullshit."

"Bullshit?" He slants a teasing grin my way. "You mean I'm not marrying a future prince? Should I call the wedding off now?"

I whack him with my pillow. "I'd like to see you try."

"Prince Émile Cromwell."

"None of that, thank you."

"Are you going to take me to your country estate for tea and biscuits before disrobing me and plundering my flower?"

"Do us both a favor and never attempt a British accent again."

"What? That was great, innit?"

Since the pillow thing didn't work on him, I decide to try and smother myself with it instead. "Make it stop."

"Huh, lad? We in a bloody bit of a pickle here, ain't we?"

"I have no clue which part of Britain that's supposed to be from, but I can assure you it's none of them."

"Would you like some scones?"

That's *it*. I toss the pillow off and pounce on him. "Eat another burger, you ridiculous American."

"Oh, *no*, right where it hurts."

We wrestle back and forth, throwing out the most stereotypical, clichéd crap at each other, and it's when Christian gets me pinned, naked body pressing mine into the mattress, that I realize he's laughing.

It fills my chest with this unexpected warmth. "See? Almost back to normal."

The smile slips from his face. "How the fuck am I going to go back out there?"

189

"Presumedly the same way you always do."

"You don't get it." He collapses, face back in that glorious place in my neck. "Josie saw everything."

"Your cousin?" It's the first time he's mentioned that.

"I think that's why I was so nervous. She showed up, and I wanted to do good, but I fucked up under the pressure. And now I'm worried I've ruined it for the whole team. Do you know we've had some really good reviews this week? Reece mentioned possible investors. That's, like, a dream. For all of us, and thanks to me, it might not even be an option anymore."

While Christian slept last night, I bought tickets to today's performance. I was going to surprise him by sitting in the audience, giving him the comfort that someone he knew was there for him. Turns out I read that wrong.

"If one person is enough to take all that away, it was never there to begin with. You're not the only one on that stage."

His face reappears, frown weighing it down. "That's true, but I'm the only one who ruined the show."

"All publicity is good publicity. I can't imagine what you went through, especially because you're prone to being embarrassed at the drop of a hat, but these things have a way of working themselves out."

"I guess we'll see …"

He still doesn't look totally convinced, but it's not the kind of thing you believe simply because someone's told you. The *everything will be okay* platitude is an empty one, because frequently everything is *not* okay. But I have a feeling in this case, it will be. And he'll believe it once it happens.

"For what it's worth, I'm very impressed you're going back today."

He pulls a face and rolls off me to climb out of bed. I take a moment to drink in that perfect round arse before he pulls on a pair of underwear. "Yeah, well, Reece messaged me approximately a hundred times last night, and then again this morning, threatening to send me out in assless chaps if I didn't show up."

"Now *that's* a show I'd pay to see."

He flips me off but there's a slight smile that accompanies it. "Josie left me a few messages to check I was okay too."

"As she should," I say.

"I'm nervous as hell."

"How many times have you done this show?"

"Uh …" He stares at the wall, eyes squinted. "Like … ten, I think?"

"And with rehearsals?"

"I dunno, a lot more than that."

"And how many times have you fallen into the backdrop and puked on the stage?"

"Okay, okay. So the odds are on my side. I get it."

"You're incredibly lucky to be marrying such a smart man."

This time he takes a moment to run his eyes over my body, and I helpfully kick off the sheets so he has an unobstructed view. "Fuck me."

"Already did."

"I still have no idea how the hell we got into this mess, but I don't regret it."

"Good. Because if I have it my way, we'll be in this mess for a very long time." The words are hard to get out, because as much as we might talk about attraction, and support each other through our family shit, we never specifically mention feelings. As in, the feelings I'm having for him; as in, the feelings that are making it harder and harder for me to *want* to go through with this marriage. Which is stupid and dumb and completely irrational. Giving up helping a lot of people because I think I'm a little bit smitten with this ridiculous human would be the epitome of selfish.

I know I *can't* do it.

But that doesn't stop me from wanting to.

Christian shifts around, back to me, face barely in profile. I watch the way his tongue swipes his lips before he reaches up and gives his nose ring a tug. "Yeah, well, I hear planning weddings can take a while."

Not the response I was hoping for, but what the hell else could I have expected? For him to confess feelings for me? For him to talk about forevers like this is some damn fairy tale? I can't forget that I'm paying him to be here, and even though we slip occasionally and have incredible sex, he's still cagey when it comes to actually talking about it all. About what this means for us.

If he's still firmly in our agreement, I wish he'd tell me, but since he hasn't said anything else, I have to go on continuing to assume that's the case.

Christian leaves me with my thoughts while he showers and gets ready, and it's not until he's finished messing about with his hair that I climb out of his bed and dress too. I'll head home for a shower before heading to his show, and then I can take him out for dinner after.

I don't mention my plans because I don't want to put that pressure on him, but in a way, I'm not even solely doing it for him. The thought of something like yesterday happening again, and me not being there to comfort him, is too much.

I need to be close.

I need him to know I'm his biggest supporter.

And, sure, he's got his friends, who know him a hell of a lot better than I do, but I want to be *more*.

Everything.

The one person in this entire world who's his. Who he doesn't need to worry about leaving him. Who he knows he can always count on.

Christian deserves it.

His phone chimes and he reaches for it, taking a moment

to read whatever message has come through. When he looks up again, his face is white.

"What's wrong?"

He opens his mouth, then snaps it closed, turning back to the message to read it again.

"I … umm …"

"You know I speak American, but I'm going to need a few more words than that, love."

"It's my mom," he rushes out. Swallows. Glances back at the message and then at me again. "She … she …" He presses a palm roughly into his eye socket. "She wants to meet up."

Chapter 26

Christian

Somehow the message from Mom doesn't fuck with my head. I get through my performance without a single goddamn screw up, and when we come off stage, I'm surrounded by a sweaty group hug. Even overwhelming body stench and heavy makeup can't ruin the moment, because … thank god.

"Who was right?" Reece asks.

And I'm more than happy for him to say I told you so.

The moment is made even better by Émile showing up backstage and taking me out for dinner. It's sitting there, listening to him talk about how blown away he was by the performance—and sounding like he legitimately means it— that I realize something.

In a choice between screwing up my performance for Josie, or for him, I'm glad it happened the way it did, because … I *think* I care more about his opinion than any of my so-called family.

At least, that's what I tell myself until Sunday night when I'm due to meet my parents.

Émile picks me up looking like a million dollars while I'm trying not to sweat through yet another shirt I've borrowed from Rush. If I'm going to continue meeting up with people in fancy places, I should probably do the guy a favor and buy a few things of my own.

"Please breathe," Émile says from the driver's seat.

"I'm breathing."

"Yes, but it's very shallow. Do I need to point out that passing out from lack of oxygen may not be the best way to get this dinner underway?"

I huff.

"That's better."

"That wasn't me breathing, that was me being exasperated."

"I don't care what you need to be to get some air into you. Just bloody do it already."

"I'm trying."

He's quiet for a moment before he says, "I know this is what you've been hoping for … but don't let them off easy. If this is some kind of reunion, make them work for it. You deserve it."

As much as I wish I could agree with him, I know full well that if they offer an olive branch, I'll plant that fucker and do whatever I have to in order to make it grow.

The restaurant they've asked to meet at is some fancy upscale place in downtown Seattle. There's valet parking and a foyer and, *goddamn*, I do not belong here. There's an enormous gulf standing between my life from a month ago, and this pala-tial dining room, and while I might have been dirt poor and not entirely happy, at least I was safe. Life was predictable. Everything stayed the same, and as much as I might have wanted it to change, I didn't want it to change *this* much.

I'm definitely only ordering water and a starter from this place, that's for sure.

Émile's hand finds my clammy one, and I immediately suck in a long, deep breath. Maybe my first one all day.

That wave of pressure fades and reminds me that not all change is too much.

In fact, Émile might be exactly enough.

For a very long time.

I push the shadow of his words out because there isn't enough room to obsess over them right now. Maybe he meant what I kinda thought he did, maybe he didn't. All I know is that it's only a matter of time before he disappears on me, and I'm not going to hope for anything different when history has given me no reason to.

"You ready for this?" he murmurs as I lock eyes on my mom.

She's sitting beside Dad, both of them having moved their chairs closer together and I hope it's from nerves at seeing me again, and not because they, I dunno, don't want to catch the gay or whatever.

They notice us a second later, their gazes flicking from me to land on Émile.

Instead of answering him when I'm not sure exactly how I'm feeling, I say, "Thanks for coming with me."

"What are fiancés for?"

"Regular orgasms?" It's a joke to try and stop the tension from suffocating me.

"I'll keep that in mind."

"Your table, sirs," the server says, before leaving us to the dry greeting of my parents' stares.

I clear my throat. "Uh, hey." They're the only two words in my brain, but luckily Émile jumps in as though there isn't a glacier building in my gut.

"Mr. and Mrs. Kilpatrick. I wish I could say it's an honor to meet you both, but I'm not fond of lying."

"E-excuse me?" Mom asks.

Fuck. "Uh, Mom … Dad … this is my, umm—"

"Fiancé."

I almost laugh at how fast he fills in that word considering what he just said about lying. "Yes, fiancé. Émile." Then I hold up my hand with the ring on it like I've been told to prepare evidence.

Mom nods, gaze still sizing him up. I can't see either of her hands, but I know exactly the way they'll be linked in her lap, thumbnails driving into the sides of her forefingers.

I've seen it so many damn times. I hate that I remember the details.

Émile pulls out a chair for me, and I hurry to sit, hoping it will help with the nerves.

It doesn't.

Neither does taking a gulp of the water Émile pours me, and it's even *less* helpful when I dribble the water down the front of me.

"Shit."

What does help is Émile's soft chuckle, the one he's always holding back, and the way he gently dabs my shirt with a napkin. "It's only water," he reminds me. "I know it's milk we're not supposed to cry over, but the message here is the same."

I allow some of his calm to take over me. *Make them work for it.*

Dad still hasn't said anything, and Mom is scowling. I can feel the way Émile is trying to sink into the background to let us have this moment, while making sure I know he's still here. For me.

Because I deserve it.

And hell, I'm still not sold on that, but with each painful, silent moment that passes, I'm looking at these people, and instead of the relief I'd expected at being here again … all I am is pissed off.

Dad's got new glasses, and Mom's more blonde now, but Dad's moustache hasn't changed and Mom's eyes are still as deceivingly warm as ever.

And I wonder if they look at me and see the familiar and the different and ache for the lost years the way I do.

"Perhaps we should look at the menu," Émile suggests.

"That's a great idea," Dad rumbles, and the fact he's said more about a menu than to me is what it takes to push me over the edge.

"Why did you message me?"

I'm met by two shocked faces.

"You had to know I was gonna ask that, surely?" Though, maybe not. As a kid, I did whatever I was told. Including get out of their house. Not try to contact them. Not try to contact the family. I gave them space at the wedding, and it's setting in that everything, *everything* I've done is to make things easier on them.

"We … have been talking," Mom says as though it's difficult for her to get the words out. "You're our son. And the years have been … this whole …" She waves a hand from me to Émile. "It's hard on us."

"And kicking me out when I was seventeen wasn't hard on me at all."

Émile chokes on a laugh beside me.

"Now that's hardly fair," Dad says, and he looks me in the eyes for the first time. I feel like a kid again, the one desperately trying to keep them happy, to make them proud, knowing deep down there was something really wrong with me. "You sprang this thing on us with no warning. One minute you were happy to go out with all the girls, and the next, you're telling us you want to live in—"

"If the next word out of your mouth isn't *happiness* or *authenticity*, I'm getting straight up and walking out."

"Uh …" He exchanges another look with Mom who glances at Émile again, before turning to me.

"We simply mean, it's been a challenge. To know that someone we love was on a path that we might not have chosen for him. And we've been working on it." Every one of her words is stilted. "And if you'll have us, we would like to try to be part of your life again."

The words are everything I've hoped to hear for the last ten years. I fantasized about it before the wedding, begging my phone to ring for years after I moved out. The first few months were the hardest, being so convinced that every text was them, every knock on the door. Telling myself over and over that they're my parents and they have to come around.

They didn't.

Until now.

And instead of sobbing and hugging them like I'd always assumed would happen, I'm … kinda empty. A little hungry. Palm still a lot clammy with poor Émile still clinging to it resolutely. And even though I'm not gonna be dramatic and think he loves me or anything, he's shown me more unconditional love in the short time I've known him than my own family have in the last decade.

You deserve this.

Fuck … maybe … maybe I do.

"Why now?" I thought I'd regret asking, but I don't.

Especially not when Mom's eyes flicker—so fast I almost miss it—toward Émile and away again.

What.

The.

Fuck.

"It's time, son."

I look Dad dead in the eyes, refusing to feel like a disappointing kid anymore. "I'm not your son."

"Oh, snap." The words puff gleefully from Émile as red splotches stain Dad's cheeks.

"You ungrateful little shit. We raised you, gave you a home and a future, and you threw it all away ten years ago, and now you're doing it all over again."

"Why. Now?"

"We want to know you," Mom tries again, and to her credit there are fat tears building in her eyes. I get the feeling they're less to do with me and more to do with Dad's rising voice and the people close to us looking our way.

"Try again."

"We've just … we've heard so much about you. From Josie. From Barbara. And seeing you at the wedding … we … we *missed* you."

"And it has nothing to do with me?" Émile asks, casually leaning back in his chair and releasing my hand to stretch his arm around my shoulders.

"Why would it?" Dad snaps.

"Maybe because earlier in the week every news source in Seattle ran the story that Christian and I are engaged, and the very next day a text from you showed up. Forgive me if I'm jumping to conclusions here, but it's coincidental timing."

Émile's hit my sinking feeling on the head. The hunch that I knew, deep down, was the only reason they reached out at all.

Émile is a somebody.

And they might have the money, but they don't have a family name that commands respect in the way his does.

"You don't know what you're talking about," Dad says, but I ignore him.

This has been a total waste of time. And I'm sorry Émile had to endure this.

"When we get married," I tell him, "I'm taking your name. I don't belong with these people anymore."

"Well then, what do you say to getting out of here and grabbing Mexican on the way home?"

"I love that idea."

"Wait," Mom says, voice hitching desperately. "We were prepared to give you another chance, you seriously won't do the same for us?"

"This was your second chance. And you blew it."

"If you walk away from this table—"

Émile cuts Dad off. "I'm afraid he must. You see, I plan to have him extremely naked within the next half an hour and if we don't leave, the waitstaff might ask us never to come back. And how else will we celebrate the anniversary of the day my fiancé told his good for nothing parents to fuck off if we're no longer welcome here?"

Dad chokes on air. Mom's eyes almost fly from her face. But I'm still stuck on that last bit.

"I don't think I actually said those words."

Émile waves a hand in their direction. "No time like the present."

"Fuck the hell off, and don't ever message me again."

For the first time in my life, I really really mean it.

Chapter 27

Émile

My place is closer. But still, after stopping for the fastest meal in history, it's twenty-nine minutes before we stumble through my door.

The apartment is dark, long shadows thrown through the space from the light spilling in my large windows, and somehow Christian and I make it down my hallway and into the living room without separating our desperately groping hands from each other.

"That was"—he cups my face—"so fucking"—his tongue dives into my mouth—"terrifying and amazing"—teeth grasp my bottom lip—"I'm still afraid tomorrow I'll realize I messed everything up, but for now …" His hands hook under my arse and he hauls me off my feet. "You promised I'd be naked in half an hour, and I'm still wearing these fucking clothes."

"Someone's impatient."

"I'm getting the feeling I'll always be impatient for you."

The words are everything I could hope for from him. This pit of emotion sitting heavy on my chest. We're both claimed by the adrenaline of his confrontation, and okay, a whole hell of a lot of horniness. Turns out, seeing Christian stick up for himself is a complete turn-on, and if I have it my way, he'll be doing a whole hell of a lot of it in the future.

"That way," I direct him, before threading my fingers through his hair. I lean in, mouth grazing his throat, his neck, until I rip open his top button and sink my teeth into the place his collarbone runs along his shoulder. I'm goddamn obsessed with them. With the taste of his skin. Maybe this has an end date, and we're doomed to crash and burn, but I'll start the goddamn fire myself if it means getting to have this time with him.

I've never craved someone as much as I crave him.

I've never had that need to show someone how perfect they are. Never felt that burst of pride and satisfaction over them finally glimpsing some self-worth. And, frankly, never wanted to bounce on one cock as desperately as I want his.

He crashes through my door, hiccups a laugh, before tossing me onto the bed. I land heavily before he crawls up over me, and we're all hands and mouths and ruined buttons as we try to dispose of these clothes as quickly as possible. Each strip of skin that's revealed to me, each muscle, each taut tendon, gives me a dizzying contentment that this divine man is choosing to be here. With me.

He hasn't stopped smiling once since we left the restaurant, and I bury my nose into the curve of his lips. Breathing in his happiness, committing his soft sighs to memory.

He breaks away from me for long enough to yank my pants down my legs and clumsily kick off his own, before he's back, all warmth and soft kisses and tangled limbs.

I let out a satisfied hum before I can catch it.

"That sounded heavy," he says, nuzzling my jaw.

"Not sure that's the word I'd use to describe it."

"Then ..." His soft blue eyes meet mine and positively *melt* me. It should be a crime for one man to have that much power with a single look. "What word would you use?"

"I'm …" I break eye contact, watching the way his hair twists between my fingers. "This feels right." My breath catches, refuses to release as I reluctantly return my gaze to his.

That permanent smile is gone, and I curse myself over being the one to steal something so precious from him.

Until he says the four most perfect words I've ever heard him speak.

"I feel it too."

Air rushes from me, and his smile is back, and that ballooning in my chest is getting deeper and more insistent.

Our mouths crash together, smile against smile, building laughter threatening to burst from me. I have no clue what's going to happen from here, but I allow myself the moment to hope. Hope that once we've unmessed the mess, we can work out something real.

"Can I be inside you tonight?" he asks. "I just, I have all this … so much energy. I need—"

"Yes. Fuck me."

He ruts against me, cock dragging precum over my own. "Holy shit, you're intoxicating."

"Take whatever you need."

He groans, dipping his head to bring our mouths together into a deep, filthy kiss. All tongue and teeth and primal grunts. My legs wrap around his waist, and he brings us together over and over, a pulsing, hot need growing deeper, burning through me, until I'm hot and sweaty and going out of my mind. His skin is almost feverish, perfect, sculpted body moving over me in a way that's sure to drive me over the edge.

"Please. Now."

"Condoms?"

I open my mouth to tell him they're in the drawer, but those aren't the words that come out. "Fuck me bare."

He pulls back, eyes hazy with lust. "What?"

"If you want to. I just … I want it. So much. Nothing between us."

"*Nrg* … Keep begging me like that and we won't even make it that far. Lube?"

"Drawer."

He jumps off the bed, yanks the bedside table open, and grabs the tube. My gaze drops to his very hard, very erect dick, and electricity sweeps from my spine to my balls, making my thighs clench.

He grunts when he crawls back over the bed. "Do you have any idea how hot you are?"

"Funny, I was thinking the exact same thing."

He hums, barely listening, and ducks his face to rub his scratchy beard over my cock. It's a war of pleasure and pain over the sensitive skin, but before it can get too much, he grabs both thighs, hooks them over his shoulders and dips his head lower.

Oh kill me now. I'm in heaven.

There's no preamble as Christian drags a long, wet lick over my hole. My head drops back onto my pillow, and I know without a doubt I'll never recover from this moment. From his scruff between my cheeks, his tongue and mouth and teeth doing things that make me lose my mind. I try every trick I know to stop myself from shooting too early, but when Christian presses a finger to my hole and slowly pushes inside, I have to dig deep. Every trick isn't enough for the things this man is doing to my body.

"More," I beg, maybe sob, who knows? At this point I don't really care to distinguish between them as long as it gets me what I want.

And he doesn't play games. A second finger joins the first,

and then a third. All moving and stretching and nudging that bundle of nerves that has every cell in my body buzzing. My fingers claim Christian's hair in a vice grip, while my other hand holds on to my balls for dear life. His tongue is wicked, his fingers so thick and filling. I almost want to go off like this, but then I picture him over me, cock pulsing inside my body and my mind does a one-eighty. *That's* what I want.

"Stop."

His face immediately reappears, fingers still, but filling.

"I'm so ready."

"Yeah?"

"Dear god, just fuck me already."

His fingers disappear, leaving me so empty and wanting as he props back onto his heels. I watch greedily as he slicks up his cock, and then he surprises me by taking my hip and rolling me onto my side.

"What are you doing?"

"I want to hold you but still be able to see your dick."

This man.

He lies down behind me, one arm wrapping under me as the other reaches for his cock.

"Prop your top leg forward a bit," he instructs, and I do as he says, then bear down when the fat head of his cock rubs against my entrance.

He slips inside, bare, and thick, and almost too much, but I breathe through it and press back while he slides forward. The burn is exquisite, stoking that fire deep in my gut, and when he bottoms out, presses our bodies together, and pulls my top leg back to hook over his hip, I stop trying to control myself.

Christian wraps his hand around my cock, and the first hard thrust forces me forward into his fist. His nose is buried under my jaw, his bottom arm wrapped tight, his body pressed so firmly against mine it feels like he wants to claim me. And I'd let him. If he did. If he wanted to call me his and take my name and let me pick up all of his broken pieces and keep them safe until he was ready to fix them again, I'd do it. I'd be everything he needed, and the only thing I'd want in return is him. Here. With me. Open and honest and hopefully one day full of a type of love neither of us has ever experienced before.

He moves inside me, a steady rhythm that fills that aching need I have for him. His grip on my cock is a perfect mix of firm and loose, making me leak, but not tight enough to set me off. Each deep grunt by my ear, each murmur of *perfect* and *oh, shit* and *your tea-obsessed British ass is going to wreck me* has me smiling and gasping and choking back that ever present laugh over and over again.

His thrusts get harder, deeper, more purposeful. The grip he has around my shaft tightens and it's all too much. I can't concentrate on his cock turning me inside out when every thrust is sending my cock into heaven. That buzzing electricity is building under my skin, zapping along my spine, sizzling in my balls. My body is begging for me to let go, but then it will be over and if there's one thing I want more than release, it's for this to go on forever. His lips, his sweat, his chest pressed to my back. His arm pulling me close. The way his beard is scratching my shoulder and his teeth are grazing my neck, and the moment he ducks his head and sucks on the dip where my neck and shoulder meet.

Every heightened emotion is merging with the next, building into a sea of *yes* that completely takes over.

And for the second time tonight, Christian gives me four gloriously erotic words, "I'm going to come," and he does.

His cock pulses deep in my ass, filling me up, and knowing there's nothing between us is my breaking point.

I moan through my release, each spurt taking me higher and higher into my lusty haze.

I come back to reality with small kisses and soft hands and a steady arm wrapped around me. But I don't let go too quickly. Don't force myself to move on to the real world when one exists where Christian just fucked my bloody brains out.

My eyes fall closed and when he goes to pull out, I grab his hip. "Not yet. Just give me another minute."

This time, six words. That's all he needs to turn my soul to jelly.

"I'll give you anything you need."

Chapter 28

Christian

With performing in the show, and Émile warming my bed at night, and my friends always wild and crazy and around, I've never been happier in my life. Especially when Reece gathers the *Not My Enemy* cast and tells us he's got an investor from Rosswell House interested in meeting with him.

Since my epic fail on stage last week, our shows have been selling out. Which ... it's wild. Almost enough of a positive that I don't totally regret what happened.

Nerves wobble in my gut, from knowing I didn't completely ruin everything, and this reluctant type of happiness takes over. The kind of happiness I wouldn't normally let myself have. The kind where I think ... *I think things might turn out okay.*

Failed show after failed show, all those countless hours. The years of unpaid time sunk into productions that never made it off the ground and now ... we only have the shows this weekend left, and I'd be lying if I said I wasn't exhausted as fuck, but I don't want it to end.

And it might not.

I'm struggling to hold on to that idea.

As soon as I walk out of there, I call Gabe and give him the news since he's been there for me through everything. He's ecstatic, and when we hang up, warmth floods me that I have someone else in my corner I can call. I've never had that before.

Émile answers almost instantly.

"Reece just broke the news that we've got interest in the show, and the investor is talking multiple cities—maybe even New York—and they want as much of the original cast on it as they can."

There's a beat of silence, and I wouldn't be surprised if he's trying to figure out what the hell all that word vomit was about. When he answers me, his voice is soft. The most genuine I've ever heard from him.

"Wow. You are so damn incredible."

I huff, turning my face down and kicking the pavement. "It was a team effort."

"In the nicest way possible, I don't give a fuck about any of them. I want to say I'm proud of you, but that holds a claim I have no right to. So ... yeah. I think you're incredible."

This lump builds in my chest, eyes and nose prickling with emotion that I press back. "So, it umm, it means I might have to travel. All over ..."

"We'll work it out."

We'll work it out.

So simple, said with the kind of confidence I've never felt a day in my life. And ... I believe him.

"We will?"

"Of course we will. I ... I've grown quite fond of you."

A shaky laugh falls from my lips and I duck my head again. "I'm, uh, *fond* of you too."

"I think we should probably talk about some things."

I nod at the sidewalk, because he's right. Our original

arrangement was supposed to be pretend, no feelings involved, but I'm definitely feeling a whole world of emotions for him, and now I don't know what that means moving forward.

Do we still get married? If we don't, what happens to his money? To his plans? The agreement of him paying off my debt long disappeared as a possibility when I decided to keep sleeping with him, but that doesn't mean this should all be for nothing.

"Can I see you?" I ask.

"You can, but …"

"But you're with your other fiancé tonight?"

"Boyfriend, actually."

I grin. "Well, he'll have to get in line. I'm demanding priority."

"Damn, love. Who knew assertive could be quite so sexy on you?"

"Don't get used to it."

His laugh floods me with goodness.

"Look," Émile says. "I'm going to this thing Gran is hosting. I can pick you up on the way, but I know you've just done two shows so it'll be a lot for you to come out and be social. I'd love you there, but there's absolutely no pressure on my end."

"Normally it'd be a no, but I'm riding this high. Can you pick me up? I just have to head home and get changed."

"Do you have a tux?"

"I can borrow one from Rush."

"So, I'll see you in an hour?"

"Perfect."

THIS "THING" his gran is hosting turns out to be a games night. And not the type of games night we have in Big-Boned Bertha; there are no Monopoly boards here.

Émile drives us to what looks like a seedy basement bar in downtown, but when we walk downstairs and through the heavily guarded front entrance, we walk into something out of a Bond film.

Dark wood walls enclose a room dimly lit by a few enormous chandeliers. Hundreds of people in tuxes and fucking *gowns* gather at tables hosting poker and roulette and black jack. Screens toward the back have yet more games running on them, and the whole area is filled with loud conversations and the smell of cigar smoke.

My eyebrows are at my hairline as I turn to Émile. "Is this legal?"

His eyes pinch in the corners as he surveys the room. "When you're rich, everything is legal."

"That sounds ominous."

"It's best you don't think about it too deeply." His hand finds mine. "So what shall we dump buckets of money on first?"

"Well, do we have to play?"

"We don't, but it helps to avoid conversation."

"In that case … black jack looks easy enough."

He pulls me in the direction of those tables, before I tug him to a stop. "I don't … have, uh—"

Émile holds up his free hand. "You're doing this for me so of course I'm not going to allow you to spend your own money. And don't try to argue with me on that point, because you'll lose. You're here now." He boops me on the nose. "Try to enjoy all this, because once I give my money away, I'll be cutting ties. I'll have my trust, but I'd prefer not to use it."

It's lucky the room is so loud and no one is paying us attention. "Then I guess that makes two of us."

"And that's still okay with you?"

The fact he's even asking me that question hurts. Not for

me, but for him. He's worth so much more than that. "Will we be happy?"

"I certainly hope so."

"Then I think we'll be okay."

This time, I let him drag me to the table and we do exactly what Émile said—lose a lot of fucking money. I'm terrible at it, he barely knows what he's doing, and the whole time we're playing, I do what he said and try not to think too hard about it. The amount of money in this room could pay off mine and all my friends' debts tenfold, but none of these people care about us. That money would never have made its way into our pockets. And while it's a stupid, corrupt system that allows people like this to treat money so carelessly, while the rest of us suffer, I remind myself of why I'm here.

I've got myself a good one, and he's actually *wanting* to make real change.

Even though we try our hardest to avoid conversations, people catch up with Émile anyway. They ask about wedding dates and my play, when Émile's planning to head back overseas and will I go with him.

"Having fun playing off Emmy's money, eh?" Clifford asks, concerningly red in the cheeks as he gulps down his wine.

The question turns my stomach, but Émile jumps in before I can.

"The opposite, actually. I'm milking Christian of all he's worth. Soon he'll be a pauper and we'll have to move into state-funded housing. Could you imagine?"

Clifford lets out a choking sound.

"You'll still visit us there, won't you?"

"Certainly not."

"Ooh, in that case, I wonder how much faster we can blow through these millions."

"I will never understand your humor, cousin."

"I wasn't joking." Émile cups his hand over his mouth. "I think Christian might have a gambling problem."

Clifford hurries to excuse himself as I turn big eyes on my … boyfriend? Fiancé? "What did you say that for?"

"Elle and I use nights like this to start as many rumors as possible. You should try it. It's the only way to get through it and keep your sanity in check."

"It's true," Elle says, converging on us in a massive sweep of cheek kisses and DKNY perfume. "I told Neil I'm thinking of flying to Utah. Mormonism is a fascinating religion."

I laugh. "You do this all the time? And people still believe you?"

"It's in the delivery, darling. Say it with enough conviction and people don't know whether to call you on your shit or not."

"Watch this." Émile grasps a man's arm on the way past, and before the guy can get so much as a word out, he says, "Do you mind finding an attendant for me? I'm not feeling the freshest and I just painted the inside of a toilet bowl. Rotten thing wouldn't flush, so I'd advise against using the loos—the stench is horrible."

The man yanks his arm from Émile's grip with a disgusted snarl, and marches away from us.

Émile turns back and Elle politely applauds him. "Fantastic effort."

"Let's see how many people nearly piss themselves because they don't want to risk the smell."

"I'll keep a tally."

I leave them to their game and wander over to roulette to take a turn that I immediately lose on. When I turn back, the two of them have been swallowed by the crowd. Instead of going after them, I head to the bar to grab drinks for us all first, because as amusing as their games are, I can't see myself joining in the fun. There's no way I can pull off that kind of dry British humor.

"Christian?"

I fix what I hope is an easy smile and turn toward the voice. Émile's relatives all know me, even if I have no idea who any of them are.

Except, this person I know.

His mom. Fuck.

Her cold blue eyes run over me. "Do you have a minute?"

"Ah, actually … I was getting drinks, so …" I make a half-assed attempt at indicating over my shoulder, knowing that there's no way in hell she's cornered me by myself for anything good.

"Drinks can wait. Follow me please."

And because I'm a spineless idiot, I follow.

She makes her way into a small back room where there are already two people waiting. Émile's dad is sitting forward, elbows on his knees and hands clasped in front of his mouth, and his gran is standing with her arms crossed.

Both of their attention lands on me the second I walk in.

"Ah, hi …" I say cautiously, even though the clawing in my throat feels like I'm being led to my execution. *Why are they all so scary?*

"Sit down," his gran instructs.

My legs fold under me like a card table. Me, in one chair near the door, with his mother just behind me, and his dad and gran in front.

Maybe I was being dramatic about the execution thing before, but … fuck. What if they *actually* kill me?

Anything is legal with enough money.

Please let Émile be looking for me.

"It's nice to see you all," I try.

"I wish I could say the same."

Okay, well looks like his gran isn't interested in playing nice.

"Look, I know you don't like me, but Émile does—"

"Keep my son's name out of your lying mouth," his dad snaps. "I was prepared to overlook this impetuous, ridiculous union until—" He thrusts his arms toward Émile's gran.

"You lied to us all," she says. "I have no idea if Émile is privy to the knowledge that you're estranged from your family, or that you live in a commune, but you have exactly sixty-eight dollars in your bank account right now and over a hundred thousand dollars in debt."

...

...

Fuck.

My jaw drops, and I hope something comes out. Some excuse or reason or ... or ... *anything* that will make all of this go away. But I'm only capable of one word, and basically, I would have liked it to be just about anything else. "Fuck."

His gran sniffs delicately, but I can tell that she's happy with my response.

"That's all you have to say to us?" his dad snaps. "Profanities? After trying to swindle my son out of his money."

"I didn't." Yes, thank you. Words. "I never lied to—" Shit. Not those words.

"He *knew*?" His mom gasps.

"Ah, *no*. I mean ... maybe. Look, I really think he should be here for this conversation."

"That won't be necessary." His gran's voice is cold. Commanding. "I've seen and heard enough. You can leave. And once you've left, you will contact Émile and tell him it's over."

What the hell? And maybe I wish he was here, and maybe I wish I could hide behind his confidence and hope this all goes away, but I know exactly what he'd say in this situation. "I'm not going to do that."

"Yes, you bloody well are."

His gran holds up a hand, silencing his dad. "It's ... admirable you think that. That you would want to hold tight to this ..." She waves her hand like she's searching for a word. "Fallacy. However, I don't recall giving you an option. Now, I suggest you leave with little fuss and no contact with my grandson. I assure you, Darcy will ensure he's taken care of."

"He doesn't want Darcy."

"He doesn't want you, either. Not deep down. He's going through a rebellious phase, and I will not let his impulsive decisions ruin his life."

"I would never."

"So you agree then?"

And even though every part of me wants to shrivel and die under her cold stare, I grit my teeth and shake my head. "I won't leave him until he asks me to go."

She sighs heavily, but my bullshit sensors are on high alert. It's then she holds out her hand and his dad places a piece of paper into it.

"I didn't want to do this, Christian, but you've left me no choice."

"Do ... what?"

She clears her throat and says, "Does the name *Rosswell House* mean anything to you?"

Fuck.

There's that word again. My heart starts hammering madly. "N-no."

"Are you sure? Because it says right here that they're planning to acquire rights to the production *Not My Enemy* and given all the media focus surrounding the show lately, it's come to my attention that *you* are a part of it."

My gut hollows out at her mentioning the musical, because it can't be good. I have no idea how she's gotten her hands on that information, but it's confidential. And I have the feeling she's about to fuck me with it.

"I am, but—"

"Were you aware that Carlisle Rosswell often attends my tea parties?"

I can't answer.

"Fine fellow. Good friends with our Darcy, in fact. It would be … well, quite a shame, if someone close to him pointed out what a terrible investment this would be."

Bile rises in my throat. "No."

"I'm simply pointing out facts, Christian."

"That's not a fact. It's a good investment and he knows it."

"It's a good investment, *now*, however, I can't imagine too many people will be wanting to rush out and buy tickets to your show if every publication across the country rates it poorly."

"You can't do that."

She lets out a tinkling giggle that I swear will haunt my dreams. "Oh, I didn't say? Darcy is the heir to MediaCorp. I'm quite friendly with his father and if I say the show is second rate, what do you think he'll be publishing all over America? What do you think will grace every television set?"

I'm drowning. That has to be the feeling rising over me. She doesn't need to say what she means explicitly for me to catch on. I break things off with Émile, or she'll put the show in the ground.

I want to call her bluff.

I want to tell her she's a bitter old hag who can shove her threats up her ass, but …

Reece. The rest of the cast. The relief and excitement we all felt this afternoon when the news came that this could, actually, finally be happening.

My own future I can gamble with.

But not theirs.

Frustrated tears sting my eyes. "Why are you doing this?"

"I don't like you. I don't like your behavior, your attitude, or the fact that ever since my grandson met you, he's been the focus of petty gossip and splashed all over the Internets. That's *not* where a Cromwell belongs. But also …" She holds out both hands. "I'm doing it because I can."

"Fuck." I scrub at my face. "So that's it? You just … you expect me to walk away?"

"Don't worry, dear. If this show does as well as it's predicted to, you'll have enough of your own money that losing my grandson's won't be such a shock."

I've never, ever wanted to harm an old lady, but this one deserves a flying face kick.

"And Émile?" I croak.

"He'll be taken care of."

"What if I don't do it? What if I tell him everything you've said and we get married and he gives me the money to fund the show myself? You wouldn't be able to stop me then." I know he'd do it, too. Know that he'd be that selfless, because that's who he is.

"Of course you're welcome to try. But my loving husband knew Émile too well. He left a clause in the will that expressly states I must approve of the union or the money will go to darling Clifford instead." She pauses for a second, like she's letting that bombshell sink in. "What? He failed to mention that?"

His dad sneers. "My son never was much good at reading the fine print."

The words fall around me and it's only once silence hits that I realize I'm shaking. How have I gone from feeling on top of the world to … to … *this*?

If I stay, he loses his money, I lose the show, and everyone

I've spent the last few months working with loses their chance. If I go, I lose Émile.

It should be simple. So, so simple.

But *fuck* I want to be selfish.

"We need an answer, Christian." Her voice has softened, eyes turning sincere. Because she knows there's only one choice here.

I swallow roughly, and nod. "You win."

"I always do."

Chapter 29

Émile

Christian's disappeared on me. I don't think much of it at first, he's a grown man and he can navigate a room, but the longer I go without seeing him, the more unsettled I become.

"Have you seen Christian?" I ask Elle, and her gaze pings away from me to scan the room.

"He was right here, wasn't he?"

"That's what I thought, but I haven't seen him for a while now."

We both push onto our toes to search the room, but I can't spot him anywhere. He'd be easy to spot too, with those wild curls on top of his head.

"Should I be worried?" I ask, even as concern clogs my throat.

"Of course not." She doesn't sound convinced. "Maybe he went to the bathroom?"

"For this long?"

"It's possible your lie to Bernie jinxed him?" I think she believes that as much as I do. But we check the bathrooms, and

I even go so far as to look into the toilet stalls, and to check the shoes on the person in the occupied one.

Not him.

I walk back out, raking my fingers through my hair. "You don't think he's left, do you?"

"Call him?"

It's loud in here, but I still make out the phone signal over all the noise. And the moment it cuts to his voicemail.

"No answer."

"Okay, now *I'm* starting to get worried." Elle's runs her hand over her head. "Why would he leave?"

I pointlessly look around again, because there's no reason he would have. He was happy to play along, maybe even enjoying himself so far as you can get enjoyment out of a night like this.

Did someone say something to upset him? If they did, surely he would have come to me instead of running off. It's our thing. He gets upset, I comfort him and remind him everything is going to be okay.

"Fuck, what if there was an emergency?" I ask.

"Why wouldn't he tell you before he left?"

"Well, if one of his friends got hurt, or …" I'm grasping at straws, but it could happen. It would be the most likely explanation, given his sudden disappearance and not answering my calls. It comforts me for all of two seconds and then I feel like a shit for hoping that's the case, when it means something dreadful.

"Émile?"

I turn to find Darcy approaching. He looks like a million dollars in his tux, and while I'm sure we could have had a perfectly plain and boring life together, I'd rather disappear off the face of this earth than make my family happy by marrying him.

I give him the most polite smile I'm able to, given the

circumstances, and he leans in to kiss my cheek before doing the same to Elle.

"I must say, I'm surprised to see you here."

At first, I look around to find out who he's talking to, until he continues.

"I thought you'd be at home, mending a broken heart." His words and the sympathy dripping from them doesn't make sense.

"I'm sorry?"

"Your engagement was called off?" He darts a look to Elle and back to me again. "Wasn't it?"

"No, it bloody wasn't." I scan the crowd again, suddenly feeling sick. "What are you talking about."

"I'm … I'm so sorry. I must have misinterpreted."

"Misinterpreted *what* exactly?" Elle asks, planting her hands on her hips.

"Uh, I'm not … I'm not sure I want to say."

"You better start speaking."

Darcy glances back over his shoulder, hands raised. "I'm not looking to get in the middle of anything …"

"No, you just, what? Decided to swoop in and help yourself to the carcass of their allegedly ruined relationship?"

"That's not it at all," he throws back with more bite than I've seen from him. I'd be borderline impressed if I wasn't reeling over whatever the hell this all is. "I'm here as a concerned friend. Nothing more."

"I appreciate your concern, but it's for nothing. I'm still very much engaged, thank you."

Confusion ripples his brow. "Of course. You would know more about your relationship than anyone else would, but … perhaps you should talk to your mother." He gives me a significant look.

And before I can ask anything else, he turns on his heel and walks off.

Elle watches him go. "Chances that this is one of those things we do where he's making up a rumor to fuck with us?"

"When have you ever known Darcy Ritcherson to have a sense of humor?"

"Bloody hell. Why would Mom say something like that?"

"I don't know, but it isn't filling me with the warm fuzzies where my relationship is concerned."

"Think she said something to Christian?"

Considering I haven't seen him for close to an hour now? "Almost certainly."

"Let's go burn the wench."

"Maybe we should find out what actually happened, before we contemplate arson," I suggest.

"If you want, but if the years of being raised by them doesn't make you jump to the worst possible conclusion, you're far more emotionally adjusted than I thought." She slants a look at me. "I don't think I can trust someone who has their shit together."

"Luckily the man I *will* be marrying is chaotic enough for us both." I hope. The ache in my chest is building by the second though.

"You couldn't have picked me a more perfect brother-in-law."

"Of course. Because the whole reason I'm marrying Christian is for you."

"It seems the most plausible reason." Elle waves a hand. "Who cares about money and poor people when you could be making me happy?"

As much as I want to laugh, I can't. My insides are knotting themselves toward an ulcer. "I need to find Mom."

Elle falls into step behind me as I push my way through the crowd. The room is starting to feel cluttered and overwhelmingly suffocating. Too much smoke, too much noise, too many people.

"There." Elle points to the other side of the room where Mom and Dad are talking with the Clarkes.

I storm right up to them, and without waiting for a break in the conversation, I demand, "Where is he?"

Four shocked pairs of eyes blink back at me.

"Excuse me," Dad says. "We're in the middle of a conversation."

"Well, I appear to be missing a fiancé, and I've been led to believe you know where he is."

"Don't be ridiculous, Émile. Christian was just here."

"I know where he *was*, my problem is that it's suddenly not where he *is now*."

Mom lightly sets her hand on my arm. "Careful, dear. You're starting to sound frightfully possessive."

I shake her off with a scowl. "What did you *say* to him?"

"You're making a scene," Dad snaps.

"Your father is right, this isn't the place for this conversation. Go back to the games, dear, and we'll talk to you later."

"There is no *fucking way* I'm going anywhere until I know what you've said to Christian."

A hush falls around us, and I'm hit with the hysterical thought that I've somehow absorbed Christian's backbone when it comes to our parents.

Dad's voice lowers dangerously. "I will not be spoken to like that."

Before I can reply, my phone ringtone cuts through the tension between us. Christian's name lights up the screen and I flip it so they can see. "Never mind. I'm about to find out everything anyway."

I quickly swipe to answer as I march away from them.

"What the hell happened?"

There's a long stretch where Christian doesn't answer and when he finally does, his voice sounds strained. "Uh, sorry I left."

"You're not the one who should be sorry. Did someone say something? Is everything okay?"

Again, no immediate answer and then, six words. Stilted. On a gravel tone. Six words that make me feel deeply like the others, but in all the wrong ways.

"I'm sorry, Émile. This isn't working."

Chapter 30

Christian

By the time I get home, my guts feel like they've been hollowed out, and I'm hanging on by walking myself through each step like it's a monumental task.

Lift foot, stretch forward, set it down.

Over and over until I reach the front door. Until *hand on handle, turn, push, lift foot …*

My entire body feels like a sigh. An impassioned waft of air just passing through.

"How much longer are you planning on leaving it?" Madden asks whoever the hell he's talking with.

I don't care enough to eavesdrop. Don't care enough to wonder.

"You know Christian," comes Gabe's reluctant voice. "He's not having the easiest time."

"So, you're not going to say anything, and he'll come home one day and you'll be gone?"

There's a groan, but I barely catch it, I'm too busy stumbling for the doorway. "*Gone?*"

Madden and Gabe's attention snaps toward me.

"Fuck, I didn't hear you come in," Gabe says.

"*Gone?*"

He curses under his breath, hands dragging back through his light brown hair. He's still in his work uniform, hasn't even made the moves to kick off his heavy work boots, and the T-shirt he's wearing is thick with sweat and soot—it clearly hasn't been an easy night for him. "Can you ..." Gabe nods to the couch across from him.

"You're leaving." That much has sunk in so far. "Like ... moving out, or ..."

"I'm *sorry*. I've tried to tell you about a million times, but things kept coming up and then I lost track of the days—you know how forgetful I am."

"You forgot. To tell me. You're leaving." I'm not even sure how I feel about the words I'm saying, not even sure I understand them. They're just *there*. Something for my mouth to do while I stare at him like ... like ... *Gabe's leaving.*

Through high school and college and five years ago when we moved into this place. He's always been right where I needed him to be. Here.

Gabe's expression grows tighter. "A place came up for lease around the corner from the station. I'm earning good money now and it just ..." He shrugs, almost like he's angry with himself. "I can't keep taking the place here, for cheap, when I've all but given up on ever making anything from my sketches. This place was set up for struggling artists, and I'm ... I'm not that anymore. Plus, with Kismet around more and more, I'm popping antihistamines like Tic Tacs. I can afford my own place now, and I think it's time."

But even as he begs me to understand all I hear is, *I can afford my own life. It's time to get away from you.*

Like living here with us wasn't good enough for him.

Like his promises to always be there for me were only something to say until the time came when he could get out.

I take a full step back.

"Christian …" Madden goes to stand, but I turn on my heel before he can and head right back out the door. Rain clouds have set in, lit from behind by the moon, but I jog to my car with what feels like my entire life ringing in my ears.

Gabe's leaving. I broke things off with Émile. The show I've been working my ass off for is being threatened when we're so close to making something of it. I'm in my car and driving before I've worked out where the hell to go. All I know is I need to move, to *do*, to keep running because if I stop, I'll have to process and this is all way too much for me.

I wind up at Gas Works Park, deep ache hitting my chest as I stumble out of my car and into the street. It's late and sprinkling rain so finding a close parking space was easy and as soon as my feet hit the path, I follow it past the rusted metal structures and to the lookout where I came that day with Émile.

It's impossible not to think about him here. Ice cream and rail lines and flying kites on the hill away to my right. I'm *aching* for him. Wishing he was here and would let me explain so he could pull me in close and remind me that he can make anything better. Making things better is *his* thing. Without him, I'm just blindly knocking into my problems, directionless and drowning under the weight of it all.

Another sob threatens to shiver from me but I push it down as well. My cheeks are already wet, and not from the rain, and I'm struggling to figure out how I'm supposed to go home and move on and pretend to be okay.

I never thought I deserved a whole lot in life, but I always clawed at the chance to be happy. To have people who fucking cared about me.

But my family left.

Twice.

Émile's family never cared.

Gabe's running away—the one person I thought would always be there.

And Émile … my heart twists painfully. We could have had something, because I believed him when he said we'd figure it out. I believed that he was starting to feel for me what I was feeling for him.

But it wasn't enough.

I never am.

My arms fold over the railing and I bury my face in my elbow, trying and failing to ignore my tears. *Only girls cry,* Dad would say, and I know it's all bullshit, but it's a hard lesson to un-learn.

A hand lands on my back and I jump about a mile as I spin around.

"Émile." I trip over his name, caught totally off guard by him being here. His blond hair is darkening in the soft rain, hazel eyes hard-edged and assessing.

"What are you doing here?" he asks.

"I … I …" I shake my head. "It's … it's over."

"You didn't answer my question."

"Because I don't know what to say. Because I don't know if I should tell you that I'm here because I'm scared. Because it's raining and I'm lonely and I'm worried I'm going to feel that way forever. That if I didn't come here, I'd end up in bed for a week or back in my car heading for your place. That I've been broken a lot in my life, but I don't think I've ever been as broken as I am right now. Tonight. I don't know if I can tell you that."

"Well, it's lucky for me that you still can't hold in your thoughts." He lifts his hand like he means to cup my face but I jerk back away from him.

"Don't."

"Christian …"

"Please. I c-can't."

Émile's expression turns to stone. "What did they say to you?"

I'm so prepared to make up some bullshit excuse, that it takes me a second to process his words. "Huh?"

"I know they made you leave, I just don't know what the hell they could have on you to actually make you do it."

My shoulders sag. "The play."

Understanding lights up in his eyes. "Those motherfuckers."

"I had to."

"They found your price, love. Tell me everything."

So I do. One, big, explosive vomit of words I don't even follow enough to make sense. They just keep coming. A stream of everything. Tonight, forever, the darkness that constantly haunts me. "And now I have no one again. No best friend, no family, no boyfriend or husband, fake or whatever the hell we were. I have nothing."

"That's where you're wrong."

I snort, but Émile ignores me, just steps forward and rests his hand on my chest.

"Turn around."

A splashing noise reaches my ears, almost drowned out by the low rumble from overheard. And then I turn.

And there, jogging along the path through the rain …

Xander and Seven. Rush. Madden. Aunt Agatha. Gabe. Gabe who doesn't stop when he's close enough. Gabe who slams into me and covers me in the smell of smoke and of the deodorant he keeps at the station.

"You big, dumb idiot," he says, voice sounding rough. "You made me worried and shit."

My eyes are leaking again and when he pulls away, I hurry to wipe them off on my shoulder.

Émile moves in close again as Gabe steps away, and then

his fingers are slotting in between mine. Exactly where they belong.

"I thought you said you didn't have a family," he says in his best teasing voice.

"Better not have said that," Aunt Agatha says, and I know exactly what's coming next. "Otherwise you'll be out of the will."

"Yeah, what the hell?" Seven snaps. "You guys are the only family I have. You just fudging try and take that away from me."

"Families don't always live together," Gabe points out. "It doesn't make them less of a family."

Goddammit, there goes my eyes again.

"How did you guys find me?"

Gabe shrugs. "Well, you're no tacos, but we've been training for this for a while." He spares a glance at Émile. "And turns out your boyfriend knows you pretty fucking well."

"I ..." I turn to Émile, surprised to find true worry looking back at me. "We're not boyfriends though, right?"

"What do you want us to be?"

Bitterness burns in my gut. "It doesn't matter what I want. I can't have it."

"Of course you can. You just need to work out how."

I drag my teeth over my bottom lip. "What do *you* want?"

He doesn't even need to think about it. "I want to get married and to keep falling for you, and I know it normally happens the other way around, and if you want to do things the traditional way, we can. But the traditional way isn't exactly our thing, and I *like* that. I like that we're chaotic and messy and don't always know our next move. I like that we're making things up as we go along, and that I might have fallen for you by accident, but now I want the chance to keep falling for you on purpose. And I know that I don't want my family to win. Not with the will. Not with this."

232

"If we do that, you'll never see the money. They said there's this clause where your gran has to approve whoever you get hitched to."

"They lied."

"What?"

"There's no clause. I've had a lawyer go over it twice. Pa knew what he was doing."

"And yet, he still wanted you to get married for it."

Émile's smile starts out slow. "It's almost like he knew."

"So, is it still happening?" Xander asks. "Because we wanna be groomsmen."

"I …" I look back at Émile. "I can't risk the show. How do we fix this?"

I'm sure he'll have an answer. It's his thing. He fixes my screwups, and I'm sure this is going to be like every other time before. His answer is the last thing I expect.

"I don't know."

Chapter 31

Émile

Every day away from him is exquisite torture. All I want to do is to tell my family to shove their threats up their asses, but I bite my tongue. He's right. Until we know how to play this, we can't risk his show.

Christian finishes up the weekend performances, and I secretly go to the final show and have flowers waiting for him when he's done. Watching him proves to me he belongs out there. Performing. He *shines*, and I know that he won't be in the background forever. Someone with that much talent deserves to be showcased, which makes what my parents and gran planned to do that much worse.

I comfort myself over the distance, knowing he's working hard with Reece to get Rosswell House officially signed on. It won't completely help things if Gran is planning to blacklist the show from national media, but we can only deal with one step at a time. And once Carlisle has signed and invested, it'll be in his best interest to make sure things go smoothly.

Still, it doesn't help my side of things. Every time we talk,

I *know* Christian is looking to me to find answers, but … *what*? I'm clueless and it's not a feeling I'm well acquainted with. I can talk out of my arse with the best of them, but apparently solving a relationship-ending debacle is beyond me.

Every time I look it over, they have us kneecapped.

We could get married, I'd get the money, and then pay for the show myself. But that doesn't solve the problem of it being trashed in reviews thanks to my family's influence. Not only that, Christian would never let me. No matter how passionate he is about this, he'd never sacrifice my plans for that money for his own happiness.

I haven't given up hope that there's *something* we can do, I'm just struggling to work out what exactly it is.

All that on top of finalizing this charity ball for Alzheimer's, and I'm officially tapped out, mentally. I do need to find a solution though because this ball is coming up fast, and I've already bought Christian a matching tux to wear. He's going to be my date to that thing whether my family likes it or not.

"Are you *still* moping?" Elle exclaims, looking up over the top of her pink highlighter. "I've told you a million times, Christian is crazy about you. Call him."

And while I one hundred percent trust Elle not to say anything, if she accidentally let it slip that he didn't walk away, we'd be screwed, and Elle would feel terrible. I don't trust my family, and my paranoia is growing. If they'd go so far as to threaten my fiancé, who's to say they wouldn't plant bugs in my apartment or my car … the only thing I know is safe is my phone. Partly because I always have it on me, but mostly because I had it checked out. Dear God, I've become a James Bond movie.

All I know is that we have to keep our relationship secret because the second Gran gets wind that we still plan to marry, she'll do everything in her power to stop Carlisle. And I *do* plan to marry him. We're just scrambling to work out *how*.

"I've tried," I lie. "He's not taking my calls." Because as if I'd leave something like that to a phone call. That night, when I realized he'd left because of *them*, I'd gone straight to his house only to find his roommates worried sick and him already gone. Thank fuck for that day by Lake Union and my brain categorizing every little thing he's ever told me.

"What are you going to do then?"

"I'm going to throw the greatest charity event that Pa deserves, and think about it all later."

"I think that's a mis-*take*," she sings.

"Consolidate that guest *list*," I sing right back, though I'm not sure if you can call butchering every note *singing*. I try to keep the moping to a minimum for the rest of the afternoon. It's not as though we've actually broken up. It only feels that way.

Christian can't risk the play. I support him on that. But having someone who's still my fiancé, who I can't see and touch and spend time with, who I can't claim for the world, it's *torture*.

Elle keeps throwing me looks over the table we're working at and I keep pointedly not noticing her do it. We're here to work. We're *not* here to discuss blindingly vulnerable boys with soft eyes and big hearts.

"I wish I knew what they said to him!" she explodes.

"You're not going to drop this, are you?"

"No, I'm bloody well not. This isn't fair on either of you. And sure, I'm not all about the happily-ever-afters and what-ever—*for me*—that doesn't mean I didn't believe in it for the two of you. It's impossible to think otherwise after seeing you together for two point five seconds."

"What do you mean?"

"It's like he gravitates toward you. Whenever you're around."

I only let myself think about that for a second. "Yes, because he's possibly the most nervous, unconfident person I've ever met."

"He wasn't unconfident in his show."

"You *saw* his show?"

She frowns. "Of *course* I saw it. I couldn't not support my future brother-in-law."

I slump, feeling like a right shit for not telling her what's going on. "I legitimately think you might be the greatest sister anyone has ever had."

"You shouldn't sound so surprised. It's also why I absolutely cannot let you give up on him. You can't keep my wonderful sisterness all to yourself."

"No, no, keep talking. You're helping restore my original image of you."

"And what's that? I suggest you're careful with your answer."

"Ah …" I turn to my phone, pretending to read something of *much* importance. "So sorry. I forgot what we were talking about."

She all but rolls her eyes but when she turns back to what she's working on, she says, "You best do something about him. Otherwise I will."

"Just once is it too much to ask that my family not interfere?"

"'Fraid so. But don't worry, dear brother. I'll be gentle."

Chapter 32

Christian

"Christian! The British are here!"

I glance up, hearing Rush's voice from where I'm sitting cross-legged in Xander's studio. We stare at each other for a beat, his tiny freckled face pale under his blue hair.

"There's no way he'd come here, right?" I ask, and Xander shrugs.

"You both are adorably dumb for each other."

I throw a dirty paintbrush at him, which bounces off his head, leaving a blackish streak from his hair down to his jaw.

Xander gives me a blank look. "Thanks for that."

Before I can tell him he's very welcome, the door to the room bursts open and it's not Émile who walks in. It's Elle.

"You *have* to take him back. I'm sorry, Christian, but I'm not leaving here with no for an answer."

Rush cringes. "Never mind consent then."

"Consent?" She jabs a hand dramatically my way. "Are you really going to attempt to bullshit me that your boy isn't half in love with my brother?"

Madden chuckles, coming to see what all the shouting is about. "No one would be that dumb."

Elle's smile widens. "Well, hello, cutie."

"Gay." Madden throws her a cheeky grin. "Sorry, babe."

Thankfully he must have known we have visitors because he's pulled on some loose gym shorts.

"Is it my turn to be fitted yet?" Seven asks, bulldozing into the room.

Rush sighs. "I *said* I'd call you when I'm ready for you."

"Yeah, but when are you ever on time for anything?"

Elle meets Madden's eye, holds up a hand, and then points to Seven from behind it. Madden gives her a double thumbs-up.

She grins and turns to Seven. "Well, hello, cutie."

Dear god.

Seven does a double take like he somehow missed her when he walked in, and then he slowly looks her over. "Who in my pansexual-fever-dreams are you?"

I clear my throat, breaking up … whatever that is. "I know you came here for your brother, but you're kinda failing at the whole crusade bit, honestly."

She waves a hand, finally stopping to take in the room. "What's all this?"

"Rush is making us groomsmen tuxes," Xander says, bouncing on his knees. Out of all of them, I swear he's the only one actually—externally, anyway—happy for me.

"Groomsmen … who's getting married?"

I lift my hand. "Before you get all mad, Émile told me he hadn't had a chance to tell you. He's gotten a bit paranoid since everything happened."

"Tell me what?"

"We talked, we're still getting married, we just, uh, don't know when or where or how or basically anything yet."

"You're still …" She throws her hands up. "So all this was for bloody nothing."

"It was cute to see you all defensive for him if that helps."

She sniffs. "It does, thank you."

"Besides, I don't think it was for *nothing*." Seven winks, and I drop my head into my hand with a groan.

"*No* hooking up at the wedding. Please. Too weird."

"Christian, you're a doll." Elle pats me on the head. "But you cannot presume to think you have any say over what I do. Especially when we have planning to do."

"Planning?"

She laughs, but it's more derisive than humorous. "I went to boarding school, pet. I know my way around a good scheme. Now, what are our problems?"

And maybe I shouldn't be sharing it all with her since she's from the family actively trying to fuck with my life, but Émile trusts her, so therefore I do by default.

By the time I'm done talking her through everything her parents said, she a) does not look shocked or surprised in the slightest, which I try not to be concerned about, and b) has slumped to the floor beside me, where she's tapping her chin, eyes narrowed.

"How far away are you from having Carlisle Rosswell sign?"

"They haven't mentioned. Reece said all of the meetings have been going well, and our ticket sales totally sold out after my, uh, *incident*. That's gone a long way toward proving the show can be profitable with the right marketing. I mean, I didn't realize I was vomiting up money at the time, but hey … apparently my humiliation was good for something."

"Okay, so you're getting him signed. Then we need to, what, wait out the cooling-off period?"

"Even with him on board, your gran said they'll trash the show in the media. We'll never make back the money, so it'd be for nothing anyway and then no one will ever want to work with us again."

Elle frowns and it's stupid how pretty she looks when she does it. "And how does she plan on doing that? All of the offense to my gran, because *none* of her friends are the types to own a mobile phone, let alone troll a production from it."

"Darcy. They said he owns some media thing?"

"Yeah, and Carlisle is his best mate. There's no bloody way he'd trash something his friend was working on. In fact, it'll probably lean ever so slightly in your favor."

I give her my best doubt-filled expression. "You really think Darcy is gonna do something that helps me?"

"Why not?"

"Because he wants to marry my guy."

She blinks at me. "Oh honey, you're lucky your talent lies on the stage. Darcy is about as interested in marrying Émile as my brother is about marrying him. I cross my heart and hope to die, needle, eye, all that stuff, that Darcy will not be an issue. If that's their only threat, carry on."

"Why wouldn't Émile know that?"

"Maybe because my darling brother has spent the last few years actively avoiding everyone here except for me. He's never bothered to get to know Darcy, whereas I have. Every time I've tried to convince my brother that Darcy isn't all bad, he doesn't listen. He's a champion at ignoring a problem until it goes away. But trust me, Darcy won't fuck this up for you. Rossy would murder him."

"Okay." My heart feels lighter. "Okay. So. We get Carlisle signed on and then …" I'm trying to remember all the things. "The production is safe. Émile is sure his money is safe. That's …" As much as I want to be excited, there's something holding me back. "It feels too easy."

"Isn't that a good thing?" Xander asks.

"For us, yeah. But even if we get married and he gets his

money … they've done a lot of shitty things—" I hold a hand up toward Elle "—no offense, and they're going to get away with it all."

And that's the biggest thing for me. I'm going to be happy with Émile. I'm entering this marriage knowing we're doing it purely for one end goal—the money—and that once he has that, our attention will turn to the relationship. It's backward, yeah, but like Émile said, everything with us has been.

I don't care about that. Married, not married, I only want to be with him.

But it burns me up that after threatening me, after squishing Émile down all his life, that they're going to get away with it all.

They'll still be rich and untouchable.

"To be fair," Elle says. "I have a feeling they'll do a lot more shitty things. Especially if they think there's any way to stop the wedding. Dirt in your past? They'll find it. Mass orgies happening in this house? They'll know."

As if on cue, the five of us recoil. "Fuck, no."

Elle smirks. "I'm only saying, they'll play dirty. This is just the first thing they had to throw at you. They'll get reception venues to turn you away, have caterers way overcharge on food, the cars will go missing on the day, and I'm sure there'll be mishaps with the suits, the guest list, the seating plans—"

"Okay, okay, I get it." My nose twinges as I tug and twist my piercing. "Then I guess … so maybe we keep the plans to ourself or …"

"They'll find out. They always do."

I narrow my eyes at Elle. "Are you here to help?"

"What do you think I'm doing?"

Before I can snap back, Madden says, "No, she's right. We need a fastball."

"A what?"

"Like, you've just gotta get married."

I pin him with a look. "Is that all? Why have I been wasting time on planning a funeral then?"

He actually rolls his eyes at me. "You need to get married *today*."

And as dramatic a declaration as that is … "That's impossible."

"Never say never."

"No, like, there's legal shit. Marriage licenses and a venue and someone to marry us and … and …"

"Details. We get it." Elle's face is pinched in concentration.

"So, maybe not today, but how long does it take to get a license?" Xander asks.

"Three days."

"And what's the soonest you can find someone to marry you?"

"I don't know. I'd have to call around and—"

"I'll do it."

I glance over at the deep voice in the doorway and find Gabe leaning against the frame, arms crossed over his chest. "Y-you would?"

"I'm already ordained. I will literally kick your ass if you ask anyone else."

My smile is fucking painful.

"I'll organize decorations," Xander says. "I'll paint the most beautiful aisle runner. And I'll *make* flowers. Lots and lots of clay flowers—"

"I've got the suits," Rush adds.

Nerves are stirring, along with excitement, and so many other wonderful things coming alive in my gut. Maybe his gran is getting off easy, but none of them are going to be happy with me in the family, and they're not going to be happy with what Émile plans to do with his money, either.

"This … could work?"

Xander claps his hands. "Seven could design you some awesome invitations."

"But then people will know there's a wedding, and his family will have time to stop us."

We drift into productive silence again. It's like a choose your own adventure book, where every solution has five possible outcomes, and I don't know how to look that far ahead. All I know is that in life, there are no do-overs. This is our only chance to make it work.

"Why don't you run off to Vegas?" Seven asks.

Xander pouts. "I want to be a groomsman."

"No good, Émile says at least two family members have to be there to witness it. Elle obviously would be, but ..." Literally no one else would come. Especially not if we eloped.

"That's a bullshit rule," Rush says.

"Probably made exactly to avoid him doing exactly what we're planning."

"You just need to blindside them all with it."

"That's it." I sit bolt upright, mentally trying to calculate how long it will take Reece to get Carlisle to sign off. "I've had a wonderful, *fabulous* idea. And I can guarantee every member of your family will be there to witness it."

Chapter 33

Émile

Getting a cryptic call from your partner slash boyfriend slash fiancé person isn't at all concerning on the day you're holding an enormous charity fundraiser. All I could get out of him was that Carlisle had signed, Darcy was on board with some write-ups on the show, and that Elle would be by to pick up the tux I'd had made specifically for him to wear tonight.

And yet he still isn't here.

Half an hour late.

There's definitely nothing. At all. To worry about.

I let out a hollow laugh to ease the tension building in my chest and down the rest of my champagne. There are a lot of people here tonight, which is amazing for the charity and sure to bring in a *lot* of money for Alzheimer's research, but it means when Christian shows up, there's more potential for a scene.

My parents and Gran won't be happy. Which I'd care about if I actually gave a shit about their feelings, but after they casually dumped all over mine, they deserve every little bit of humiliation they can take.

"You've outdone yourself," says a familiar voice. Only it's not the one I want to hear.

I turn to Darcy. "They're all here for Pa."

"Perhaps." He takes a sip from his glass. "But you're very like him, you know? So maybe they're here for you too, just a little."

I have no clue where this is coming from. "What makes you say that?"

"Well, you too, are slightly odd." He softens his words with a smile. "You're always off traveling, have time for people, stand by your family … even when you probably shouldn't."

"I shouldn't?"

Darcy's jaw tightens, and he casts his gaze around the room. "I've been in contact with your fiancé."

My eyebrows almost fly from my face. "What?"

"Very clever, charming man. I understand what you see in him."

I blink at him. "Wait. *My* Christian?"

Darcy throws his head back and laughs. "I like you a whole lot more when I know I'm not going to be forced into being your husband."

"Then …"

Darcy leans in, stormy eyes pinned on me. "He told me. Well, he and Elle. About what they said to him and how they tried to bring my name into disrepute by doing so …" Darcy clears his throat. "My point is, I have the story, and unless they play nice, I'm going to run it. With your consent, of course."

"And if I don't?"

Darcy shrugs. "Then it doesn't see the light of day. It's merely a, uh, *contingency*."

I'm clueless with what's happening here. "You'd willingly publish something like that? Villainizing them?"

"Yes."

"But, why?"

A light hand lands on my shoulder and I turn to find Elle.

"Because they are the villains, love."

I'm not sure whether to be hurt they spilled my secret or … or …

"All we need is your yes," Darcy reminds me. "And everything would be cleared with you and Christian before I ran a story anyway."

I don't even need to think about it. "Yes." And with that one word, the weight I've been carrying around, the worry and stress and *pressure* it just … it disappears. Maybe we'll do something with the information, maybe we won't. They tried to blackmail him and that's not something they'll want to get out.

"I need to see him," I say, heart feeling like it might burst. "Where the hell is my man?"

"Come with me." Elle takes my hand, and I finally notice the pale pink suit she's wearing. It's perfectly tailored, all severe lines and pinched waist, and looks amazing on her.

"Where did you get that?" I ask, because it's not the dress she showed me she'd be wearing.

"I've recently met an extremely talented designer who made it specially for me." She steps onto the small platform that we'll be auctioning things from later and tugs me up after her.

"What are you …"

"Excuse me!" a voice bellows, and I turn in time to spot two people who could not look more out of place.

Xander, with his periwinkle blue hair, is waving people aside while Seven, with his red hair, piercings, and neck tattoos, rolls something out from the back of the room to the platform where we're standing.

The hiss and rattle of levers distracts me and I glance toward the noise, finding an enormous backdrop unfurling behind us. The words *forever and always* are painted surrounded by flowers, cakes, and an ice castle. And dotted in between them are tiny, colorful kites.

I bite my lip and throw a suspicious look Elle's way. "What's all this?"

"This is all Christian."

A throat clearing is amplified in the room and Gabe joins us on stage. His six-foot-four bulk has been squeezed into a suit, and he lifts a hand to the room. Silence falls, and he unleashes an easy, dimpled smile.

"Ladies and gentle fools, thanks a bunch for coming. I know you're all here to give generously, but before we get into all that, we want to divert your attention for a sec. Our amazing host thought, with all his friends and family gathered, it couldn't be a more perfect time to do this. And so, let's break some legs and get this show on the road."

The band starts up again, playing a soft, floaty tune as the lights in the ballroom dim until only the giant chandeliers are on. Xander appears first, at the head of the carpet they rolled out, and he walks along throwing glitter at the people on either side. Seven follows him, then Rush, then Madden, who blows kisses and throws out winks for anyone who'll look.

But I'm not.

Looking.

Not anymore.

Because right behind them, arm hooked through Agatha's, is Christian. He's got his bashful expression turned up to a thousand, blush visible even from a distance, and as Agatha walks him toward me, my heart claws its way up into my throat, and I think *I'm not falling anymore.*

His friends gather around me, and when he reaches the platform, tugging at his collar, bright blue eyes shining with the types of emotions I'm feeling, I'm drunk on the sight of him.

It's been entirely too long since I last got to check him out.

His mouth forms the word *hey* and mine follows on a *hi*.

Elle kisses my hand she's still clinging to, then she holds it out at the same time as Agatha reaches Christian's forward. His hand slots into mine, and I'm home.

He trips onto the stage, because, of course he does, and it warms me to the core. His blush, his muffled *fuck*, the way his hand tightens over mine.

"Never change," I whisper.

"Couldn't if I tried."

The music drifts off and Gabe takes over.

"I dunno about you all, but this is one sexy as hell couple." He cuffs me on the shoulder. "Pity they're monogamous, am I right?"

He chuckles at his own joke, while Christian looks like he wants to die.

And it's perfect.

Perfect the way he talks through the wedding stuff.

Perfect the way his friends heckle their way through the ceremony.

Perfect the way I can feel my parents' disapproving glare.

And perfect when I catch a glimpse of Darcy and he throws me the thumbs-up, and I never thought I'd be happy to see him on my wedding day, but I am.

All except for one thing.

"I don't want you to be a guarantee," I tell Christian. The words are out before I can stop them, and Gabe stumbles in whatever he was saying. I turn to look at the most incredible man I've ever seen and find his forehead crumpled in confusion.

"What? You don't want to do this?"

"I certainly, certainly do. But for the right reasons. I don't want you to feel like you're a guarantee or a contingency or a clause in a contract. Because you've become so much more than that to me. You're the way you dance, and how you care, those addictive collarbones, and that bloody heart you wear on your sleeve. You're absolute word vomit at the worst possible times, and occasionally real vomit, and I love both of those versions equally. You're so messy and real and sometimes broken, but always, always the very best version of yourself."

Christian's eyes have gone glassy. "Love?"

I swallow. Nod. "Yes. I'm afraid I've gone and gotten it all mixed up. I know we agreed to wait until *after* marriage, but—"

Christian hauls me into a kiss. A sweet, consuming, mind-numbing kiss. "I love you too. And I don't even feel bad about breaking the rules because you deserve it. And I'm gonna spend the rest of forever proving to you how much. Like, I think we both know I'm gonna fuck up now and then, but if you can promise to deal with me, I can promise to keep on trying."

"And I won't always have the answers, and I'll laugh at the most inappropriate times, and sometimes I'll be impossible to deal with, but if you can love me through that—"

"Always. I promise."

He's so close he's all I can see and smell and feel. My awareness is narrowed down to his nose ring and his scruff and the hidden vulnerability that pinches the corners of his eyes.

"So ..." Gabe says, breaking through the moment. "Y'all just went and did your own thing there. Lucky there's no set script for this except two things. Christian, say I do."

"I do," he echoes.

"And Émile, you're up."

"I definitely do."

"Close enough." Gabe raises his voice. "Now, if there's anyone who doesn't want the sexiest couple alive to get married, time to speak up."

"I bloody well object," Dad shouts.

Gabe looks around, and for one absurd moment, my gut bottoms out.

"Anyone?" Gabe calls.

"Yes, I *said* I object to this ridiculous joke of a marriage." Dad storms toward the stage, but Madden, Seven, Rush, and tiny Xander, jump off the stage and cut off his path. Elle, Aunt Agatha and Darcy all join them, forming a human wall between him and us.

Then Christian, my sweet, uncertain man turns and levels Dad with the most menacing look I've ever seen on his face. "Back down or I tell everyone here why this almost didn't happen, and you'd want to hope there's no one in the room with the reins to a *media conglomerate*."

Dad's gaze immediately shoots to Darcy who grins at him, and … and … holy shit.

My poor, unconfident almost-husband just fucked my family up with their own weapon. Dad backs down, and I don't think I've ever swooned so hard in my life.

"No one? Going once and all that shit?" Gabe calls, then winks at me. "Lucky. I can't hear a thing over these damn ear plugs anyway."

Christian grabs my hand and slides a ring onto my finger. "Almost forgot that."

"Shocking for us, really." It's plain gold, but the way it catches the light has my heart so bloody full. I don't need a ring, but the weight of it, the importance, is thrilling.

"I now declare Christian and Émile married!"

The band starts playing again, and his line of friends starts hooting and cheering, which of course Elle joins in on. The rest of the room fills with polite applause that I'm only too happy to ignore.

Because the only person I care about in this second is standing right in front of me.

"C'mere, husband," he says, tugging me into a kiss.

I go to him. Easily. And I have a feeling I always will.

Chapter 34

Christian

We stumble through Émile's front door, my hands buried in his hair, his cupping my cheeks. Our mouths are soft, all teeth and tongue, both of us ready to take this further but happy to take our time.

Because we have it.

As much damn time as we want.

I can't stop smiling at the thought.

All night while we went through the charity auction and the dinner, talked to wealthy benefactors and whoever else was there, Émile didn't let me out of his reach. He was as needy and clingy with me as I was with him, and I'm pretty sure everyone there tonight is already over our blatant PDAs, but if he doesn't care, then neither do I.

After all, my entire, true family was there, and not one of them was embarrassed by me or judging me. I could be myself for the first time in a really, really long time.

"Take me to the bedroom, love," Émile mutters against my lips.

I hook my hands under his thighs and lift him off the ground. The satisfied hum in his chest smothers my burning need in happiness. Contentment. Whatever feeling makes my insides too big for my outsides. Makes my body thrum with excess energy, and my arms feel like they might float away.

Émile's room is a mix of soft gray linen, blue walls, and his own intoxicating scent. I'm surrounded by him everywhere in here and when I drop him back onto the bed, I take a moment to catch my breath, even though I'm hungry for him. *In love.* I want to take him in my hands and never stop touching.

Émile laughs, so golden and perfect. "I assure you, it'll be much more enjoyable if you join me down here."

"In good time." One corner of my lips hooks upward, and I lean down and unbutton his shirt. Each one I flick open is followed by the soft caress of my thumb and then the barest of kisses over his sternum, his diaphragm, his stomach. Émile's long fingers twist into the bedsheets and the semi I've been rocking for half of the day, thickens behind my fly.

I peel open his shirt and let out a shaky breath. Fuck, he's beautiful. Broad shoulders, narrow waist, tiny bit of golden chest hair, and perfect, flat nipples.

"I can't believe we're married," I say.

His smile is soft. "For real."

"And if I have it my way, forever."

"I love finding a man with similar life goals."

I duck my head to press a kiss to where his pants have slipped down and his hip bone is exposed. As slowly as my unravelling control will allow, I pop the buttons on his pants and draw his fly down over his straining erection.

Even though my mouth is watering over the idea of blowing him, I redirect my attention to his pants. Pulling them sensually over his thighs, his calves, before I toss them unceremoniously to the floor.

I can't be fucked to take my time with his briefs and once

I've yanked those off, my self-control snaps. I lean in and swallow him to the back of my throat.

We moan at the same time. My eyes roll back. He tastes and smells so incredibly like *him*, and my cock is throbbing with need.

"Fuck," I gasp, pulling off and starting on my buttons. I'm in such a hurry it takes me an impossibly long time, so while I work on that, Émile sits up and works off my pants. I kick them and my briefs away, grab the lube from his bedside table, and slick myself up.

"Lie back."

Émile shuffles back onto his pillows and lets his legs fall open. I will never understand how someone can say the male body isn't the sexiest sight. I mean, sure, I'm biased. And I'm gay as fuck and allosexual, and I'm here with *Émile* so maybe my opinion is skewed, but *damn*.

I want to consume him.

My underwear is closest so I use those to clean the lube off my hand, then crawl up over the top of him.

He looks up at me, all liquid hazel eyes and gentle mouth, and my heart does the familiar stutter is always gives me around him.

I lower myself until we're pressed together and Émile wraps his arms around my neck. His lips find mine. Soft, slow, over and over. His breath smells like cherries from the drinks he had earlier, and I probably taste like Coca Cola and bourbon, but apparently he doesn't hate it. His fingers reach for my hair, tighten, as I press into the kiss harder and taste every lingering flavor on his tongue.

Émile wraps his legs around my waist and brings our hips together. My dick slides against his, and he better have a round two in him because I don't plan on this lasting long. I don't want it to. All I know is that I'm turned on and full of emotion, and something's gotta give. Right now, my cock is insisting he's it.

I roll my hips, bringing us together over and over. His velvety hard length feels incredible crushed against mine, and when I break the kiss, forehead pressed to his, hand stroking his cheek, I catch a glimpse of the ring on my finger. It's the same one he gave me when he proposed, but this is the first time I've looked at it and known it *means* something. Something great and heady and invincible.

I untangle his left hand and hold it in mine, seeing the gold band against his soft skin almost makes me choke up.

Émile groans. Squeezes my hand, rolls his hips against mine. "Lord, that turns me on."

"Me too."

I catch his mouth again, hungrier this time. Our hands still entwined and crushed between our chests as we madly frot together, desperate for that finishing line. His tongue is demanding, and mine is just as needy. I chase every grunt, every pant, even his *lord, save the king*, which I'm certain he just says to fuck with me.

I'm rocketing closer to the edge, movements less skilled and refined, more frantically seeking friction. His precum is leaving a sticky mess between us, my balls drawing up, becoming over-sensitive. And then Émile curls one hand around my nape, fingers biting into my skin as he throws his head back.

"*Nrgh*, Christian." His cock jerks under mine, releasing, spilling over the both of us, and I work myself harder against him, trying to follow him through. His body still moves with mine, sweaty, warm, perfect, his steady hand at my nape doesn't shift, only grips tighter.

"Come for me, love," he rasps.

And one look into those beautiful eyes is enough to make it happen. The building pressure releases, and I keep grinding against him, milking out every last drop until that frenzied need slowly ebbs into nothingness.

I collapse against him. Émile's tight grip loosens and his fingers work their way into my hair. I lie there, completely sated, letting him stroke me as I drift in and out of consciousness. I could easily fall asleep here, for days, and catch up on all the sleep I've lost ever since I met him.

"We have a lot to talk about," he says.

"Yeah, I guess. But we don't have to do it now, do we?"

He chuckles. "No, now is for recovery so that we can go again. I simply mean that tomorrow we'll have time to get the money details squared away and then … we start making plans."

"And your family can't do a thing about it."

His nod is hesitant and I can tell there's something on his mind. "Is it wrong of me to hope?"

"Hope what?"

"That they learn from this?"

I'm so not the person to be asking that question. "Hey, if I can hold out hope for a decade that my parents aren't as shitty as I remembered, I'm not exactly going to judge you, am I? In my case, my family were shitheads. The damage they've done is irreversible, and I'm glad I can finally see that and be okay with it. What your parents and gran did to me … that was pretty shitty. They could have ended it. I'll never forgive them for that, but they have a chance to step up now. And even if I never forgive them or like them or whatever, I could learn to have a level of respect for them if they really do change."

"Yeah, I think that's what I'm hoping. I've never had a high opinion of them, but I'd like to believe that they're not completely fucked up."

I kiss him lightly. "All we can do is wait and see."

"That's true.

"And have a lot of sex in the meantime."

Émile smirks. "Well, that's a given."

I smile and kiss him again, and again. The man who proved to me that I can be loved wholly, unconditionally, and that just because I don't have the family I was born with, doesn't mean I don't have one at all. He's there when I need him, completely unruffled by my mishaps, and loving me in spite of them.

I don't care if things are early.

I don't care if we've done everything the wrong way.

Because all of those wrongs gave me the biggest right of my life.

Him.

And I'll hold on to him forever.

Chapter 35

Émile

The complete freedom is messing with my head, but it's not like I can say it's a bad thing. Every day I wake up, convinced it will be another day of playing a part, but then I roll over and Christian's there, and every good thing comes crashing down on me again.

Gran tried to nullify the will by scaring our family into saying they didn't attend my wedding, but even ruling with terror doesn't guarantee you the win and in the end, both Mom and Elle signed off on their attendance. Even if they hadn't, it wouldn't have mattered. Thanks to Seven, we had plenty of photo evidence.

I haven't heard from any of them since.

Unlike me, Christian has been catching up with his cousin every week. At first I was standoffish, worried she was the same as the rest of them, but she's grown on me. It certainly helps that she's been putting the homophobes in her family in their place.

Christian rolls over and throws his arm across my chest.

"Happy money day, now please don't divorce me," he says, still half asleep.

I chuckle and kiss his shoulder. "I suppose I can keep you."

"Huh?" His head jerks up, eyes blinking into consciousness before his expression relaxes. "Good morning." He yawns. "Did you say something?"

"Yes, I was answering you but apparently you were sleep talking."

"Uh-oh. What did I say?"

"You begged me to stay with you forever and ever. It was pathetic, really. Turned me completely off."

"Which is why you want to keep me, then?"

Should have known he heard me. "Turns out needy and clingy does something to me."

"Explains so much."

I bop his nose. "You know, I've been thinking about what I could do with my inheritance."

"And you know that you're not obligated to do anything, right? You want to do good, and I know you will, but you have time to figure that out."

"Well, yes, but …"

The arm across my chest tightens. "You know I don't care whatever you decide."

I do know. When we got married, I truly thought Christian was going to be someone special, but I highly underestimated how much. He says I'm his rock, but he's that and more for me. Without him in my corner, I doubt I'd be able to think anywhere near as many impossible thoughts as I do when I'm with him.

"I'm paying off your loans—"

"Émile—"

"Non-negotiable, I'm sorry."

"But—"

"You don't need me to, you're earning your own money,

etcetera, I know. I've heard it all before. And I don't care. I'm more than prepared to give the money away to people I don't know because of guilt and a sense of responsibility. Let me first give a little to someone I love because it'll make me happy."

"It's a lot of money," he says, weakly.

"And it barely makes a dent in what's coming to me. But that's my priority and then … I want to start a charity. Not for profit, not tied into the family business, just something that will genuinely help people. I haven't worked out the details yet, but I want to do something that will help the most amount of people I can."

Christian's big hand runs over my hair. "Fuck, I love you."

"Good, because that makes asking this next question easier. Can I come with you? In a few months when you leave and you're traveling around with the play, I want to be there. I can make plans for my business while we're gone and whatever I come up with, I'll make sure it allows me to be wherever you need to be."

"You'd do that for me?"

"I'd do anything for you, love."

He ducks his head, hiding the smile I know is on his lips. It warms me, reminds me of all the things about him that I've fallen for and continue to fall for.

"I still find it hard to believe we found each other."

"I like to think that everything that's happened was always meant to be."

"Hard to argue with that when I'm looking at a life with everything I've ever wanted."

Little does he know I plan to give him everything. The things he wanted and the things he never would have dared to dream about.

Epilogue

Christian

Nine Months Later

Getting back to Seattle after a long time on the road was an enormous relief. I loved our time away, I loved performing and getting to see different cities and towns all over America, but I missed my friends and I missed home.

It helped that Émile was with me. I'm not sure I would have made it without him.

Which is wild when a year ago, I would have said I'd do anything to go on tour with a show. It's funny how dreams change. Every time I look at Émile I'm reminded of it.

After talking to Reece about it, we came up with a plan. He's written another production Rosswell House have bought the rights to, and I get to stay in Seattle to train the cast.

Choreography, fitness conditioning, nutrition, and consulting on rehabilitation plans for injured dancers will all be part of my role.

Permanently.

In Seattle.

"I still can't believe you dragged me out of the house at seven in the morning," Émile says as I pull into a parking space at Gas Works Park. It's hard to fight the happiness trying to break free as I turn off the car and jump out. The last few weeks have been a lot of back-and-forth communication with my Bertha family—including Gabe who's moved out, and Molly, the guy who took his room—organizing this surprise for Émile, and, fuck, I hope he likes it. It's like, no matter how many times I tell him how I feel, it's never enough. Not really.

He's the most incredible person I've ever met.

"This is cute," Émile says, joining me on the path. His free hand slides into mine as his other grips his coffee. "A morning stroll."

Something like that.

But instead of leading him to Lake Union like he expects, I veer to the right, toward the hill. And where all my friends are waiting.

A cheer goes up the second they see us and at first I think it's because they're excited—it's been a while, but then—

"What the hell is that?" I ask, eyeing the *enormous* dragon-looking thing that's taking up half the damn hill.

Xander holds up a tiny finger. "In our defense, you said you wanted something impressive. And I asked myself, *Xander, what do you find impressive?* And of course my answer was big dicks, so …" He gestures toward the monstrosity like a magician revealing his assistant. "Big kite."

"A kite?" Émile repeats, craning his neck to get a better look.

Gabe throws him a dimpled grin. "I think the word kite is generous."

"It didn't seem this large deconstructed."

Seven looks up from where he's attaching … a wing, maybe? "It definitely did."

"I did my *best*, okay?"

Madden laughs from where he's flopped on the grass, loose gym shorts leaving nothing to the imagination. "Considering Christian gave us a week's warning—"

"Three weeks."

"—I'd say you pulled it together pretty well."

Xander thrusts an arm in his direction. "Thank you!"

"Fuck, sorry I'm late," Rush says, as though any of us expect anything different from him by this point. He pulls his jog up suddenly. "What the hell is that?"

Xander throws his hands in the air. "I give up!"

Before he can go to storm off, Seven tackles him and smooshes his face into the grass, while Molly, the new guy, watches them, looking out of place. "Relax, I'm sure Christian has something he wants to say to us all. Especially you who worked so damn hard on this." The glare Seven throws my way has me stumbling over myself to reply.

"He's right. Thank you. You did an amazing job, and I'm so appreciative of this, uh, kite, that we are definitely going to be able to get off the ground because I have zero doubts over its aerodynamic … *ness*."

Madden waves his hand at me to continue.

"And I'm so lucky to have you all?"

"Close enough." Gabe pulls me into a hug, smacking a loud kiss on my cheek, before doing the same to Émile.

It's not until Émile extracts himself that I get my first good look at his face. And his glassy eyes.

"You did this for me?"

I try for a smile that doesn't stick. "Yeah, I wanted to surprise you, but I don't … is this okay?"

"This is fucking perfect. Are you kidding?"

I let out a long exhale. "Okay, good. Because it looks like you're going to cry, and I wasn't sure …"

He laughs and pulls me into a long kiss that turns my friends into high schoolers again.

"To be clear here," he says. "This is perfect, and I can honestly say it's the most wonderful thing anyone has ever done for me."

"So far."

He cocks his head. "What?"

"The most wonderful thing *so far*. You're an amazing person and you deserve amazing things always."

"Such a sweet talker."

Not hard when I'm only telling the truth. Émile shows me what it's like to be married to a partner, a supporter, someone who's always in my corner and willing to go to the ends of the earth for me. I never have to worry about him letting me down. I never have to worry about disappointing him. And because he shows me that daily, I want to return it. And I'll never stop trying when it comes to him.

"Let's go see if we can get this thing off the ground," he says, setting his coffee on the grass and pushing up the arms of his long-sleeved T-shirt.

"One more thing." I grab him before he can run off. "I love you."

But it's not only Émile's voice that answers me.

Five others join in.

"*I love you, too.*"

THANKS SO MUCH FOR READING THE FIRST BOOK IN MY ACCIDENTAL LOVE SERIES!

Look out for more chaotic men accidentally falling in love later this year

My Freebies

Do you love friends to lovers?
Second chances or fake relationships?
I have two bonus freebies available!

Friends with Benefits
Total Fabrication
Making Him Mine

This short story is only available to my reader list so follow the
below and join the gang!

https://www.subscribepage.com/saxonjames

Other Books By Saxon James

FRAT WARS SERIES:

Frat Wars: King of Thieves

Frat Wars: Master of Mayhem

Frat Wars: Presidential Chaos

DIVORCED MEN'S CLUB SERIES:

Roommate Arrangement

Platonic Rulebook

Budding Attraction

Employing Patience

NEVER JUST FRIENDS SERIES:

Just Friends

Fake Friends

Getting Friendly

Friendly Fire

Bonus Short: Friends with Benefits

LOVE'S A GAMBLE SERIES:

Good Times & Tan Lines

Bet on Me

Calling Your Bluff

CU HOCKEY SERIES WITH EDEN FINLEY:

Power Plays & Straight A's

Face Offs & Cheap Shots

Goal Lines & First Times

Line Mates & Study Dates

Puck Drills & Quick Thrills

PUCKBOYS SERIES WITH EDEN FINLEY:

Egotistical Puckboy

Irresponsible Puckboy

Shameless Puckboy

Foolish Puckboy

FRANKLIN U SERIES (VARIOUS AUTHORS):

The Dating Disaster

And if you're after something a little sweeter, don't forget my YA pen name

S. M. James.

These books are chock full of adorable, flawed characters with big hearts.

https://geni.us/smjames

Want More From Me?

Follow Saxon James on any of the platforms below.
www.saxonjamesauthor.com
www.facebook.com/thesaxonjames/
www.amazon.com/Saxon-James/e/B082TP7BR7
www.bookbub.com/profile/saxon-james
www.instagram.com/saxonjameswrites/

Acknowledgments

As with any book, this one took a hell of a lot of people to make happen.

The cover was created by the talented Rebecca at Story Styling Cover Designs with a gorgeous image by Michelle Lancaster, and edits were done by Kathleen Payne, with Lori Parks proofreading the bejeebus out of it.

Thanks to Charity VanHuss for being the most amazing PA I could have ever dreamed up. Without you I'd be even more of a chaotic disaster and there isn't enough space to cover the many hats you wear for me.

Eden Finley, you constantly under-sell yourself but I've learned so much from you. You're the bestsest disaster bestie I could ask for, and a queen of a co-author. You're also stuck with me. Lucky you.

To Louisa Masters, thanks for constantly reining in my spirals of doom and reminding me to "stop borrowing trouble". I'd be an anxious mess in the corner at least half of the time without you.

AM Johnson and Riley Hart thank you so much for taking the time to read. Your support is incredible and I really appreciate it!

And of course, thanks to my fam bam. To my husband who constantly frees up time for me to write, and to my kids whose neediness reminds me the real word exists.